WITHDRAWN

Praise for
DEBORAH RANEY

"Raney has fashioned a startlingly honest portrayal of love, commitment, and redemption in the midst of tragedy that will appeal strongly to fans of Janette Oke and Neva Coyle."
—*Library Journal* on *A Vow To Cherish*

"Raney immediately draws the reader into the story. Well-defined, empathetic characters have true-to-life motivations, and the strife-filled country of Haiti is depicted so that readers will feel compassion rather than despair."
—*Romantic Times BOOKreviews* on *Over the Waters*

"*Over The Waters* is a poignant and memorable look at love and sacrifice."
—Karen Kingsbury, bestselling author of
One Tuesday Morning and *Beyond Tuesday Morning*

"[Her characters] slipped from the pages of [*Beneath a Southern Sky*] and into my heart. I experienced all their heart-wrenching emotions and rejoiced as they triumphed by God's grace. Bravo, Ms. Raney!"
—Robin Lee Hatcher, bestselling author of
Return to Me

D1450303

"Readers will lose their hearts to the characters in this jewel of a story. Polished and excellently plotted...engrossing from start to finish. 4.5 stars, Top Pick."
—*Romantic Times BOOKreviews* on *A Nest of Sparrows*

"Deborah Raney's writing is always full of warmth and hope."
—James Scott Bell, Christy Award-winning author of *No Legal Grounds,* on *A Nest of Sparrows*

WITHIN THIS
Circle

DEBORAH RANEY

Steeple
Hill®

Published by Steeple Hill Books™

STEEPLE HILL BOOKS

Steeple
Hill®

ISBN-13: 978-0-373-78594-0
ISBN-10:   0-373-78594-1

WITHIN THIS CIRCLE

Copyright © 2007 by Deborah Raney

Printed in U.S.A.

To my husband, Ken
With all my love

Many thanks for help with research to: the Denver Police Department, the police department of McPherson, Kansas, Tamera Alexander, Pat Black, Eileen Key, Donna Meier, Mary Rintoul, Max and Winifred Teeter.

To my wonderful pre-readers who are also friends (and in some cases family), Kim Hlad, Tobi Layton, Terry Stucky, Max and Winifred Teeter.

To my dear friend and most excellent critique partner, Tamera Alexander; my fabulous editors, Krista Stroever and Joan Marlow Golan; and my agent extraordinaire, Steve Laube. You all make me look good.

With love to my family, near and far, who are always so supportive and encouraging. Special thanks to my "baby" sister Beverly for the wonderful care package that came during crunch week. It made all the difference!

If you are involved in the selfless task of raising your grandchildren, you will find help and support at GAP (Grandparents As Parents). GAP's mission is to provide programs and services that meet the urgent and ongoing needs of grandparents and other relatives raising at-risk children. Helpful information can be found at their Web site at www.grandparentsasparents.com or write to: GAP, 22048 Sherman Way, Canoga Park, CA 91303.

Chapter One

~◆~

The sharp blare of a horn jolted Jana McFarlane from her chaotic thoughts. She peered up through the windshield of her little white Ford Escape at the traffic light swinging in the wind overhead. Green for some time, judging by the chorus of honks that swelled behind her on South Michigan Avenue.

"Okay, okay, give me a break." Muttering under her breath, she glanced both ways and eased through the crowded Chicago intersection. She stole a glance in the rearview mirror, checking on Ellie in the car seat. Her daughter's thumb was in her mouth, eyelids drooping, head listing to one side.

Great. If Ellie fell asleep this late in the day, she'd be up wanting to play at 4:00 a.m. again. Weren't kids supposed to sleep through the night by the time they turned three? She sighed. So much for that hot-bath-and-early-to-bed-with-a-book fantasy she'd entertained all day.

She merged onto I-55 as the clock on the minivan's dashboard flipped to triple fives. She was late. Again. They were supposed to meet with the investors in Mark's restaurant in an hour. He would be furious. Well, he'd just have to get over it. It wasn't as though he was winning any husband-of-the-year awards lately, either. And hey, this was Wednesday night. Whatever happened to the Wednesday family nights Mark had designated? Ever since he'd opened the restaurant last September—almost a year now—their life had been one big, not always fun, roller-coaster ride. It only promised to get worse and her fear that her mind was slipping, that something was off-kilter, made the ride that much scarier.

The news she'd learned at lunch today hadn't helped her mood any. Her thoughts returned to her encounter with Sandra Brenner at Buca di Beppo. Jana and a coworker from the museum had gone out for a late lunch. She'd been surprised to run into Mom's old friend on the way out of the restaurant. She hadn't seen Sandra in almost four years. At Mom's funeral. She swallowed hard. It still seemed impossible that her mother was really gone.

But what Sandra had mentioned so casually as they chatted on the sidewalk outside the restaurant shook Jana to her marrow. All afternoon, she'd tried to fabricate a way that Sandra could be mistaken. But the more she thought, the more it all added up too neatly. Why hadn't she seen the truth all along? In her mind, she'd confronted her father fifty different ways. Would Dad defend himself when she told him what Sandra had revealed?

An aching sadness simmered inside her, and with every mile, the grief and disappointment boiled until it resembled something closer to rage. She clenched her jaw and pounded the steering wheel with the heel of her hand.

She had tried to embrace her father's new wife. Even though Jana and her brothers had thought things moved a little too quickly with Dad and Julia, they'd all agreed he deserved some happiness after everything he'd been through. It wasn't as though Mom were coming back.

She bit the inside of her cheek. Why hadn't she seen it before? *Dad's friendship with Julia had begun while Mom was still alive.* Sandra implied they'd had…an affair. Jana could scarcely make herself think the words, much less believe them.

The emotions of those excruciating months before her mother died pressed in on her. And the more she remembered, the more doubt crept in and found footing amid the painful memories. She remembered her brothers commenting about how much happier Dad seemed after admitting Mom to Parkside. Brant and Kyle assumed it was because the burden of Mom's care had been taken from Dad's shoulders. At the time, it confirmed for them that Dad had done the right thing.

Jana's focus sharpened. Dad's happiness hadn't been caused by the relief of his burden at all. It had been Julia. He'd been seeing someone else! No wonder he'd wanted Mom put away.

How *could* he? Fury boiled up inside her. She—they all—had put John Brighton on a pedestal for his long-suffering devotion to Mom. And he'd smugly perched there, letting them think he deserved the adoration they'd showered on him. Her stomach churned and heat flushed her face, as if the shame were her own.

Julia was no innocent in all this, either. She'd had to know about Mom. Know that Dad was still married. Jana shook her head. Had everything she'd ever believed about marriage been a sham? If Dad hadn't been able to remain faithful to Mom, where was there any hope?

Somewhere a horn blared and Jana tried to focus on the congested highway. The Jeep in front of her merged left and Jana sped up, glad for a little space. But when the car behind her swerved into her blind spot, she saw the reason for the lane changes. A construction barricade loomed mere yards in front of her. Her brain registered the speedometer inching past sixty. She slammed on the brakes.

The squeal of tires echoed a shriek from the backseat. Something smashed hard against the back of her seat, then tumbled beside her between the bucket seats. *Ellie!*

The Escape lurched, bucking forward as her foot slipped off the brake. She tried to move her right arm, but it wouldn't obey her brain's command. Gripping the steering wheel with her left hand, she watched her knuckles pale from pink to white.

She stomped the air wildly, searching for the brake pedal. She finally connected with a force that caused the vehicle to tilt, then come to an abrupt halt inches from a low wall of cement.

Everything went silent except for the *whoosh whoosh* of cars zipping by on the freeway to her left. The Escape rocked and swayed in the wake of passing traffic.

Jana tried again to move her arm. Pain shot down her forearm. She looked down and gasped. Ellie's car seat was upside down, wedged between the front seats of the vehicle, pinning Jana's arm to the back of the seat.

"Ellie!"

Raising up in the seat, she stood on the brakes with her full weight and yanked her arm free. She cried out in pain as the molded plastic scraped her skin. The gearshift went easily into Park and she scrambled to her knees in the seat to gain some leverage on the car seat.

"Ellie!" She screamed her daughter's name again. "Please God...please God...please God..." She breathed the words in and out like air.

She wrestled the carrier into an upright position and propped it on the passenger seat. Ellie faced forward, her face chalky, her blue-gray eyes round, staring straight ahead. For one awful instant, Jana thought her little girl was dead.

But then Ellie sucked in a frayed breath and belted out the most beautiful scream Jana thought she would ever hear.

She turned off the ignition and quickly unsnapped the carrier's seat belt. As she did so, she turned to stare at the rear seat belt in the Escape. It rested flat against the side panel of the vehicle.

Her breath caught as she realized what she'd done. She had buckled her daughter into the car seat at the day care center, but she'd completely forgotten to fasten the car's seat belt around the carrier. She shuddered and her hands started to tremble. *That stupid mistake could have been fatal!*

As quickly as she'd had to stop, it was a miracle Ellie hadn't been ejected from the car. Only the back of the seat had prevented her from hitting the windshield.

Numb, Jana lifted the screaming three-year-old and inspected her from head to toe. No blood.

Gingerly, she palpated her daughter's limbs through the little hooded sweater and denim overalls, searching for broken bones or other signs of injury. What if Ellie had internal injuries? Her wails sounded like a typical terrible-twos tantrum. But what if she was wrong? She'd heard horror stories about children who died of unseen injuries minutes after seemingly surviving an accident.

Jana hugged her child close and Ellie's sobs subsided as her thumb went into her mouth. The air in the car grew sultry and stale. After several minutes, Jana eased Ellie back into the car seat.

Ellie didn't resist, but popped her thumb out of her mouth long enough to look into Jana's eyes. "Mommy?"

Jana brushed the fine auburn curls from her daughter's high forehead. "It's okay, baby. We…we had a little bump in the car. Here…lift up your arms. Let Mommy check you out." Ellie cooperated in silence while Jana stripped off the little undershirt and training pants. Not surprisingly, they were soaked. Probably would have been even without such a scare. Potty training hadn't been going very well lately.

She reached behind the seat and rummaged in the diaper bag until she found a spare undershirt and a disposable diaper. Ellie was still in diapers at night, but this one was left over from her infancy and was at least two sizes too small.

"Ouchy, Mommy!" Ellie bucked and squirmed, trying to escape the car seat. "Ouchy!"

Jana struggled to loosen the diaper's tape fasteners. "Stop it, Ellie. Hold still!" She slapped the pudgy bare thigh, then rocked back, appalled at what she'd just done. She'd nearly killed Ellie and now she was spanking her? What was *wrong* with her?

Forcing her voice down an octave, she willed a soothing tone to her voice. "I know, sweetie. I'm sorry. You're getting too big. We'll get some new clothes when we get home."

"I want Daddy!" Ellie's wails crescendoed.

"Ellie! Stop it. *Shut up!*" Without warning, the awful, out-of-control feeling that had dogged Jana the last few months came over her again. It fell heavy on her, like a scratchy wool blanket in deep summer. A terrifying thought gripped her. Was this what it had been like for Mom when the Alzheimer's first started eating away at her brain?

Jana clapped her hands over her ears. "Ellie! I said stop it!"

She hadn't meant to scream, but the words came out shrill and earsplitting.

Ellie stopped crying, and stared wide-eyed, as though seeing a stranger.

A laugh bubbled up Jana's throat, but before it could escape, a sob took her voice hostage. What finally came from her throat was the haunting cackle of a lunatic. She saw herself as if she were watching from someplace outside her body.

She was going crazy. Losing her mind. Just like her mother.

She stopped short, grappling to gain control of her emotions. *Deep breaths.* She should take Ellie to a hospital. Have her checked to make sure she was truly okay.

No. If she did that, she would have to admit her irresponsible mistake. The nurses might even report her to Child Protective Services. And who could blame them. She could have killed her little girl! She dropped her head in her hands as a new thought struck her. How would she ever explain this to Mark? What kind of a mother was she anyway?

Cars whizzed past on the freeway and Jana huddled against the window, hiding her face from her daughter, putting as much space between her and Ellie as the confines of the vehicle would allow.

She could not let anything happen to Ellie. She might be on the edge of insanity, but she would keep her precious little girl safe if it was the last thing she ever did in this life.

In the periphery of her vision, the traffic blurred into an abstract streak of color. Jana concentrated on breathing, breathing, breathing, while her mind expended its last fragments of sanity on a plan.

Chapter Two

Julia Brighton rolled over in bed and squinted at the hazy light seeping beneath the curtains. The tops of the trees wore the first purplish hint of autumn and even through the closed windows, she could hear the birds twittering outside.

Stretching, she pulled in a deep breath and caught the heavenly aroma of fresh-brewed French roast.

She heard John rattling around in the kitchen, opening and closing cupboard doors in quick succession, but she resisted the urge to crawl out of bed and help him find whatever it was he was looking for. A smile tugged at the corners of her mouth. If she were patient, her sweet husband would soon appear in the doorway with a breakfast tray.

She fluffed her pillow and propped herself on one elbow. Even after two and a half years of marriage, John had kept this Saturday-breakfast-in-bed ritual with all the devotion of a newlywed.

As if on cue, he appeared in the doorway, bearing a loaded tray and the grin that still kicked her pulse up a notch.

"Good morning, sunshine." He set the tray on the dresser and went to draw back the curtains.

Julia rubbed her eyes against the light, then scooted upright in the bed and leaned back against the headboard waiting for him to place the tray across her lap. "You are a wonderful man. Do you know that?"

"Well, I try." He kissed the tip of her nose, then shook out a paper napkin and tucked it into the neckline of her nightgown. "We must be out of strawberry jam. I hope you can live with orange marmalade."

"I wouldn't dare complain," she said over a bite of still-warm bagel. "And hey, why are you so dressed up?" Instead of his usual weekend uniform of sweatpants and T-shirt, John wore crisp Dockers and a polo.

He grimaced, as if aware he was in trouble. "I have to run by the office for a little while this morning…sit in on a short coaches' meeting."

"John," she moaned, "you promised…" The man hadn't taken a real day off from his job as superintendent of schools since their honeymoon. And even then, he'd called back to the district office at every port of call where he could get a cell phone signal. The weekends were supposed to belong to her. To them.

"Half an hour." He held up a hand in defense. "Not a minute longer. We just have to iron out the game schedules."

She rolled her eyes.

"More coffee?"

She grinned up at him, shaking her head. "Don't think you can appease me with a mere cup of coffee. Let's see—" she scratched her temple "—I think an evening at the ballet might make amends."

"Okay, okay… Uncle!"

She laughed and waved him off. "Go to your stupid meeting."

He leaned to kiss her. "I'll tell them to cut it short or they're all coming to the ballet with me."

"Hey, do me a favor and stop by the cleaners on your way home, would you? I want that silk blouse for church tomorrow."

"Will do."

He started from the room, but the telephone on the nightstand stopped him. "It's probably Alexander. I'll take it in the den."

The phone rang again and Julia leaned to check the caller ID display. "No, it's Jana."

John gave her a pleading look. "Would you take it, babe?" He tapped his watch, whispering as if his daughter could hear him on the other end of the line. "I really need to run. Tell her I'll call her back when I get home."

She nodded and reached for the phone, blowing him a kiss with her other hand. "Half an hour," she mouthed.

He snapped a sharp salute and headed down the hall.

She waited until the kitchen door slammed before clicking the phone on. "Hello?"

"Julia?" The deep voice belonged to Jana's husband.

"Oh… Mark. Hi. I was expecting Jana. How are you?"

"Is Jana there?"

"Here? No… Was she supposed to—"

"Can you put John on, please?"

She heard the muffled grind of the garage door closing at the other end of the house. "He just left for a meeting. Mark? Is everything okay?"

"No." His voice broke. "It's Jana."

Her pulse thrummed. "What is it? What's happened?"

He didn't answer for a moment. Then a deep sigh came across the line. "She's left me."

"Left you? What on earth are you talking about?" Like any young married couple, Mark and Jana had had their spats, but there'd never been a hint that anything was seriously wrong between them.

"I got a call from the day care to come and get Ellie. Jana… never showed up to get her."

Confusion knit Julia's brow. Why was Ellie at day care on a Saturday anyway? "Where is Jana? Is she working?"

"No." This time Mark's sigh hinted at frustration. "I don't know where she is. She left me a note. That's all."

"Oh, Mark. Are you sure? Maybe she's just trying to get your attention." Julia bit her lip as soon as the words were out. She hadn't meant to imply that Mark was to blame. But he did work long hours at the new restaurant he'd opened. It was a strain on a young couple, and Jana complained often enough to John that she sometimes felt like a single mom. But that was the way new businesses were, and Julia and John had both reminded Jana that once things were running smoothly she'd get her husband back.

Jana tended to be a bit of a drama queen, and Julia had never given her comments much weight. Especially since she knew all too much about what it actually felt like to be a single mom. Had it really been almost a decade since her beloved Martin died on that rain-slick street in Chicago?

She shot up a prayer for wisdom, regretting that she hadn't let John answer the phone. She was only the stepmother here—and an in-law at that. Hardly the person Mark would want to confide in. "What does Jana's note say? If you don't mind me asking. Did she give you any hint where she might have gone?"

"It just says she can't take it anymore…that—that she has to have some space." Sarcasm punctuated his words.

Julia forced a chipper note into her voice. "Oh, I'm sure she'll be back before you know it, Mark. She probably just needed to get away for a couple hours. You know she has a tendency to overreact sometimes. Raising a toddler can be a little overwhelming. Do you want us to come and get Ellie? We could keep her for the weekend? Give you two some time alone…" Julia slid the breakfast tray off her lap and eased her legs over the side of the bed. So much for a leisurely Saturday at home.

"You don't understand. This…this happened Thursday night."

It took a moment for Mark's words to process, for the seriousness of the situation to sink in. "What do you mean…? You haven't seen Jana since Thursday?" A frisson of alarm skittered up her spine. With an effort, she softened her tone. "Mark, you should have called."

"I thought…I just kept thinking she'd come home. She's left before…for a few hours. But this time, I'm not sure—" A muffled sob halted his words.

A lump rose in Julia's throat at the thought of her burly, six-foot-three son-in-law in tears.

She reached into the closet for her bathrobe and shrugged into it as she paced the length of the bedroom, trying to connect the dots in her mind. "I'm sorry, tell me again… You haven't seen Jana since Thursday? You haven't heard anything at all from her since then?"

"No. I've tried to call, but she's not answering her phone."

"Oh, Mark. What's going on?" She thought of Mark and Jana's precious little girl. "Is Ellie with you? How is she dealing with all this?"

"She's fine. She's asleep right now. But she's been crying for her mama. I don't know what to tell her. I'm worried, Julia. I— I'm afraid something's happened. We had a meeting with the shareholders Wednesday night. She was late and I—I let her have it about that. But she—she was acting really weird. I didn't think much of it. Until Thursday."

Julia tugged at the comforter with her free hand, going through the motions of making the bed, but making a lumpy mess of it instead. Her mind raced, exploring frightening possibilities. "I'm sure there's some explanation. She's probably just trying to get your attention." She hoped her words did more to encourage Mark than they did her. "I'll call John…the minute I hang up. He'll know what to do. Did you call the police?"

"I did, but they can't really do anything—because of the note."

Julia had watched enough *CSI* to know that was true. If Jana left of her own volition, the police were not going to get involved. "Do you want to come here, Mark? To Calypso?"

He sighed into the phone. "I'd better stay here…in case she comes home…or tries to call. I think she has her phone, but she— she didn't take her PDA or her laptop with her."

Julia's concern ratcheted up a level. Jana was rarely without a briefcase full of fancy electronic gadgets—the latest model PDA, the laptop Mark had bought for her, and Julia didn't know what all else. Jana was the one they all went to for technical help. Even Sam and Andy, Julia's sons, sought Jana's advice when they had a computer problem.

There was something Mark wasn't saying. Something that went far beyond anything they knew of John's daughter. She remembered a night a couple months ago when Mark and Jana had come over for dinner. Mark had been animated and attentive to Jana, but she'd seemed distant, and a little cool toward all of them. Julia never had quite won John's daughter over. After all, no one could ever take her mother's place. Julia had chalked it up to that. But now, she suspected it was something more.

"I'll call John," she said again. "We'll come and get Ellie if you want us to." She looked at the clock. "We could probably be there in a couple of hours."

"Julia? You need to know that Jana was…"

She waited, cringing at the anguish in his silence. But after a long minute, she started to think the line had gone dead. "Mark? Are you there?"

"I—I'm afraid she might do something…to hurt herself."

Chapter Three

John passed the stapled schedules around the boardroom table. Two of the coaches hadn't shown up, so they probably could have met in his office, but the guys—and Barb Garrison who coached boys' tennis—looked pretty relaxed in the cushy, high-back leather chairs.

Mitchell Bender regaled them with one of his famous blonde jokes and John chuckled along with them, even though he'd heard this particular tale before. Mitch could have read a grocery list and made it seem funny.

When the laughter died down, he glanced pointedly at the clock on the wall across the room. "Let's get started, shall we?"

While the group silently looked over the schedules, John's cell phone rang. He slipped it from his pocket and flipped it open. Julia. He checked the time again. She surely wasn't calling him home yet. Agitated, he excused himself and stole into the hall outside the boardroom. "Julia, I'm in the middle of things here. Can this wait?"

"John, you'd better come home. It's Jana."

"Jana?" He didn't like the tremor in Julia's voice.

"I just talked to Mark. She's left him."

He glanced over his shoulder toward the boardroom and lowered his voice. "What are you talking about?"

"She left a note saying she needed some space. She never picked Ellie up from day care Thursday and Mark thinks—"

"Thursday? She's been gone since Thursday?"

"That's what Mark said."

He cradled the phone on his shoulder and kneaded the space between his brows. "Where's Ellie? There's got to be some kind of mix-up. Jana wouldn't do that. She'd never leave Ellie. Where *is* Ellie?" he asked again.

"She's with Mark."

"Let me wrap up this meeting. I'll be home in a few minutes." He flipped the phone shut without saying goodbye.

Something was fishy. Jana would never just up and leave Mark, especially if it meant leaving Ellie. Besides, wouldn't she have talked to him if they were having problems? He *was* her father.

He dropped his phone into his pants pocket. Struggling to compose himself, he stepped back into the boardroom.

Somehow he managed to rush through the meeting, and twenty minutes later, he slipped out to the parking lot. He drove too fast, his mind concocting worst-case scenarios. When he pulled into their driveway, Julia was standing on the front porch waiting for him. He left the engine running, jumped out of the car and ran to her side.

"What is going on?"

Julia's crinkled forehead made her look older than her fifty-one years. "I'm not sure, but Mark's worried sick. The way he talked it sounds like he thinks she's practically…suicidal."

John stopped in his tracks. "You're not serious? Jana?"

"Mark said he was afraid she might 'do something to hurt herself.' That's how he put it."

John harrumphed. Mark had bit off more than he could chew with the new restaurant, but surely his son-in-law wasn't so out of touch that he actually thought Jana would harm herself. Jana might be a little moody now and then, but his daughter was not suicidal. He went around the car. "Would you mind driving? I want to call Jana…try to get to the bottom of this."

Julia came down the steps toward him. "Mark doesn't know where she is and he said she's not answering her phone."

He shook his head. "That can't be right. Jana's never without her phone."

"Mark said she's not answering his calls. He thinks she has her phone with her—at least it's missing. But she didn't take any of her other electronic stuff with her."

Julia's expression frightened him. This wasn't making any sense at all. "We need to talk to him. Are you ready to go?"

She shrugged and looked down at her khaki slacks and tailored blouse. "I'm ready. Unless you think we need to pack for overnight. Are you thinking we'll bring Ellie back with us? I offered…"

He scratched his head, still trying to fathom how Jana could have just up and left her family. "I don't know…" It was a good hour-and-a-half round trip between Calypso and Mark and Jana's house. And Ellie wasn't the best traveler.

"I think that would be the best way we can help Mark."

She waited, but John sensed her impatience.

"What do you want to do, John?"

He tensed his jaw. "I want to talk to Mark. That's what I want to do."

"John… Don't be too hard on him. This has got to be killing him and it—"

"You don't think it's killing *me?*" His words boomed like an explosion.

Julia flinched as if he'd raised his hand to her.

"I'm sorry." Instantly regretting his words, he closed the gap between them and reached for her. "I'm sorry, Julia. I didn't mean to take it out on you."

She received his embrace, but she was stiff and silent in his arms.

"I'm sorry your weekend is ruined," he said.

She pulled away. "John. Stop. That doesn't matter. Not now. The kids need us."

His heart swelled. She hadn't said "*your* kids." One more reason he loved this beautiful woman. He felt terrible for shouting at her. Why did he do that? He pulled her close again. "Let me take my briefcase in. We'll talk on the way."

* * *

"Grandpa, where's my mommy?"

With a catch in her throat, Julia watched John's expression. Ellie sat on his lap, her pudgy hands on either side of her grandpa's face.

He brushed a curl back from Ellie's forehead and cast an imploring look at Mark.

"Ellie." Mark came to John's rescue. "Why don't you show Grandpa the awesome drawing you did at day care yesterday."

"It's a *painting,* Daddy. Wanna see, Grandpa?"

Julia breathed an inward sigh of relief that the diversionary tactic worked.

"You bet I do." John lifted her gently from his lap. "Run and get it."

The little girl padded down the hallway, and John turned to Mark, barely concealing the edge of hostility in his voice. "What have you told her?"

Mark dropped his head briefly before meeting John's eyes. "I told her Jana's on a trip." He shrugged and held out his hands. "I didn't know what else to say."

Julia got up and came to stand behind the overstuffed chair where John sat. She placed her hands on his shoulders, hoping her touch could somehow calm his rising ire.

She turned to Mark. "That's what we'll say then…until we know something more."

"Where have you looked?" John's voice remained tight.

Mark shrugged again. "Everywhere I can think of. I've called all her friends, her boss at work, the day care—"

"What did they say?" John may as well have pounced on Mark, his words held such force.

"She called in sick at work on Thursday morning, but she took Ellie to day care at the usual time. No one seems to have seen her since then, and no one—not her coworkers or anybody at the day care—seemed to have any idea she planned on going away. I checked her cell phone records and she hasn't used her phone since that day. There wasn't anything unusual on there that I could see."

"What about Ellie's day care? Surely Jana made arrangements—"

Mark wagged his head. "No. She didn't put in for vacation, didn't arrange for Ellie to be gone." He shrugged. "I didn't know until late Thursday night that she hadn't even shown up for work that day. That's when the day care finally got hold of me. They said Jana told them *I'd* be picking Ellie up." He shook his head again. "She never said anything to me."

"Are you sure? Maybe she told you and you were distracted. Maybe—"

"I'm sure, John." Mark glared at John, his nostrils flaring.

John glared back. "None of this seems odd to you? That nobody has a clue where your wife could have gone? There has to be something you're not thinking of. I think we need to get the police involved." John's voice shook.

Julia squeezed his shoulder. She'd already explained to him what Mark had said about the police.

"I did contact the police." Mark combed his fingers through his hair. "I went in again last night to talk to them. And to show them Jana's note. Apparently that pretty much guaranteed they wouldn't get involved except to put her on a list."

"What do you mean?" John was still in combat mode.

"They said since I had a letter from her, obviously in her handwriting and obviously not written under duress, the only thing they could do is put her on a BOLO list."

"What's that?"

"It stands for 'be on the lookout.' Even then, they wouldn't be actively searching for her. All it means is if she gets stopped for a traffic violation or something, they have her name and they can let us know she's okay. The officer called it 'check welfare' or something like that. But unless she gave permission, they still couldn't tell us where she was."

"That's ridiculous! She's your wife!" John pounded a fist into his palm. "What about your car? What was she driving? Couldn't they put out a search for your vehicle?"

"I thought of that. But the Escape is registered in both of our names. The officer I spoke with said technically Jana has as much right to drive it as I do. I could file a missing persons report, but with the letter…unless we suspected foul play…" He shrugged.

"How do we know there *wasn't* foul play?" John's tone was accusing. "This is just not like Jana. Maybe we need to hire someone—a private investigator or…something. You can't just do *nothing!*"

Julia patted his back as if attempting to calm an angry child. Couldn't he see Mark was distraught? It wouldn't accomplish anything to make him defensive. And besides, she *had* seen the restlessness in Jana of late. She hadn't given it much credence until now, but things were adding up in ways she hadn't foreseen.

She lowered her voice. "Mark, would you mind if we read Jana's note? I don't mean to pry, but maybe we'll see something you missed. Maybe there's something there that might give us a clue where she could have gone."

"Sure. I'll get it."

Mark disappeared down the hallway just as Ellie burst back into the room, flapping a sheet of bright yellow construction paper. The paper was cockled from the heavy watercolors. "I got it, Grandpa." She turned to Julia "Wanna see my picture, Go-Go?"

Julia smiled at the little girl's nickname for her. Ellie had just started to talk when John and Julia got married. The little girl's first attempts at "Grandma Julia" had come out sounding like Grandma Go-Go. The name stuck, and eventually got shortened to simply "Go-Go." It warmed Julia's heart each time she heard the endearment.

She was "only" a stepgrandparent to John's grandkids, but she'd always felt like a full-fledged grandmother to Ellie. Probably because they lived closer to Ellie than to Brant's or Kyle's kids. And since Mark's parents weren't living, she also had the distinction of being Ellie's only grandmother.

Ellie held the painting out to her like an offering.

"Oooh, this is beautiful, sweetie. Pretty colors." Julia could discern three figures in the painting, presumably Ellie's family, beside a box that resembled a house. She pointed to a blob of brown paint beside the house. "And is this a doghouse?"

Ellie put her hands on her hips and gave Julia a look that said "silly Go-Go." "That's the *baby's* house."

"Oh? What baby?"

"The baby that Mommy and Daddy's gonna get."

John looked up at her over his shoulder and they exchanged raised eyebrows. Was there something they didn't know?

Mark returned just then, a folded note in hand. "Is she telling you about the baby's house?"

"Yes…" Julia let her voice trail off, waiting for Mark to explain.

Mark squatted on his haunches and spoke to his daughter. "Remember, Ellie, we don't know if we'll get a baby."

"I know, I know… We're *prayin'* to God for a baby someday." Ellie recited the obviously rehearsed—or coached—answer, then turned to Julia. "But I told God I wanted a baby brother tomorrow."

John laughed, the muscles in his jaw noticeably relaxing. He ruffled Ellie's curls. "I think you'd better give God a little more time than that, punkin. Babies take time. Lots of time."

Mark lifted the little girl into the air and blew raspberries on her tummy. The giggles that followed were pure music.

Watching them, Julia wondered how Jana could just walk away from her child? There had to be something more to all this than they were seeing.

Mark set Ellie down and patted her back. "You run and play in your room for a little while, okay? I need to talk to Grandpa and Go-Go for a little bit."

"About Mommy?" Ellie's blue eyes studied Mark's face for a moment, then darted to John's. When her gaze bored into Julia's eyes a second later, Ellie's expression seemed to hold a knowledge no three-year-old should have to carry.

Mark ignored his daughter's question, and handed John the note, before herding Ellie back down the hall to her bedroom.

Chapter Four

Jana's note was written on letterhead from the museum where she worked. It was folded once, and from the limp paper and the sharp crease down the middle, Julia imagined Mark had handled it many times. Or perhaps it was Jana who had pressed the crease shiny, trying to decide whether or not to go through with her plans. What could she have been thinking?

John unfolded the worn sheet of paper. Julia came to perch on the arm of the chair beside him, reading over his shoulder.

> Mark,
>
> I'm sorry, but I need to get away for a while. I can't keep on the way things have been. I have to sort things out. I don't know when I'll be back, so please don't try to find me. Tell Ellie I love her, but Mommy has to go away for a while. Everything is all mixed-up and I just need some time. I know you'll do the right thing, Mark, but right now, it's just best that I go away.
> Jana

Julia scanned the note again and turned to see if John had the same reaction to its terse lack of emotion.

The pain in his eyes and the deep lines marring his forehead told her the note spawned more questions than it answered for him, too. He shook his head. "It doesn't even sound like she wrote it."

She looked at him askance. "But that's Jana's handwriting."

He turned the letter over, folded and unfolded it, inspecting it as if he might discover some secret code to explain everything. "I don't know. I guess I never paid much attention to her penmanship."

Mark's voice came from down the hallway. "It's definitely her handwriting."

"Well if it is, she doesn't sound like herself." John shook the letter at him, causing the paper to crackle.

Mark held his ground. "It *does* sound like her, John. At least lately. She's been stressed out about work, about Ellie, the restaurant…everything. Look at this place—" He held his hands out, encompassing the room where they sat.

The apartment where Mark and Jana had lived until Ellie was born had always been tidy and charmingly decorated. In this place—what a Realtor would have called a "nice starter home"— the few pictures scattered haphazardly about the walls and a silk flower arrangement on the coffee table were the extent of the decor. There were stacks of newspapers, magazines and unopened junk mail scattered about the room, and Ellie's toys littered the carpet.

"We've been here three years," Mark said. "and we still have boxes to unpack downstairs. I know she's got her hands full with Ellie and with work, but it's like she doesn't even care anymore. And lately she's been on this kick—" He glanced at Julia, something like apology in his expression. "Jana is convinced that she has Alzheimer's disease—that she's in the early stages of—"

"Oh, good grief!" John came out of his seat. "That's baloney!"

"I know…" Mark nodded.

"Why in the world would she think that?" Julia asked.

John started pacing the length of the small living room. "It's ridiculous! She's thirty—?" He looked to Mark to fill in the blank.

"She's thirty-four."

"Right…of course. Thirty-four. Ellen was in her late forties before there were any symptoms at all. Why would Jana think such a crazy thing?"

Mark shook his head. "It's just little things. She forgot a couple of appointments, sometimes she forgets to give Ellie her vitamins, stuff like that. Nothing that should be a big deal."

"Well, of course not," Julia said. "What parent of a three-year-old isn't a little out to lunch sometimes?"

"That's exactly right." John stopped and glared pointedly at Mark. "Especially when she has full responsibility for Ellie the majority of the time. Did you ever think of that?"

Mark's voice rose in defense. "I've tried to get her to go to the doctor…get it checked out if she truly thinks she has a problem."

"And?" Julia was starting to understand what might have prompted John's daughter to go off the deep end. She knew if one of her parents had suffered from the dreadful disease, it would have been difficult not to dwell on the fact that Alzheimer's appeared to be hereditary, especially the early-onset type Ellen had suffered from. Died from.

"She wouldn't go to the doctor. She refused." Mark glanced at John. "Said she didn't want to know, that once her mom knew what she had, it was all downhill."

John stood in front of the sagging drapes and raked a hand through his hair. "That's only because by the time Ellen was diagnosed, she'd had the disease for months, years maybe."

Julia hadn't noticed how much the gray had taken over her husband's thick head of hair. Ordinarily the frosting of gray made him look distinguished. Today, it only made him look old. She touched his arm, trying again to calm him. "We need to find Jana. Somehow we've got to convince her to go to the doctor."

"Mark, you haven't noticed any symptoms have you?" John's eyes held fear.

Mark shook his head. "Nothing that would make me think Alzheimer's. But she *hasn't* been herself. Not for quite a while now. She's been under a lot of pressure at work, but I wonder if maybe she's in a depression, too. You know—clinically depressed. She went through something similar a few years ago. But it didn't last long. It just kind of went away finally."

Julia glanced down the hallway, making sure Ellie wasn't in

hearing distance. "You said on the phone that you were afraid Jana might do something to hurt herself. Do you think she's suicidal?"

"I don't know. I…I was probably overreacting."

The creases in John's forehead deepened. "Are you sure? That's not something to mess around with. Has she ever made threats? Has she talked about how she might…accomplish that?"

"No. No, nothing like that. She's just…she's been different lately, that's all. She seems so sad all the time. Sad or mad. Or stressed out."

"Has this all been since you opened the restaurant?" John's voice was even, but Julia sensed the accusation behind his words.

Judging from Mark's expression, he didn't miss it, either. "We've both been busy, John. Between Jana's job and the restaurant and Ellie, it's been crazy. I admit it. But no more than a lot of our friends' lives. And they're not run—" He held up a hand and shook his head.

John's lips firmed into a tight line, but after a minute he reached to put a hand on Mark's arm. "That wasn't fair. Let's just concentrate on finding her. That's all that matters right now."

Julia turned to Mark, and voiced what no one had mentioned yet. "Is there any chance Jana is…with someone else?"

Mark's eyes widened. "You mean that she's having an affair? I'm absolutely positive she isn't. For starters, she wouldn't have time. Every minute she isn't working, she's taking care of Ellie." He hung his head, as though accepting the burden for that. Or maybe considering the possibility Julia had raised?

"But what about at work?" Julia tried to make her words gentle. "Is there anyone there she might have been involved with?" She hated to worry Mark over a possibility he obviously hadn't entertained, but she knew—she and John *both* knew— how easily such a friendship could form, even when neither party intended for it to go beyond friendship. She felt a twinge of guilt, but she brushed it off as if it were lint on a sweater, and willed her mind elsewhere. There was no reason to dwell on that. God had redeemed the mistakes of their past and blessed her and John's love more than she could have imagined.

John's voice broke through her thoughts. "What about the boys? We should call Brant and Kyle. Maybe she went to one of her brothers'." His voice was bright, as if he'd just hit on the solution.

But Mark frowned. "I called them already. Just after I talked to Julia this morning. Neither of them have heard from her."

John's sons lived with their families in Indiana. It seemed unlikely to Julia that Jana would have gone there.

"She wouldn't call Sam or Andy, would she?" John asked.

"I don't think so." John's children and her two sons had been grown by the time she and John married. While their kids got along fine, they had never been particularly close. "Still, we should call them anyway. They'll want to know."

"Who else? Who else could we call?" John vaulted to his feet and stomped across the room, then came back and collapsed beside Julia with a sigh. "What about her friends at church?"

Mark looked at the floor. "She…we've kind of lost touch with a lot of them. It's been hard. I have to work most Sundays and it's just not worth the hassle for Jana to try to get Ellie ready—"

"Well, who else could she be with?"

Mark sank into a chair across from the sofa. "Jana had a few friends at work—women she had lunch with sometimes, that sort of thing. I called the office and talked to a couple of Jana's co-workers yesterday. Laura Abriano was out of town, but they gave me her cell phone number. She and Jana had lunch together on Wednesday—the last day Jana worked."

John sat forward. "Did Jana tell this Laura anything? Did she have any idea what might have been bothering Jana?"

Mark shook his head. "Laura didn't know anything. She didn't think Jana seemed upset that day. Apparently Jana ran into a friend there at the restaurant. Laura said Jana seemed pleased to see the woman and they talked for a while. She thought Jana was a little preoccupied after that, but nothing that made her think anything was out of the ordinary."

"Maybe we should talk to this Laura again." Hope brightened John's voice. "Maybe she's thought of something since you talked to her."

Mark worked his tongue along the inside of his cheek. "I don't know if Jana confided much in any of her friends. She's a pretty private person. I really think Laura would have called me if she thought of anything else."

John gave Julia a searching glance, and she knew he wanted her to take up his cause. She looked away. She didn't blame John for being defensive of Jana, and it was only natural that he was worried sick about his daughter. She was worried, too. But she wasn't going to interrogate Mark as if Jana's disappearance were all his fault.

She scrambled to think of something that would calm John down. Ellie. She should be everyone's first concern anyway. She looked up at Mark. "Do you have a bag packed for Ellie?" Without waiting for an answer, she turned to put a hand on John's forearm. "We probably ought to get on the road. It's going to be a long day for her."

"I'll go get her things together." Mark hurried down the hall, calling Ellie's name.

Julia patted John's cheek, love and concern for her husband welling within her. "Let's get Ellie home and try to keep things as normal as possible for her."

John eyed the hallway and lowered his voice. "You don't really think Jana could be having an affair, do you?"

"I don't know. I believe Mark—at least that he doesn't think Jana was involved with someone else."

"I'll admit, I was angry when you first suggested that possibility, but now I don't know what to think." He pressed two fingers to his temple. "I never in a million years thought Jana would leave Ellie. Do you think Mark is being up-front with us?"

"Of course! He's just as scared as you are, John. I'm not saying he hasn't made some mistakes where Jana is concerned, but I think he only wants the best for her."

John sighed, and she tucked her hand in his, trying to squeeze some reassurance into him. "I have a feeling she's just over-whelmed. Let's give her a little time to sort things out. I remember feeling that way once in a while…overwhelmed and like I desperately needed some time away."

He studied her. "But you never would have left your boys like this."

With one sentence, he dismantled the meager defense she'd built for Jana. "No," she admitted, "I don't think I could have ever done that."

Chapter Five

Mark stood in the doorway and watched the Explorer creep down the street. He could see Ellie's head of curls bobbing in her car seat in the back. Julia sat angled in the passenger seat, talking animatedly to Ellie in the seat behind her.

He watched until the SUV disappeared around the curve of the subdivision street, then closed the door and leaned his head against the warm wood. Ellie was in good hands. John and Julia were both wonderful with her, and she'd gone with them happily. He knew it was best for Ellie to be with them now, but when Julia had asked him to write out a note of medical release before they left—in case anything happened to Ellie while she was in their care—it had nearly undone him. He'd felt as though he was signing her over for adoption. Of course, working at the nursing center, Julia would naturally think of the release. It was a wise precaution.

In his heart, he knew Ellie would be safe and happy with John and Julia. Still, it hurt to let her go, especially right now with everything so messed up.

He locked the door and walked through the house, gathering up Ellie's little shoes and the trail of toys she'd strewn through the house. It was too quiet. The kitchen clock counted off the seconds like an executioner's drum.

He didn't know where to begin. Jana was gone. He didn't know how long it would be before he'd see her again. And what frightened him most was that he'd somehow grown so out of touch with the wife he'd once loved more than life itself, that he couldn't think of one place where she might have gone. Or whom she might have gone with.

Julia had suggested Jana might be having an affair. The thought had never crossed his mind. But was it possible? He didn't know. And maybe that was the crux of the problem. *He didn't know Jana anymore.*

Down the hall at the doorway to Ellie's bedroom, he tossed her toys into a wicker basket at the end of her bed. He went to her closet and placed the tiny sandals on the floor beside a whole row of little girl shoes. Ellie came by her love for shoes genetically. His own closet had a similar row of Jana-sized shoes—a row that was always edging over into his side of the narrow closet.

He'd searched Jana's closet and dresser, trying to discover if she'd packed for a few days or a few months. There were empty spots in her drawers where she'd obviously taken clothes out, but he couldn't have named one specific item she'd taken with her. He assumed she had her cell phone with her, since it wasn't in the charger on the nightstand. But she wasn't answering his repeated calls and text messages. Her laptop, PDA and the new iPod she was so proud of were all neatly tucked in her briefcase as if she'd just packed for work. It worried him that she hadn't taken them with her.

They'd grown apart. He hadn't wanted to admit it until now. There'd barely been time even to concede the fact. But it was true. He saw it now. Their schedules were different; they rarely had a conversation that didn't involve Ellie or work. They hadn't been on a date in he didn't know how long.

He scooped up a handful of dirty clothes from Ellie's floor, carried them down the hall and stuffed them in the overflowing hamper in the master bath.

A new wave of hopelessness rolled over him as he entered their bedroom. Their king-size bed almost filled the small room.

Until the past year, they'd met often in the middle of the expansive mattress, making love, snuggling together long afterward. Even when they finally rolled over to sleep, they would reach across the divide and find each other's hands, happy just to be joined by their fingertips.

But it had been a long time since he and Jana had even gone to bed at the same time. His hours at the restaurant were grueling and Jana was almost always asleep by the time he got home.

They'd both known when he opened the restaurant that it would be rough at first. But Jana had been his biggest cheerleader, encouraging him to follow his dream. Even though it meant sacrificing the financial security that had been just within their grasp.

But somewhere along the way something had changed. She'd started obsessing about her mother's death and hinting that she would meet the same fate. She'd seemed overwhelmed with caring for Ellie. Even though Ellie was in day care all day. It wasn't as if she was working overtime to keep the house immaculate. And he brought home food from the restaurant almost every night so it wasn't as if she had to cook very often, either. He didn't know what else he could have done to take the pressure off.

He and Jana weren't the only ones who'd made sacrifices to turn McFarlane's into a reality. He had his investors to think of—five men from their church. Successful men who believed in Mark and entrusted him with their money—life savings in a couple of cases.

Jana's father had helped him out with the start-up costs, too. John hadn't invested nearly as heavily as the others, but still, it was no small sum.

He was grateful to all of them. He'd been so incredibly pumped to see his dream finally coming true before his eyes. And so relieved to be free of the boring, mind-numbing engineering job he'd been stuck in for most of their marriage.

He was indebted for Jana's support. "I'll make it up to you. I promise," he told her the night they went to dinner at Kiki's to celebrate the approval of the loans. She'd looked so beautiful in the candlelight. He couldn't remember ever loving her more.

Now, he slumped onto the unmade bed and dropped his head in his hands. What a terrible difference a year made.

"God, I don't know what to do!" On a whim, he reached for the phone on the nightstand and dialed Jana's cell phone. It rang four times, then clicked over to voice mail. Her recorded message—in her formal, professional tone—only deepened his pain. He'd left umpteen messages there already and text messaged her several times. He didn't know how many messages their service would allow, but he wouldn't stop trying till it shut him down.

He waited for the tone. "Jana. It's me. Please call me. I love you. I miss you, Jana. Please…" Eyes burning with unshed tears, he clicked off and replaced the phone in its cradle. Almost immediately it rang. He picked it up. "Hello?"

"Mark?"

"Jana!" He straightened at the sound of her voice—her actual voice. The phone on the nightstand was a cheap corded phone without Caller ID. He would have run to the kitchen to check the LCD screen for a number if he hadn't been afraid she'd hang up.

"Jana? Where are you?" In the background a car's engine and the familiar noises of the road droned. She must be on her cell phone. "Are you okay?"

"Is Ellie all right?" Jana spoke in a monotone.

"No, she's not all right!" He gripped the phone, wrapping the cord so tight around his palm that his hand hurt. "She needs her mother. Where are you, Jana?"

"Listen to me, Mark. I need to know Ellie is okay. Is she there? Please let me talk to her."

"She's not here."

"What?"

"She's on her way to Calypso."

"She's staying with Dad and Julia?"

"Yes. Listen, Jana, I—"

"Good. Good…she's always happy there."

As if she wouldn't be happy with her own father? "Where are you, Jana? Why are you doing this?"

"Mark, I'm sorry. But I need to get away. Please just let me go. Don't come looking for me. Ellie will be fine. I just can't do this anymore. I can't."

"Can't do what? Jana, please!" The desperation in his own voice was a counterpoint to the lethargy in hers. "Let's talk about it. Jana? Tell me where you are. We can figure this out together. We can get help. I'll do whatever you want me to. Anything. We can go to counseling. I…I didn't realize you were so unhappy. I didn't know."

"I'm hanging up now, Mark."

"Wait!" He felt powerless to reason with her. "Just tell me when you'll be back. What am I supposed to tell Ellie?"

"I don't know…" There was a long pause, then Jana's voice came back, hollow, empty. "Tell her I'm dead."

The dial tone buzzed in his ear.

Chapter Six

"Careful, Ellie. Sit down before you spill your mi—" The word died on Julia's lips as milk splashed in seeming slow motion over the lace tablecloth, onto the seat cushions Julia's grandmother had stitched, then down the polished maple table leg and into the plush carpeting. Julia bit the inside of her cheek, stemming the angry words that balanced on the end of her tongue.

"I'm sorry, Go-Go. I'm sorry… It was a accident."

She rumpled Ellie's curls. "I know it was, sweetie. But you need to sit down when you're eating. If you don't, things can get spilled." She gathered the delicate tablecloth into a soggy bunch and moved Ellie's dinner plate onto the tabletop. "John!" She hollered toward the kitchen. "John, can you come help me for a minute?"

He appeared in the doorway, smiling, two bowls of ice cream in hand. "Anybody ready for ice cream?" He stopped short when he saw Julia dismantling the table. "What happened?"

"We had a little spill. It was an accident." She threw John a look. "Can you help me here? Bring me a damp dishrag and a roll of paper towels."

He set the bowls on a dry edge of the table and jogged back to the kitchen.

Julia tried in vain to corral the river of milk. It had been a long day after an even longer night. Ellie hadn't gone to sleep until after ten last night and Julia had spent most of the morning in the church nursery trying to convince Ellie that she'd be fine with Miss Emma and the other children. To top it off, apparently the small Coke they'd let Ellie order at McDonald's for lunch contained enough caffeine to forestall her afternoon nap. Well, she had no one but herself to blame for that. She'd raised two children to adulthood. Had she forgotten everything she'd ever known?

John's voice wafted from the kitchen. "Where did you say the paper towels were?"

"They're under the sink."

"I'm not seeing them."

It sounded as though he had his head stuffed under the cabinet. Julia gave a frazzled sigh. "Stay put, Ellie. I'll be right back." She stamped into the kitchen.

John was bent over the open cabinets, peering inside. Julia bumped him aside, reached in and instantly came up with a full roll of paper toweling.

"Oh. I must have been looking right at it."

She measured her words, willing her temper to behave. "Could you bring a damp rag, please? You do know where the water is, don't you?" Without waiting for an answer, she raced back to the dining room. She dropped to her hands and knees and swabbed at the liquid seeping into the carpet.

She looked up to see Ellie standing in the chair looking down at her.

"Ellie!" She spoke through gritted teeth. "Sit down right now. That's how this happened in the first place. Now sit down!"

"Julia." John spoke her name softly. "It was an accident."

That was the last straw. John had indulged the little girl all through dinner, and then he'd started playing silly games that were not conducive to good table manners. It was no wonder the meal had ended in disaster. They'd be lucky if the house didn't reek of sour milk until Christmas.

She struggled to her feet. Not meeting his eyes, she threw the sodden wad on the milk-streaked tabletop. "I'll let you finish up here." She took Ellie into her arms. "Come on, little one. Let's get you ready for bed."

"It's not dark! It's not dark outside, Go-Go." Ellie started kicking at Julia's legs.

"Yes, but it soon will be, and you've had a long day."

Ellie quit kicking, but her lower lip jutted out and she stiffened in Julia's arms. Julia felt a twinge of guilt putting her to bed at seven o'clock. Especially when she knew Mark and Jana let her stay up until well after dark. But it *had* been a long day and Julia was seriously considering going to bed early herself.

She heard John running the vacuum in the dining room and her irritation subsided a little. She had to hand it to the man. He had a good grasp on the concept of extra credit.

"Do you want a bubble bath or a rainbow bath tonight?"

Ellie's pout curved into a smile. She arched her body away from Julia, a spark of mischief in her eyes. "Can I have bofe of 'em?"

"Bubbles and colored water?"

Ellie's chin bobbed in an exaggerated nod.

"That's a lovely idea!" Julia said, choosing to join Ellie in her much-improved mood. "What color do we want tonight?"

"Green!"

"Green? Green water?"

"Wait… I know, Go-Go. Can we mix green and yellow together and make some lime-green water?"

"Ooh, that sounds bee-u-tiful. We'll try it."

"You puts two squirps of yellow and one squirp of green. That's for *lime* green."

Julia looked at her, surprised at her precociousness. "Now how did you know that?"

"Mommy teached me how."

"She did, did she? Well, you've got a smart mommy." She cringed, hoping her comment didn't bring on the "where's mommy?" questions. "You run put your clothes in the hamper," she said quickly. "I'll go get the food coloring and be right back."

The vacuum was silent and when Julia got to the kitchen, she found John at the sink, ringing milky water out of several rags.

He glanced at her over his shoulder. "Everything under control? You need help in there?"

She was hit with a wave of guilt. She knew exactly what was going through her husband's mind, thanks to her little tantrum earlier. He was feeling guilty because she'd had to take on the burden of *his* granddaughter. She would have felt the same way if Ellie were Sam's or Andy's child.

She came up behind him and wrapped her arms around his waist. "Thanks for cleaning everything up. I'm sorry I lost my temper, John. I was the one acting like a three-year-old. Will you forgive me?"

He turned and pulled her to him. "Already have. And I'm sorry I got her all wound up. I'm probably the one who deserves a spanking."

"There will be no spankings tonight. But you *are* invited to a rainbow bubble bath down the hall." She extricated herself from his embrace and rummaged in the cupboard behind him for the food coloring. "Party starts in five minutes. Be there or be square."

He laughed. "You *do* act like a three-year-old sometimes, you know."

She mimicked Ellie's pouty face but she could only hold it for a second before a smile broke through. "Maybe we can have our own party later. Just the two of us." She did that wiggly eyebrow thing he called "the look."

He did it right back. "Mmm…I'm liking the sound of this."

He tried to pull her into his arms again, but she laughed and tagged her sweet husband, then took off at a jog down the hallway. "Last one in's a rotten egg."

Chapter Seven

The rocky road narrowed and Jana slowed and shifted the SUV into second gear. Daylight was fast waning and she wasn't sure she'd recognize the place after dark. Slowing down, she bent over the steering wheel and peered out through the tinted windshield.

A rustic sign jutted out from the woods ahead and she turned the wheel to shine the headlights on the edge of the road. She was on the right road. Of that much, she was certain. But nothing looked the same. Of course it had been spring when they'd been here before. She didn't miss the irony of it—running away from her husband to the place where they'd spent their honeymoon.

She didn't dare think too long about what she'd do if someone was already staying at the cabin. A new thought hit her. It had been thirteen years since their honeymoon. What if the place wasn't even there anymore? Or what if it had changed owners? She brushed the thought away, but it was quickly replaced by a more disturbing one.

What if she'd dreamed up the whole thing? She'd done that lately. Been absolutely certain that she'd mailed a bill or canceled an appointment—had a vivid memory of performing the task—only to discover later that she'd done no such thing. What if she'd dreamed up the cabin? What if they'd spent their honeymoon in the Bahamas or Cancún, and her damaged brain had somehow invented a cabin in Colorado. But…

No. Until they moved out of their apartment after Ellie was born, they'd gotten an invitation from the owners each year—a discount rate for returning guests. They talked about going back every time that little flier with the photographs and the map arrived in the mailbox. She remembered that.

And she had vivid memories of shopping in Denver just a few miles up I-25. They had souvenirs proving they'd been here. The salt and pepper shakers with the columbine motif that now sat on the table in the breakfast nook. The coffee cups from Le Central in downtown Denver. Mark had begged their waiter to let them buy a set of cups and saucers when Jana fell in love with the restaurant's dishes. She wasn't dreaming that.

A flash in the headlights' beam brought her back. Beside the road on the left, the lights illumined a ramshackle shed that was guarded by an eight-foot-tall carved black bear holding a sign that said Gone Fishin'. She could have cheered.

She and Mark had used that wooden bear as a landmark for their turnoff. It would be just ahead now. She slowed the car and spotted the sign, letters burned into the wood. She could barely make out the words, but it looked like Atlas Springs. That didn't sound right. She pulled over on the shoulder in front of the sign. *Alta* Springs Road. Yes, that was it. She remembered. Relief flooded through her. She was almost there.

She turned left, onto a trail barely wide enough for the car. She rolled her window down and folded the rearview mirror snug against the side of the vehicle. The tires rumbled across a rickety bridge. It was all coming back now. This was right. This was the place. She hadn't dreamed it up.

She crept forward, and a minute later, the outline of the steeply pitched roof came into view. The Escape labored to climb the trail, the engine kicking into overdrive. She glanced at the 4WD knob on the dashboard. Did simply turning the knob kick the SUV into four-wheel drive? She recalled Mark telling her about it when they'd first bought it, but she hadn't thought she'd need to know until winter, so she hadn't paid attention. Her brain barely had room to remember what day of the week it was. She couldn't waste precious cells storing useless data. Now, she hoped she wouldn't regret it.

The A-frame sat high on the mountainside, looming against the darkening sky. Jana expelled a jagged sigh. The sliding security doors—what looked like old barn doors—were bolted across the front door. That meant the cabin was empty. She'd have a place to sleep tonight.

After dropping Ellie off at day care, she'd hidden out at Laura Abriano's apartment, knowing her coworker was in Minneapolis on business until Sunday night and Laura's daughter was staying with her ex-husband. Jana knew where the keys to Laura's apartment were hidden from when she'd watered the Abrianos' flowers while they were on vacation last summer. But she'd slept on the sofa in their living room, not daring even to unfold the afghan on the back, or use the shower, for fear once the news got out that she was missing, Laura would suspect she'd been there and call Mark.

She looked down at the rumpled khakis and sweatshirt she'd lived in for two days now. Touching a hand to her head, she cringed. Her hair felt like it belonged to a mangy dog. She'd tried to pull it into a ponytail at Laura's, but the chic layered cut she'd paid so much for a few weeks ago at Roque Salon wasn't long enough to stay in the rubber band. She'd have to buy some supplies soon.

She'd cashed her paycheck Thursday and used her credit card to fill the tank up with gas and stock up on snacks and supplies at Wal-Mart. Mark wouldn't get around to checking the credit card for a day or two, but she determined not to use it once she was on the road. She didn't want him knowing even what direction she'd gone.

She'd tossed and turned on Laura's sofa, her brain overloaded and in chaos. She had enough trouble processing ordinary thoughts lately, but the thoughts that assailed her that night left her in turmoil. She was losing her faculties for rational thought, but cruelly, she could not forget the near accident with Ellie. Every time it flashed through her memory, the knot in her stomach twisted tighter.

Ellie wasn't safe with her anymore. The knowledge killed her. But she knew now that if she didn't take care of matters, she would end up like Mom. And if she waited too long, she wouldn't even have the presence of mind to take things into her own hands. She could not let it go that far. *Poor Mom.*

She'd left Laura's in the middle of the night and started driving. She drove for fourteen hours, not having a clue where she was headed, stopping only for gas and caffeine to stay awake. Somewhere in western Iowa, she'd hatched this plan to come to Colorado. To the cabin.

She'd eaten up her limited funds paying cash for gas along the way. A thousand miles she'd put on the Escape. But she was here now, and she still had enough to live on for a while. If her courage didn't betray her, it would be enough.

Leaving the engine running, she climbed out of the car, then reached back in to flick the headlights on high-beam. They cast an eerie light on the cabin. In the distance, the river roared. She'd heard a clerk at the last gas station say the river was running higher than usual for September. The air was brisk, and so clean it almost hurt to breathe it in.

If she could get a fire going, she could heat enough water to wash up. She'd figure out the generator and hot water heater tomorrow.

She tipped her head and gazed into the night sky. Giant firs bowed in the mountain breeze. She stood transfixed, watching the last breath of light fade before her eyes. The star-crusted sky—nonexistent in the city—had been utterly romantic when Mark was here with her. Now, it was just plain spooky.

She took a deep breath and eyed the SUV, where her cell phone was tucked in a side pocket of her purse. She staved off the sudden urge to call Mark again. She couldn't do that. Wouldn't. There wasn't anything he could change.

He'd called her ten times since Thursday, and left as many messages. She wouldn't let herself listen to any of them. She'd finally turned the phone off somewhere in Nebraska. She wasn't sure why she'd even brought it with her, but somehow she couldn't make herself unplug it from the car charger, either.

Shivering in the chill of twilight, she clambered up the flight of steep, wide steps to the cabin's deck. She ran cold-numbed fingertips along the top of the door frame. A heavy key clunked to the wood floor, followed by a smaller chain with several keys attached. They bounced several times, flashing in the beam of the headlights. The larger key spun and tottered over a wide gap in the floorboards.

Gasping, she went down on all fours, scrabbling for the keys. She came up with them, and stole a look over her shoulder toward the road. Empty. She had no reason to be nervous. If anyone questioned her presence here, she knew exactly what to say. "Ron and Edie told me to let myself in." She was familiar enough with the place from their brief stay to be convincing.

Still, her hands shook as she unlocked the heavy padlock. She manhandled the bulky timber doors that served as a security gate, sliding them away to reveal the cabin's front door and to the right, a bank of glass set to frame a picturesque view of the mountains.

One of the smaller keys turned easily in the door and she let herself in. The air was stale and musty with dust and old pine ashes. The headlights from the Escape painted patchy shadows on the walls. She fumbled for a light switch, but wasn't surprised when it failed to trip. They'd had to run a generator much of the time they stayed here before.

They'd felt like such adventurers, she and Mark. They'd been proud when they figured out how to build a proper fire in the massive stone fireplace that took up the whole west wall of the A-frame. They'd managed to cook eggs and sausage over the smoldering embers the next morning.

Tonight it didn't feel like such an adventure. She found a flashlight on the top of the bookcase by the door and flicked it on. Nothing. The flashlight was heavy with batteries, but apparently they were dead.

As her eyes adjusted to the dim light reflected through the window, she spotted an oil lamp in the center of the large round oak table where she and Mark had played gin rummy that first night. They'd dealt cards, hand after hand into the night, putting off going to bed because neither of them had ever made love and they were timid, each uncertain what the other expected. She smiled at the memory, suddenly aware of the unfamiliar muscles working to turn up the corners of her mouth. How long had it been since a genuine smile had touched her lips?

She and Mark worried for nothing that night. Their lovemaking was gentle and unhurried, and Mark had sealed himself into her heart with his tender words of love. "You're so beautiful," he'd told her. And she'd believed him. She *had* been beautiful then. But it was as if her mind harbored the memories of a stranger. She didn't know who those people were anymore. Did Mark ever think about that night? Did he compare her now to the young Jana with whom he'd been so smitten?

Mark had changed, too. Thirteen years later, they were like two different people. Her mother's slow decline with Alzheimer's had taken a toll on all of them. Mark had supported her as she made weekly trips to Calypso to help her father care for Mom, but she wondered now if his resentment simmered beneath the surface where she couldn't see it. They'd all made sacrifices during the long years while her mother was dying.

What irony if their marriage was a casualty of Mom's illness, while Dad and Julia's thrived. Her conversation with Sandra Brenner played in her mind like a damaged CD, skipping to repeat the haunting words over and over.

"I'm not sure your dad believes me," Mom's friend had said, "but I never blamed him for finding comfort in Julia. He was so good to your mom through it all."

Jana had stood there on the sidewalk outside Buca di Beppo with a plastic smile molded to her face, her mind roiling with the implication of Sandra's words.

It was crazy that no one had put two and two together. Julia worked at Parkside, where her mother had lived during the final years of her illness. She cast about now to remember what Dad had told her and her brothers about how he met Julia. She seemed to recall something about running into her at the park in Calypso while he jogged. Had he just made that up? Dad and Julia walked at the little park every morning, so it was believable. But he'd apparently left out a minor detail of the story: he'd met Julia while Mom was still living.

Poor Mom. Her mother hadn't even had enough awareness to know the ultimate betrayal. Sandra's voice echoed again through her head: "I never blamed him for finding comfort in Julia." *I never blamed him... I never blamed him...*

She slammed the heel of her hand hard on the table. Sandra may not have blamed him, her mother may not have had the mental capacity to blame him, but Jana blamed him enough for all of them. Did Dad not think his betrayal would hurt anyone? *If he only knew.*

It was the last straw for her. Nothing she believed in—*nothing*—felt true anymore. If even her saint of a father couldn't stay faithful, then how could she ever think Mark might? Especially now that she was clomping around in her mother's shoes, a horrible thing eating away at her brain, gobbling up her sanity, her ability to take care of her little girl. Who would blame Mark if he sought someone else's arms after she—?

She stopped herself. This was different. She had Ellie to think about. She couldn't let things go on as they had for Mom. She didn't have that luxury. She wouldn't *let* Mark be put to the test. It was best for everyone if she just exited gracefully.

She crumpled onto a ladder-back chair at the table in front of the window. What was Ellie doing right now? Mark would probably let her remain with Dad and Julia for a while. That was fine with her. Ellie would get more attention at their house anyway.

Did her daughter miss her? Jana wrapped her arms around herself. She'd been so out of it lately that it was probably a relief for Ellie to have her gone.

She pushed the cold oil lamp aside. She could see well enough from the headlamp beams of the Escape to use the bathroom and get settled for the night. Thank goodness there was running water, icy cold, piped from the creek. She could worry about starting the generator tomorrow in the daylight. The cabin was chilly, but she'd be warm enough in the sleeping bag.

She looked up to the loft. She couldn't see through the darkness, but she knew the bed was there. The bed where she and Mark had first made love.

Her eyes went back to the sofa in front of the fireplace. She would sleep there. At least for tonight.

She started to lock the cabin's front door, then gave a little gasp when she realized the engine of her car was still running. The headlights glared at her, accusing.

She was definitely losing it. She opened the door and jogged down the stairs, chanting reminders to herself as she went. "Turn off the car. Turn off the car. Lock it. Lock it. Get the suitcase. Get the sleeping bag."

With her mental list completed, she mounted the steps and went back into the cabin. She stowed the keys in her purse and turned the latch, locking herself inside.

It was pitch-dark and the temperature had plummeted. But she was too weary to think anymore. She'd figure things out in the morning. For now, it was enough to have a place to lay her head.

A place where no one would find her.

Chapter Eight

Mark waited for a break in the conversation before stepping up to the booth where two elderly couples were finishing dessert. "Was everything all right for you folks this afternoon?"

All four nodded in unison, smiling. Good. That was the response he always strove for. The lunch crowd had thinned and Mark moved past the wall of booths and into the shadow of a potted ficus tree beside the fireplace. He surveyed the main dining room. Several women lingered over a six-top by the window, nursing coffees, obviously savoring the tail end of a late business lunch. At Table 22, a young mother packed a baby into an infant carrier, while her husband helped their toddler wriggle into a lavender sweater.

Ellie had a sweater just like it…little butterflies and bumblebees stitched across the back, flying down one sleeve. She called it her bug shirt. For a while she'd begged to wear it every day. Jana would have to wash it each night so it would be ready. He didn't remember seeing Ellie in it lately. Maybe she'd outgrown it. He didn't know. The fact that he didn't know didn't help the ache in his chest.

He watched the little girl at 22 and longed to hold his Ellie again. Longed for Jana. His girls. The house had echoed with their absence last night. He'd come in to work early this morning and would stay until he was exhausted. Until he could be sure he'd sleep the minute his head touched the pillow.

He knew Ellie was safe and happy with John and Julia, but he was at a loss at what to do about Jana. McFarlane's—the restaurant—was the important thing right now. If he didn't give all his energy to grow this business, he wouldn't have anything to offer Ellie and Jana when he got them back.

Jana. Where was she? What was going through her mind right at this moment? She'd been distant and…weird—just flat weird lately. Still, it wasn't like her to leave Ellie. To not even call again to find out about her. He had a note by the phone in his office reminding him to call the day care center after work and let them know what was going on. And to alert him if Jana contacted them.

A crash from the kitchen kicked him out of his reverie. Great. There went another hundred bucks to replace dishes. He didn't have time to stand here and contemplate his personal life. He had a restaurant to run. And a life to build for the two people who meant more to him than anything else in this world.

He started toward the kitchen. They'd have one quiet hour before things started getting crazy again for dinner. Tuesday had become their busiest day since they'd instituted kids-eat-free-night. He'd always wanted his restaurant to be family friendly, but he hadn't exactly wanted it comparable to Denny's. But it was a way to get people in during the week and the stockholders had pressured him—in an affable way, of course.

The five investors were good guys—all friends or acquaintances from the men's group he'd attended—back when he had time for church. They had a lot of wisdom. Just not quite the same artistic vision as Mark had. But then, beggars couldn't be choosers. His gaze panned the restaurant with its pale paneled walls and soft lighting. Tasteful art on the walls, live shrubs and trees under spotlights and the massive fireplace that anchored it all—and literally warmed the place in the winter months—gave the feel of a restful retreat. He would never have fulfilled this dream if it weren't for the five men who'd entrusted him with a good chunk of their retirement.

Sometimes a stark fear welled inside him when he imagined the restaurant going under, when he thought about the possibility of losing the capital that had been entrusted to him. The statistics weren't on his side. He'd just read an article in *R&I Magazine* that said half of all new restaurants went belly-up the first year. Even those that survived only had a twenty-five percent chance of still being viable after five years. Things were good at McFarlane's so far. They'd worked hard. They'd almost made it through that first year. They were one of the lucky ones.

No. Not lucky. Blessed. Every shareholders meeting opened with a prayer. Mark had prayed long and hard before he'd even approached anyone about the money to get McFarlane's off the ground. The whole thing had been bathed in prayer every step of the way.

Still, good men went bankrupt. He believed in prayer, but it wasn't a magic penny. It wasn't a guarantee that God wouldn't use your business to test your faith or teach you to rely on Him alone.

A sudden awareness stabbed at him. He hadn't been to church in four months. Or so Jana said. He hadn't taken time to do the math. Brushing the thought away, he puffed out his cheeks and released his breath, as if he could blow all the worry and guilt from his body. He pasted a smile on his face and made one last walk through the dining room, making sure his guests were happy with the fare and the service. Satisfied, he headed on to the kitchen.

The minute he swung open the stainless steel doors, angry words assaulted his ears.

"—and I don't care what you do with it. I'm through!"

His sous-chef stormed past him, red-faced, jaw like iron. Frank Wiley had threatened to quit before, but Mark and Tanner Stone, the head chef, always managed to assuage him. Still, even at his worst, Mark had never seen Frank this furious.

Before Mark could decide what to do, Tanner swooped out of the office behind the kitchen. "What the—" He stopped short when he saw Mark. "What's going on?"

"You're asking me? I thought he got into it with you again."

Tanner shook his head. "I heard yelling. I don't have a clue what that was all about." He looked at the kitchen door, still swaying from Frank's hasty departure.

"Who *does* know what happened?" Mark raised his voice, addressing the rest of the kitchen staff, who were standing around looking at the floor.

Several of the waitstaff shrugged and inched backward. One of the cooks cleared his throat. "He's torqued because I changed a recipe."

"And why did you change it?" Mark was careful to keep his voice level. He didn't want to lose a cook, too.

"It was too heavy on the Cajun. I've had it come back to the kitchen twice this week. So I cut back. Not much. Just enough so I don't have to make every plate twice. But you'd have thought I rewrote his precious cookbook."

Mark dragged a hand through his hair and sighed. "Okay. We'll talk about it later. Let me see if I can catch Frank. I'll talk to him."

He could not afford to lose Frank Wiley—especially not now. He was sick and tired of having to baby the guy's temper through every minor disagreement, but Frank was a great chef and a good worker. It would take weeks to properly train a replacement for him. Not that cooks were exactly easy to come by, either. Interviewing to replace either one of these employees would eat up hours Mark didn't have.

He'd hoped to take a few days off to talk to some of Jana's friends, see if he could figure out where she'd gone. And he'd promised John and Julia he'd get up to spend some time with Ellie this weekend. He'd sort of let them think he planned to bring her home with him then. No way that was going to happen now. But he needed to let them know. Julia had taken a week off work, but John was just starting a new school year, which meant he was probably at least as busy as Mark.

He clenched his jaw until his teeth hurt. Had Jana thought for one minute how her rash decision would affect anybody else? As much as he loved her, as much as he longed for her to get whatever was eating her out of her system, it was a good thing she'd gone into hiding because if she walked in the door right now someone would have to restrain him from wringing her neck.

He turned on his heel and trudged back through the dining room in search of Frank Wiley.

Chapter Nine

The rusty padlock gave way and Jana went sprawling on her back in the soft earth beneath the cabin's high deck. She scrambled to her feet, looking around as if she might have an audience for that embarrassing pratfall. She'd have laughed if she weren't so bone weary.

She'd somehow managed to sleep Monday completely away. When she finally came out of her groggy lethargy this morning, it was to hazy dawn light revealing a cabin far shabbier than the one she remembered from their honeymoon. Cobwebs spanned the rafters and the wide front window was dingy with soot and dirt. Jana found a morsel of comfort in the neglected appearance of the A-frame. Apparently the Gambles hadn't rented the place out in a while—if Ron and Edie were even still the owners. That made it less likely she'd be discovered and evicted. Or arrested.

Ripples of guilt sloshed over her. But it was too late for shame. She didn't have a choice now.

She inspected the generator beneath the deck, trying to decipher the faded instructions printed on its side. Mark had been the one to start it up when they'd stayed here before. But how hard could it be? There were two huge canisters attached—propane, she assumed. She prayed they were full.

She rubbed her hands together. The air was crisp, but not

freezing. How much earlier did winter come to Colorado? They'd been having a hot spell when she'd left Chicago, but here, the frigid mountain air tempted her to start a fire in the cabin's stone fireplace.

The generator would take awhile to heat the water, and she didn't want to run it any longer than she had to, but a hot shower would be welcome therapy. First she had to get the monstrous generator started. Even if the propane tanks were full, she had no idea how long they might last.

She turned the key in the generator's ignition and pushed the starter button. Nothing. After fifteen minutes of trial and error, the engine finally sputtered to life. A strange thrill went through her at the anemic *putt-putt-putt* of the motor. She'd done it. Figured something out on her own. Made sense of the directions and gotten the thing to work. She wanted to cheer.

She gathered a handful of twigs and small branches for kindling before climbing the stairs to the deck. Back in the cabin, she swept out the fireplace, replacing the ashes with a hefty log from the small pile of wood stacked in the corner near the hearth. She'd noticed a good supply stacked under the deck across from the generator. She wouldn't have to play lumberjack any time soon.

The fireplace matches in the jar on the dusty mantel crumbled on impact, but she found a box of matches in the tiny kitchenette and managed to get a modest fire going.

What she wouldn't give for her morning Starbucks right about now. The thought brought a quick smile to her lips. But just as quickly, she sobered. This was no vacation she was on.

What was Ellie doing this morning? And Mark? Was he worried about her? Or was he angry? Was he out looking for her? She hoped not. He'd probably called a few of her friends. All the more reason she hadn't told anyone she was leaving.

She still could scarcely believe she'd left home. That she'd come this far. But it was better this way, for Ellie's sake. Mark would soon recognize that he was better off without her, too. They all were.

She took the bucket of ashes out and dumped them over the deck railing. The sun blazed through the golden aspen leaves, dappling the shake shingles of the A-frame in yellow and blue. A bevy of birds chattered in the branches overhead. Jana's mind registered the glorious day, but she couldn't shake the cloud of gloom that had followed her across the country.

She went to the refrigerator and stood in front of the open door. The boxy, old-fashioned appliance wasn't plugged in and it emitted a sour odor in spite of the fact that its only contents were two boxes of baking soda. Jana plugged the cord into the outlet and sighed with relief when the motor hummed. She'd fill the refrigerator and pray it would stay cold enough after she shut down the generator to keep a couple days' worth of groceries from spoiling. When she and Mark stayed here, they'd tied nylon cord around the handles of the milk and orange juice jugs and sunk them in the river to keep them cold. Oh, how delicious the icy juice straight from the river had tasted after a long hike.

Remembering a little market she'd seen a ways down the road, she checked her watch. They'd probably be open by now. If she lit the water heater now, maybe there'd be hot water for a shower by the time she got back.

As hopeless as her situation seemed, there was something freeing about being here alone. Here, if she made a mistake, did something stupid, Mark—or God forbid, Ellie—wouldn't have to pay for her mental deficiencies.

A few minutes later, she locked the cabin and crawled into the Escape. The route looked different than she remembered from their honeymoon, different even than it had looked in the dark the day she'd arrived. The narrow mountain roads snaked through canyons and climbed lofty ridges. Jana risked a glance over the guardrail and shuddered. Little had she known what those rails were barricading when she'd driven these roads in the encroaching darkness that first night—Sunday, wasn't it? She'd lost track of time again.

The parking lot at the market was empty, but an Open sign hung in the window. A string of brass bells jangled when she pushed open the heavy door.

"Mornin'." A bearded grandfatherly clerk waved from behind the counter. His name tag read Gus in big red letters.

"Good morning." Jana loosed a miniature grocery cart from a row lined up near the window.

"You let me know if there's anything I can help you find."

"Thank you."

She wheeled the cart through the store's narrow aisles, filling it with foods she thought would keep without refrigeration. Cans of soup, tuna, boxed macaroni and cheese, cheese and crackers, hot cocoa mix, instant coffee. She couldn't remember if there was a coffeemaker at the cabin or not.

At the checkout, the clerk made small talk. "You just gettin' in to town?"

"Last night." She pulled several twenty-dollar bills from her billfold.

"Oh? You stayin' nearby?"

She froze like a statue, while her mind scrambled for a reply that wouldn't give her away. She'd forgotten how friendly people were up here. But she was from Chicago. She'd just play the cautious city girl. She didn't owe the man any explanations. Surely he didn't expect every lone woman who rented a cabin up here to give him her address. She pretended not to hear him and waited for her change.

He seemed to take the hint and didn't ask any more questions. But as she started out the door with her little bag of groceries, he called after her. "Oh… Miss?"

She pivoted to face him, waiting.

He pointed to a pale green flier tacked up behind the counter. "Don't know if you've heard, but thought I ought to warn you. We've had several cougar sightings around here. Cats have torn up a couple of campsites. You probably don't want to be hikin' by your lonesome unless you take a firearm with you."

"Oh." The news sent a little shiver through her. "No… I hadn't heard. Thanks."

He smiled. "Sure thing."

She hurried out, afraid he'd take her few words of conversation as an invitation to pry.

On the way back, half a mile up the mountain, she spotted a

coffee shop. She was tempted to see if they made a decent caramel macchiato, but she was sobered by how much of her cash the groceries had taken. She'd better live a little more frugally until she saw how quickly the generator ate propane.

Seeing the black bear landmark towering near the shack ahead, she slowed the car, watching for her turn. Amazing that decrepit old shed was still here all these years later. More amazing someone hadn't stolen the carved bear. He'd have brought a fortune in a Chicago antique shop.

She was just turning onto Alta Springs Road when her phone played its distinctive rumba from the floor between the front seats. It'd been plugged into the car charger since she left Chicago.

She checked the Caller ID. Mark. She started to toss the phone in her purse. But something stopped her. What if something was wrong with Ellie? No. Ellie was safe with Dad and Julia. She'd be fine. Better off there than with her mommy. Or her daddy, now that Mommy couldn't be a mommy anymore.

The phone persisted. Her brain played tug-of-war with her heart. All these memories of her honeymoon had gotten her thinking of Mark the way he'd been when she fell in love with him. If only she could go back in time. She shook her head, forced herself to remember why she was here.

She reached once more to put the phone away. It rang again. She jabbed the off key, as if some outside force compelled her.

It was hard enough to think straight without constantly worrying that her phone would ring and she'd have to decide over and over again whether or not to talk to Mark. Or her father.

Slowing the car, she rolled down the window and slung the phone. It caught the light briefly, glinting before it bounced and tumbled down a ravine.

It felt right. She punched the accelerator and roared up the mountain.

Chapter Ten

John drained his coffee mug and shook out the newspaper, but his attempt to concentrate on the editorial page was futile with Ellie squawking in the background. They were happy sounds—singing, chattering to herself, banging some jingly toy. The familiarity of it made him smile. Ellie's mother had been the same chirpy, noisy kind of little girl. Ellen had always chided him if he tried to shush Jana. "That's just the way little girls are made, John. They have to talk." As Jana headed into junior high, he realized Ellen was right, and that it only got worse.

Thoughts of Jana leached the smile from his face. Where was his daughter right now? What had happened to that happy child that she could grow up to abandon her husband and daughter? He wished Ellen were here to offer advice right now.

The thought immediately filled him with guilt. He meant no disloyalty to Julia. She had handled Ellie's sudden entry into their lives with the same graciousness she brought to everything. But she wasn't Jana's mother—or Ellie's grandmother. Not by blood anyway. And somehow, he imagined Ellen would have had the answers.

That thought in itself was a blessing of sorts. He'd finally begun to remember Ellen as she'd been before Alzheimer's had ravaged her mind. Oh, how devastated she would be if she could know the trials Mark and Jana were facing now. What if Jana's fears were well-founded and she were in the early stages of Alzheimer's? But surely that wasn't possible. Ellen had been forty-seven when she was diagnosed with probable Alzheimer's disease, and the doctors had commented on how young that was—even for early-onset Alzheimer's. Jana was still in her thirties.

God wouldn't do that to them… Would He? It had to be something else. But what had made his daughter question her mental state? Even if she were merely imagining symptoms of dementia, that alone signaled a reason for concern, didn't it? Normal, healthy young mothers didn't imagine themselves insane.

Or did they? He had a vague memory of Ellen as a harried young mom, in tears—nearly hysterical—at the end of a long day nursing the boys and Jana through the flu. And Ellen had always stayed home with the children. She hadn't contended with the added pressure of a job the way Jana did.

Julia came into the room, still dressed in her bathrobe, her hair damp from the shower. "Do you mind having cold cereal?"

"Again?"

Julia's jaw tensed and her eyes narrowed.

John quickly held up a hand. "I'm sorry. It's fine. Maybe I'll grab a doughnut on the way to work."

"Don't do that. I'll fix something. I'm sorry… It just takes longer to do everything with her." She nodded toward the hallway that led to the guest room where Ellie was still belting out a song with all the fervor of an opera diva.

"I understand. I shouldn't have said anything. Cereal is fine."

Julia looked pointedly at his newspaper. "You might as well just put that in the recycle bin when you're finished. I haven't read a paper in four days. Anything newsworthy I should know about?"

"Gas went up another three cents."

She gave a little snort. "Like I've had an opportunity to drive anywhere lately." She moved to the sink and turned the hot water on last night's supper dishes, piled high.

Julia had volunteered to take a week's vacation from her job at the nursing center. She had several weeks of vacation built up at Parkside, and she'd told John she welcomed the chance to use it. But something in that unladylike snort didn't seem quite so accommodating now.

"Do you want me to come home from work early tonight so you can get out?" The words no sooner left his mouth than he remembered a meeting he couldn't cancel. He winced. "Never mind. I can't get away before five tonight. But how about tomorrow? Can you hang in there till then?"

Julia seemed not to hear him. Ice cream bowls and spoons clattered in the top rack of the dishwasher. She shoved the door closed with one hip and turned to face him, arms folded rigidly over her stomach. "What you can do, John, is help out a little around here. Ellie is a full-time job even if I am home all day. And then I've got dishes and laundry and this pigsty—" Her voice fractured and she flung her arms out to encompass the toy-strewn floor in the adjoining family room.

He pushed back his chair and went to her. "What can I do, Julia? I'll help. Just tell me what you need."

She stiffened and wriggled away from his touch. "I need you to just pitch in. Can't you look around and *see* what needs to be done? I don't have enough energy left at the end of the day to dole out assignments. And I don't think I should have to. You've got eyes, haven't you?"

Ouch. He wanted to gather her into his arms, apologize and be done with it. That's how it would have worked with Ellen. But Julia wasn't that way. He'd learned that he needed to give her a little more space. She thawed more slowly than Ellen had. So instead of saying anything, he went into the family room and started collecting toys.

When his arms were overflowing, he started out of the room only to realize he had no idea where the toys belonged. Some of them Ellie had brought with her, but others Julia had picked up at garage sales so they'd have something at their house when Ellie came to play. He opened his mouth to ask Julia, but thought better of it. Instead he went down the hall where Ellie was playing. Her aria had ended, and now she knelt on the carpet with her back to him, whispering to a collection of dolls and stuffed animals, her brow knit in a manner much too serious for a three-year-old.

She apparently didn't hear him come in and he stopped in the doorway to listen.

"—and that's okay 'cause she doesn't mean it, she's just cranky, right Sparky?" She picked up a floppy pink dog and gave it a squeeze. "You don't never get cranky, do you, Sparky? 'Cause you don't has to work so hard and do dishes and do laundry and—"

The floor creaked as John shifted his weight. Ellie turned and, spying him, her face lit. She bounded across the room to wrap her arms around his knees. "Grandpa! I thought you goed to work."

"Not yet, punkin. Pretty soon, though. Can you be an extra good girl for Go-Go today?"

She eyed him as though he'd just offered her a dubious bribe. "I wasn't gonna be bad."

Laughing, John knelt to wrap her in a hug. "I know you weren't, sweetie. You're always a good girl. But Go-Go is tired so if you could just try to play really quietly and keep your toys picked up. Would you do that for me?"

She parked her fists on her narrow hips. "When are you comin' home?"

"I'll be home in time for supper." He puffed out one cheek and tapped it. "Where's my goodbye kiss?"

She gave a gleeful laugh and planted a wet kiss on his cheek.

He turned to leave the room, making a mental note to stop off and pick up something for supper on the way home from work.

"Grandpa?"

Ellie's tone made him turn back and kneel beside her. "What, sweetie?"

"Do you know where my mommy is?"

He sucked in a deep breath and released it slowly, trying not to let his anxiety show. "Honey, your mommy is still on a trip. She'll be back just as soon as she can."

How much longer could they put Ellie off this way? But the truth was too cruel. He couldn't make her understand what he didn't understand himself.

Ellie popped her thumb in her mouth. "I hope Mommy doesn't miss my show-and-tell day."

"Oh? When is it your turn?"

"I dunno, but Teacher said it's pretty soon."

He scooped Ellie into his arms. "Let's go see if Go-Go wants to go get doughnuts with us for breakfast."

"Grandpa! I still have on my nightie." She held out the ruffled skirt of her flannel nightgown.

"That's okay. Krispy Kreme has a drive-through."

"Krispy Kreme!" A smile smoothed her forehead and she looked three again.

He felt like a heel, deflecting her question with the promise of doughnuts. But he was not about to tell this little girl that her mommy wouldn't be at her show-and-tell. He'd hunt Jana down himself before he let that happen.

Chapter Eleven

The smoke alarm let out an abbreviated blast, then went silent again, but the haze in the kitchen grew thicker. Mark waved a chef's apron at the ceiling, praying the alarm wouldn't sound in earnest. If they didn't get this thing under control now, they'd be forced to evacuate the restaurant. That was the last kind of publicity McFarlane's needed.

"Get that fire out now!" He kept fanning while he glared over his shoulder at his two cooks who were frantically moving pans off the cooktop and tossing salt on the small skillet that was creating all the havoc.

They finally got things under control, leaving guests in the dining room none the wiser. But by the time the dinner rush was over, Mark was at his wits' end. Worse, he'd promised John and Julia he'd call Ellie to talk tonight, but one glance at the clock told him she'd gone to bed two hours ago.

He huffed out a leaden sigh. This was Thursday. He'd have to catch her tomorrow. *Thursday.* Jana had been gone over a week now. His pulse quickened when he remembered that he hadn't called her cell phone yet today. She hadn't answered his calls since he'd talked to her Saturday night, but still, he left a brief message for her each time he called, just in case she was checking.

He ripped off his apron and wiped his face with it before flopping it into the laundry cart with the one he'd used to fan the smoke.

Heading for the dining room, he flipped his phone open and pressed Jana's speed dial number. Her voice mail picked up on the first ring as it had for the last three days. She had a charger in her car, but she must have turned her phone off. He waited through her prim-but-cheery message—the old Jana—and moved to an empty corner of the south dining room where he could speak without being overheard. "Jana, it's Mark. I—" All at once he was at a loss for words. What could he say that he hadn't already said every day she'd been gone?

Yesterday, he'd spent off and on all day in his office on the phone to Jana's coworkers and friends. He called every person he could think of that she might have gone to stay with, or that she might have confided in about her plans to leave him. With each one, he'd recited his litany of questions: "Have you talked to her since Thursday? Did she say anything to you about being unhappy? Do you have any idea where she might have gone?" Across the board, he got a resounding "no" to every question. It seemed that no one really knew his wife very well. And the Jana they did know was the well-adjusted, happy woman he thought he'd married.

He swallowed hard. "I love you, Jana. I…miss you. Ellie misses you. Please come home. Please call me." He held the phone to his ear for a few seconds before disconnecting. But he'd given up days ago on her ever picking up again. He wasn't sure why he kept trying.

The phone flashed 11 p.m. before the screen went dark. He didn't dare call John and Julia now and risk that they'd already gone to bed. He was on probation with John as it was. They were probably expecting him to come and pick up Ellie for the weekend, but with one of his cooks gone, there was no way he could take the weekend off. He'd half considered bringing Ellie to work with him, but this evening's fire reminded him that a restaurant kitchen was no place for a three-year-old. He couldn't leave her in the dining room, either. She was just precocious enough that she'd roam the floor and make friends at every table.

A few might find it charming for the owner's tiny daughter to make the rounds. Others would be annoyed and never come back.

He went in search of Tanner and found him in the lobby chalking tomorrow's specials on the easel menu board. McFarlane's head chef was a jack-of-all-trades and master of most. Mark seriously feared losing the young man to one of his many other talents. Probably his art. Jana had once threatened to take the menu board home and frame it after Tanner sketched a particularly beautiful border around a seafood special.

"Hey, boss." Tanner wiped chalky fingers on his chef's pants and straightened, giving Mark his full attention.

"Are you still okay with working all weekend?"

"Sure. I could use the money."

"Thanks. I can help out in the kitchen if we're swamped."

"So Frank's not coming back?"

Mark shrugged. "I assume not. He's not answering my calls." The parallel struck him. *No one* was answering his calls these days. Maybe there was a message of some sort in that, but if so, he wasn't sure what it was. "I'll start doing interviews Monday. If you know anyone…"

"Sure." Tanner picked up a hunk of lime-green chalk and went back to work.

On the way back through the dining room, Mark almost crashed into his part-time assistant manager, Denise Kelligan, and the new evening hostess, Rhonda something-or-other. "Whoa!" He sputtered an apology as the two women laughed nervously.

"Don't apologize. I wasn't watching where I was going." Denise had one arm in a sweater and wrestled with the purse and backpack slung over her shoulder as she tried to wriggle into the other sleeve.

"Here…" He held the sleeve out for her while she adjusted her bags and slipped her other arm through. He doubted the thin sweater would go far toward warding off the September chill.

"I'm checking out a few minutes early tonight." She gave a little cringe, one that made her pretty features all the more so. "I hope that's okay, since we're not too busy. I need to go in to the office early tomorrow." Denise had a day job as office manager for an engineering firm. He envied her energy.

Turning over his wrist, he checked his watch. "No problem. It's almost closing time. You go on." He turned to Rhonda. "Is everything going okay? Are you starting to feel comfortable up front?"

She nodded, giving him her "cheery hostess" smile.

"Thanks, Mark." Denise waved, and she and Rhonda hurried on through the lobby and out the front door.

Watching the two women leave, a sinking feeling settled in his gut. He would go home to an empty house. Again. He missed his wife, ached for Jana with a physical longing that made him want to bury her memory to stop the pain.

He hurried on through the kitchen to his office, the disturbing emotions coursing through his mind. He slogged through some paperwork for the next hour, grateful for something to put off his exit. Finally, he turned out the lights and locked up the empty restaurant.

Tomorrow he'd start the routine all over again. Was this really what he'd been so excited about a year ago when they cut the ribbon on McFarlane's?

He walked to the car with his head down against a northerly wind that already had the bite of winter in it. He hoped Jana was someplace warm tonight.

A yellow flame flared up from the kindling, then fluttered out as quickly as it had been born. Jana rubbed her hands together and arranged more twigs beneath the log in the fireplace. There must be more to the art of building a fire than Hollywood made it seem.

Each night she'd managed to get enough of a blaze going to take the chill off, but none of her fires lasted through the night, no matter how much wood she piled on. She awakened on the couch every morning shivering and aching with the cold. And it was only going to get worse.

She'd made another trip to the little market this morning and heard on the radio that temperatures were expected to drop into the twenties tonight. The jugs of milk and orange juice she had cooling in the stream would be frozen solid if she didn't remember to bring them in.

She would've asked for fire-starting advice from the overly friendly clerk at the market but she was afraid he'd offer to come and start a fire for her, so she kept her distance.

Apparently, September was past the prime tourist season. She'd driven past the market this morning down to the little tourist trap of shops and eateries. Many of the stores had Closed—See you in the Spring signs hanging in the windows.

It was a ghost town and she was the lone customer. But it meant she could quit worrying about someone showing up at the cabin wanting to spend their vacation there.

The log snapped and shifted and Jana stuffed a wad of newspaper under the grate, blowing to fan the flame. She was too tired to turn the generator on, but maybe she'd warm up some soup if she could ever get a decent fire going. There was a propane tank hooked up to the cookstove in the kitchenette, but she hadn't been able to get it to light, and she was afraid to mess with it anymore.

She examined her fear and marveled that her mind could let her worry about setting off an explosion and at the same time ponder whether a propane leak might be mercifully lethal. The prospect sat on her shoulder like a squawking parrot—enticing and repulsing her at the same time.

Chapter Twelve

"What am I supposed to do, Robbi?" Julia shook out a little pink sweater, and matched up the buttons before folding it.

"Oh man, Jules..." Robbi Tobias shook her head, her forehead crinkling in a frown. "I don't even know what to say. I have no clue what I'd do. You know me. I'm the one who did a cartwheel when Dustin finally left for college. I'd totally freak out if I was in your shoes."

"Some help you are." Julia smiled at her friend over the mountain of clean laundry between them on the sofa.

"I'm sorry. That was thoughtless."

"No... Hey, it helps that you think it's as horrible as I do. Seriously. Sometimes I get the impression John thinks I should be delighted about the whole thing. I mean—" she glanced pointedly toward the bedroom where Ellie was napping, and lowered her voice "—I love her. I really do. But she can be a handful." She sighed and rolled her eyes. "And in case you hadn't noticed, I'm no spring chicken."

"Well, now that's where we disagree, lady. You *look* like a spring chicken."

Julia felt the hot surge of tears behind her eyelids, but bit them back for Robbi's sake. "Oh, that's why I love you so much. You always know when a good lie is in order. But I'm too old for this,

Robbi! And if I'm *too old*, what does that make John? He'll be old enough to retire in five or six years. I've raised my kids. John and I both have been there, done that. I am so not capable of going there again. I can't do it." She spread her fingers and dragged them through her hair, which only reminded her that she'd had to cancel a desperately needed haircut yesterday.

"But you *are* doing it, Julia." Robbi spoke with the calm tone Julia had come to either appreciate or despise, depending on her mood. "And let me guess," Robbi said, "you had a few days with your own boys when you had to run and cry on somebody's shoulder?"

Julia stopped short and conceded. "Okay. You got me there. There were definitely some days back then when I felt eighty."

"See there." Robbi gave a smug grin. "And this time you've got John to help out."

She thought about that. The boys had been eleven and fourteen when Martin was killed. She'd been a single mom through the most difficult years of parenting. It hadn't been easy, but she'd had no choice. And John *had* been more helpful since she'd blown up at him on Sunday night.

Robbi put a hand on Julia's arm. "Besides, this is temporary. You said yourself you can't believe Jana could stay away from her daughter too long."

Now it was Julia's turn to shake her head. "I don't know, Rob. I'm starting to wonder. It's been over a week. I really thought she'd show up by now."

"Nobody's heard from her at all yet?"

"Just that one time she talked to Mark. And I've already told you what she said to him."

Robbi cringed. "That doesn't sound good. Do you think—?" She dipped her head. "You know…"

"Oh, I hope not. I don't know what to think. I just wish she'd let us talk to her. The way Mark talks, she got all worked up over nothing. She thinks she has Alzheimer's disease."

Robbi nudged an empty laundry basket with one toe. "Well, I can sort of understand that. They say it's hereditary, right?"

"It can be, but Jana's not even forty. It's highly unlikely she'd have any symptoms yet."

"I do remember thinking I was going insane when the kids were little."

Julia laughed softly. "*Anybody* would have in your shoes, Rob. Five kids under five? I shudder at the mere thought."

Robbi's trademark belly laugh made Julia smile. "The twins were almost my undoing. But there were good times, too. I wouldn't change a thing."

"Oh, you're right. And it's the same with Ellie. She's precious." She smiled, remembering last night at dinner when Ellie and John had giggled themselves almost sick. "Some of the things that girl comes up with. She keeps us in stitches. It breaks my heart to think of Jana missing out on even a few days of Ellie's life. Every day she comes up with something new to make us smile."

"It sounds like she's handling it pretty well then. Ellie, I mean…"

"I think so. But sometimes she gets that faraway look in her eyes and I wonder what thoughts are going through her little head. What do you suppose a three-year-old imagines when her mother disappears? She has to believe the worst. Especially these days when TV puts the most horrible scenarios imaginable out there for her to see. Things sure have changed since my boys were kids. I'm amazed at what Jana and Mark have let her watch." A shiver slunk down Julia's spine.

Robbi didn't reply. Julia matched up a tiny pair of socks and folded them together. For a few minutes the two women sat in contemplative silence.

A rustling in the hallway made Julia glance up. Ellie's shadow darted down the hallway toward the bathroom.

"Ellie? Honey? Are you awake?" She gave Robbi an apologetic smile. "I'll be right back."

Scooping the laundry pile aside, she went after Ellie.

She found her in the bathroom, standing in front of the toilet, head down, her shorts dripping wet and reeking of urine. "Oh, Ellie. Couldn't you make it to the bathroom in time?"

Ellie didn't look up. "I wetted the bed, too, Go-Go. I'm sorry." She started crying.

"Oh, honey… It was an accident. Don't cry. Here, let's get you cleaned up." She peeled off the sodden clothes and started the bathwater running. So much for being caught up on the laundry. Thank goodness they'd put a new waterproof cover on the mattress.

Robbi appeared in the doorway. "Can I help?"

Ellie scowled at Robbi from beneath thick, dark lashes. She popped her thumb out of her mouth and slapped at the air with one hand. "Don't. Go away."

"Ellie! You don't talk to my friend that way." She looked up at Robbi, trying to convey a silent apology.

Ellie's thumb went back in her mouth.

"I'd better go," Robbi mouthed over Ellie's head. "Thanks for the coffee, Jules."

Julia's spirits flagged at the thought of being left alone again, but she couldn't very well ask her friend to stay and clean up stinky laundry. "I'm sorry, Rob. The afternoon didn't go like I hoped."

"No problem. I'll give you a call later. I can let myself out."

A few seconds later, Julia heard the front door close. How long would it be before Robbi actually called? She would assume Julia was busy with Ellie. Besides, who of her friends would honestly look forward to spending an afternoon in the company of a petulant three-year-old?

A thought nudged its way into her consciousness—one that had recurred over the past few days. She'd pushed it away again and again, but it wouldn't stop niggling at her. They'd had Ellie for a week now. But what if she and John ended up with permanent custody? She couldn't let herself consider that possibility.

She tested the bathwater and helped Ellie climb into the tub. While the little girl splashed happily, talking to some imaginary friend, Julia sat at the vanity beside the tub and stared into the sudsy water, letting a fog of gloom enshroud her.

Chapter Thirteen

John pulled into the garage and cut the engine. He reached over the backseat and brought out a large bag that emitted a savory steam. Take-out from Applebee's. Julia's favorite grilled salmon dinner. One for him, too, and grilled cheese for Ellie.

With his briefcase in one hand, and the heavy bag in the other, he hurried into the house with his offering.

Uh-oh. The equally savory aroma of roast beef greeted him the moment he opened the kitchen door.

"That you, John?"

"It's me. How was your day?"

She appeared in the archway between the living room and kitchen. "What's that?" She pointed at the bag accusingly.

He put on his best sheepish grin. "Dinner?"

"Oh, no! But I made dinner." She pointed to the dining room table set with the good dishes. "Roast beef. Your favorite."

He held up the bag. "*Your* favorite. Grilled salmon."

"Oh, John!" Her shoulders slumped. "Why didn't you call? Now it's just going to all go to waste."

He looked at the floor. It seemed he couldn't do anything right. "I'm sorry… I just thought—"

"You know what?" Her countenance brightened. "Don't

worry about it. We can have the roast tomorrow night. It'll be even better the second day. That salmon smells divine."

She came to wrap her arms around him and he breathed an inward sigh of relief.

"Thank you, John. That was very thoughtful of you."

He risked breaking the spell. "So how did your day go?"

She smiled up at him and stood on tiptoe to nuzzle noses. "It went pretty well, actually. Ellie and I took a little road trip."

"You did?" He was surprised. Julia hadn't ventured out with Ellie before, claiming it was just easier to stay home.

"We went over to Naperville to the children's museum."

"You did? And it went okay?"

Julia beamed. "It was great, actually. Ellie was an angel, and I'll tell you what, that little girl is smart as a whip! They have these displays that are all about science and mathematics, and she was amazing!"

John laughed at her exuberance, but she crowed on.

"No, seriously, John, she figured out stuff *I* couldn't even work. The volunteers there couldn't believe she's only three."

"Really?" It thrilled him more than he let on to hear Julia bragging on his granddaughter. He still could hardly believe Julia had taken Ellie to the museum. She hadn't said a word to him before he left for work this morning. She was an amazing woman. He tried to tell her so with a kiss.

"Mmm. Don't get any ideas, mister. I'm exhausted." But her giggle and the kiss she gave him in return said she might just be persuaded later tonight.

"How about I do the dishes and get Ellie to bed while you relax after dinner?"

"Oh, baby. Now we're talking."

He laughed and pulled her closer. "Speaking of getting Ellie to bed, where is our little genius?"

"She's playing in her room."

"She's awfully quiet." He made note that Julia had referred to the guest room as Ellie's room. She was definitely seeing the world through different glasses today.

"I checked on her just a few minutes ago. We bought a coloring book from the museum gift shop. She was 'making art.'"

"Ah, I see. Shall I go get her for dinner?"

"Sure. I'll get the roast put away and we can eat in five minutes."

John squeezed her shoulders, feeling a colossal weight lift from his own at his wife's cheerful turnabout. He hadn't seen Julia this chipper since before Mark had called to tell them about Jana.

He went down the hall, whistling.

But when he stepped into the guest room, he stopped short. Ellie whirled to face him, holding her hands behind her back. On the wall behind her—mural size—was the art she'd been "making."

He reached to push the door closed and fought to keep his voice even. "Ellie. What are you doing?"

She rocked back and forth on her heels and bit the inside of her cheek.

"Ellie. I asked you a question."

"I made this for you, Grandpa." She brightened theatrically and turned toward the wall. "See, it's my house and there's Mommy and Daddy and Go-Go, and there's you! I made you the biggest 'cause I love you *so* much." She pointed to a stick figure that was only marginally taller than the other figures in her mural. When she flung out her other arm, she revealed a bouquet of crayons clutched in her chubby fist.

By the look in those blue eyes and the too-bright tone of her voice, John was certain the child knew what she'd done was cause for punishment. What he wasn't certain of was what that punishment should be. Neither was he sure he could keep a straight face at the creative little scamp's evasive tactics long enough to mete out said punishment.

Unfortunately, all it took to sober him was thinking about telling Julia. There would be no avoiding that, and then they'd be back to square one. Why did this have to happen? Just when Julia was warming to the idea of having Ellie around.

He tried to make his tone sober. "Come here, Ellie."

Her bottom lip quivered.

He knelt on the carpet and held out his arms. "Come here. Grandpa needs to talk to you."

She shot into his embrace and burst into tears. "I'm sorry, Grandpa! I'm sorry. I was naughty."

The desperation in her silvery voice fractured John's heart into a million pieces. He held her to his chest and rocked her.

She clung to him tightly, her spindly arms encircling his neck. "Please don't leave me, Grandpa! Please don't go away."

The only utterance his voice would allow was a choked "Shh… Shh… Shh…" He wanted to cry along with her.

He wanted to throttle Jana for what she'd done to this precious baby.

Julia's voice floated down the hall. "Who's ready for din—?" She appeared in the doorway and exploded. "Oh, no! No!" She clasped her head in her hands as if someone had just been murdered before her eyes. "Look at this mess!"

"Julia." John gave a low warning.

But she ignored him and raged on, teeth clenched, eyes blazing. "What have you done? Ellen Marie, you will scrub that wall this minute."

That did it. Now fury burned through John like wildfire. How dare she use Ellen's name in that tone—his beloved Ellen. Ellie's namesake. If Ellie hadn't still been sobbing in his arms, he wasn't sure what he might have done. But he forced himself to calm down enough to soothe Ellie. "I'm not leaving you, sweetheart." He looked pointedly at Julia. "Nobody is leaving anybody."

He set Ellie on the edge of the bed and wiped her tears with his shirtsleeve. "You stay here for a few minutes and—"

"That's it?" Julia exploded. "You're not even going to punish her?"

John kept his voice even, but he spoke through gritted teeth and turned a laser stare on the stranger standing in front of him. "Julia. Stop. Stop it this minute."

Her eyes grew wide. "Don't you take that tone—" Her face contorted midsentence and she burst into tears exactly as Ellie had moments earlier.

He opened his mouth to apologize, but she whirled and fled the room before he could get one word out.

John turned back to Ellie, forcing a soothing tone. "You stay right here, honey. I'm going to go talk to Go-Go. I'll be right back."

She nodded, eyes round, face glum.

Down the hall, the door to the master bedroom was closed. John knocked softly. "Julia?" He turned the knob. "I'm coming in, Julia."

She was sitting on the bed, elbows on knees, head in her hands. His anger softened a trace and he sat down beside her, yet not touching.

"I'm sorry. But you don't understand everything that happened in there, Julia."

She looked at him, her eyes red, her expression hard. "I understand that I'll be spending hours scrubbing and painting those walls, and you acted like it was spilled milk." Her voice rose on the final word.

"No, Julia. What Ellie did was serious. And it won't be you who cleans it up. I promise you that."

Julia crumpled. "I'm just so tired, John. I'm exhausted. All the time. And this house is a pigsty. I can't keep up with anything. I don't know how we're going to do this."

"We're going to do it one day at a time. I don't know any other way."

She nodded, sniffling.

"I'm sorry if you thought I wasn't supporting you in there." He hooked a thumb back toward Ellie's room. "But the thing is, Ellie knew she was in trouble. Her heart was broken when she realized she was caught. She started crying and begged me not to leave her. It broke my heart, Julia. I couldn't punish her after that." The mere memory stuffed a lump back in his throat.

Julia looked at him, seeming surprised by his emotion. She straightened and reached out to put a hand on his cheek. "Oh, John. I'm sorry." Her voice broke and she started to cry again. "I'm a selfish pig."

The corners of his mouth twitched. "You're *not* a pig." He put an arm around her slim shoulders and let himself grin. "We may live in a pigsty, but you are most definitely *not* a pig."

She sniffed, then looked up at him with a wobbly smile. "Go to Ellie. Poor thing. She's got to be so mixed-up. I'll come and talk to her later. Apologize for the way I acted."

"And I'll have her help me clean it up. Um…I don't think we really want her helping with the painting, but—"

Julia gave a vigorous shake of her head. But then a mischievous gleam came to her eyes. "I've been wanting to redecorate that room anyway. Maybe Ellie and I can go shopping for new curtains and bedding and—"

He dropped his jaw in feigned shock. "You double-teamed me! No fair."

She laughed and jumped up, taking his hands and pulling him up after her. "You'd better go talk to Ellie. We can have this argument later. Meanwhile, both our dinners are cold as a stone."

Chapter Fourteen

Mark scooped yet another dinner roll off the floor and forced a smile at the family of six trashing Table 32. This Tuesday Night Kids Eat Free thing was going to be the death of him yet. But tonight John and Julia were bringing Ellie in for dinner. He looked around the crowded restaurant, wondering how in the world he was going to get away to eat with them. He should have insisted they meet him at somebody else's restaurant.

Guilt shot through him at the thought of Ellie. Another weekend had gotten away from him and he still hadn't made it out to Calypso to see her. It had been two and a half weeks now since John and Julia had taken her home with them. He'd finally found a minute to call and talk to her on the phone Sunday night. Unfortunately, John had found time to call him and rake him over the coals. "I don't know what is going on," his father-in-law had said, "but you've practically abandoned your daughter. If this is what Jana was dealing with…"

John had let his voice trail off, but his implication was clear. It was all Mark's fault Jana had jumped ship. He couldn't defend himself against that. John had offered a halfhearted apology and the phone call ended in the arrangements to bring Ellie here for dinner tonight.

He sighed. He didn't blame his father-in-law. Maybe he

deserved every harsh word John had meted out. Mark's own father would have done the same if he'd still been living. A flush of gratitude that Mom and Dad weren't here to see what his life had become only deepened his guilt

He glanced at his watch. They'd be here any minute. He pulled out his cell phone and dialed Jana's number. For all the good it would do him. But at least he could tell John and Julia—and Ellie—that he'd tried.

The phone rang, but instead of her voice mail, he got a message that her mailbox was full. Well, so much for that. *Where was she?* Sliding the phone back in his pants pocket, he made the rounds again.

On a pass through the lobby, he noticed Denise was covering for Rhonda at the hostess stand. She was patiently explaining the Tuesday policy to two women, each with four kids in tow: two children eat free for every paying adult. People were always trying to get around the rules.

When the contingent turned to leave in a huff, Denise caught Mark's attention and rolled her eyes.

He laughed and leaned closer. "Excuse me?" he said, under his breath. "Are you driving my customers away?"

She threw up her hands. "Why can't people just follow the rules and be grateful they're getting a break? I do not get it."

"Hey, my in-laws are bringing Ellie for dinner tonight." He checked the clock. "They should be here any minute. Would you seat them at 16?"

"Sure. Jana's still on her trip?"

Mark flinched. He hadn't told his staff what was going on. To those who noticed Jana and Ellie hadn't been in for a while, he'd simply said that Jana was on a trip and Ellie was staying with her grandparents. He started to make something up about where Jana was, but looking into the warmth of Denise's smoky-brown eyes, he decided to come clean.

"Yeah... I guess you could say that. To be honest, I don't know where Jana is." He looked at the fancy carpet beneath his shoes.

"What do you mean?" Denise moved a step closer. "Mark?"

"Jana left me. She sort of checked out. I don't know where she is."

"You're kidding."

"I wish I were."

"You seriously don't know where she is? Have you talked to her?"

He shook his head, then glanced around the lobby to be sure no one was listening to their conversation. "She doesn't want to talk. Not to me, not to Ellie. Not even to her parents."

"What happened?" Denise put a hand to her mouth. "Not that it's any of my business. I'm sorry if that was out of line."

"No… It's okay. It's kind of nice to get it off my chest."

"Does she want a divorce?"

The word stunned him. He hadn't thought that far ahead. Hadn't had time to think. Or hadn't wanted to think about how this would all play out. "I don't know," he said finally.

"Where do your in-laws live? Is Ellie staying with them… indefinitely?"

Another disquieting question. "I don't know that either, Denise."

"I'm sorry. I didn't mean to pry."

"No. No… It's okay." He found himself wanting to bare his soul. He was tired of hiding his secret. And it was nice to have the attention of a beautiful woman. It had been so long…

Denise's words broke into his conflicted thoughts.

"You must miss her something terrible. Ellie is such a doll."

"I can't wait to see her. Ellie, I mean." He managed a weak smile. The truth was, he was nervous about seeing her again. He'd purposely immersed himself in the restaurant so he wouldn't have time to miss Ellie. And to some extent, it had worked. He fell into bed exhausted every night and left the house in the morning minutes after he stepped out of the shower. He didn't know what to expect with this visit. Would she even remember him? He rejected the thought. Of course she would. He'd been on business trips before. Never this long, but close. And his favorite part was coming home to her squeals of delight at seeing him again.

But this was different. He wasn't on a business trip. He didn't know what John and Julia were telling Ellie about their situation, but judging by the ice in John's voice when he'd called, he would've had to fake it royally to say anything nice about Ellie's daddy.

He touched Denise's arm. "I'm going to go walk through the kitchen. Go ahead and seat them if they get here before I'm back. I won't be long, though."

"Will do. And Mark?" She moved back to the hostess stand, but didn't take her eyes off him. "I'm really sorry about Jana."

He shrugged. "Yeah, well, thanks. And hey, I'd prefer you not say anything to anyone else. At least until I know what's going to happen."

"Oh, no. Of course not." She graced him with a warm smile.

He walked back through the main dining room, regretting that he'd spilled his guts to Denise—and wishing at the same time that he could tell her everything.

Things appeared to be running smoothly in the kitchen. Grilled cheese and chicken fingers didn't present much of a challenge to his cooks. When he got back out to the dining room, Denise was handing off John and Julia to Freddie, one of the new servers. John carried Ellie in his arms, but before they followed Freddie to the table, he set her on the floor.

Mark's heart did a somersault. She looked as if she'd grown two inches. He dodged tables and almost flew to meet them.

Ellie spotted him before the Brightons did. "Daddy!" She broke away and raced across the carpet to leap into Mark's arms.

"Hey, baby!" His voice caught and he had to restrain himself from squeezing the very breath out of her. "I've missed you, you little squirt! Are you having a good time at Grandpa and Go-Go's?" He looked up to acknowledge John and Julia.

"We got to go swimming, Daddy!"

"In October?" He looked to Julia for an explanation.

"Hi, Mark." Julia gave him a one-armed hug. "John took her to swim at the Y this morning."

"Ah." He shifted Ellie to one arm and reached to shake John's hand. "John."

"How are you?" John's smile didn't reach his eyes.

"I'm okay." He tried to look appropriately grieved, then pondered why he should have to feign the expression.

"Have you heard anything?" John looked pointedly toward Ellie.

"Not since that first time. Today when I tried, I got a message that her mailbox was full."

Ellie took Mark's face in her hands. "Are you talking about Mommy?"

The three adults exchanged looks.

"Yes, sweetie. I was talking about Mommy."

"If our mailbox is full why don't you bring in the mail so it won't be full no more?"

He closed his eyes briefly, aching for his daughter. "I meant on her telephone, punkin… Her voice mail."

"Oh. Did her mail voice say when she's gonna come home?"

"Not yet, Ellie." He had to explain things to Ellie soon. But what could he possibly tell her that would make sense to her three-year-old mind?

Freddie had stood patiently while his boss greeted the party of three, but now he'd moved to the corner booth and put a booster seat in place for Ellie.

Mark motioned toward the server. "Why don't we go ahead and sit down."

When they were all seated and had ordered their drinks, Ellie scooted across the bench seat to snuggle up to Mark. He put an arm around her. She felt so small and vulnerable. A sudden yearning engulfed him. He wished he could put her in his car and head for home. Call Jana and say the magic words that would bring her home, too. He wanted his family back. When had life gotten so complicated? Where had he taken the wrong turn that tore his family apart?

John and Julia perused their menus, ostensibly giving him and Ellie time to get reacquainted. But it was obvious they were listening carefully to his every word. Again, he didn't blame them. He tried to put himself in John's place. What if this were twenty years down the road and it was Ellie who'd disappeared and he was sitting across the table from some jerk who'd abandoned his granddaughter. He'd probably want to be sure of the guy's intentions, too.

He opened the kids' menu and bent his head beside Ellie's. "Do you know what you want, sweetie?"

"Can Tanner still make me ska-betti?"

He smiled. "Yep, he still makes the meanest spaghetti in Chicago."

"Not *mean* ska-betti, Daddy! I just want the reg'lar kind." She bobbed her chin and closed the menu, suddenly looking much too grown-up.

But when she reached across the table for the mug of crayons, she was three again. Soon, she was absorbed in decorating her place mat, talking to herself the way Mark remembered. She seemed to be doing fine.

A few minutes later, Ellie was squatting on the floor entertaining a baby in a carrier at the next table. The infant's parents seemed delighted with the arrangement and Mark used the opportunity to talk to Jana's parents about Ellie. Angling his body away from her, he lowered his voice to a near whisper. "So how is she handling all this?"

John and Julia looked at each other as if trying to decide who should answer the question.

John cleared his throat and spoke in low tones to match Mark's. "She's doing all right. We've had our moments, but she's hanging in there. But—" John shifted in his seat "—we—*you*—need to make some decisions, Mark. This arrangement isn't going to work long-term and it isn't good for anybody to not have a plan."

Mark sighed. "I understand. I'm sorry I haven't been able to see Ellie. I'm glad tonight worked out."

Julia piped up. "And *we* had to arrange that, Mark." She didn't say "if not for us, when would you have ever gotten around to it?" but Mark heard the words just the same.

"I know. I'm sorry. I don't know what else I could do. The restaurant isn't at a place I can just leave it."

He turned to John, weighing his words carefully. "My assistant manager is still in training and I've got investors breathing down my neck to make this thing go." That wasn't exactly true, but it would be if he slacked off for even a day. "It won't always be like this, John, but right now, it's a fifteen-hours-a-day job. Even if there was a day care that would keep Ellie that long, I wouldn't do that to her. And before I forget, I'll write you a check tonight—it's only fair to give you what we were paying for day care." He didn't dare mention that without Jana's paycheck, he could ill afford the cost of day care.

But John waved off his suggestion. "That's not it. The money is the least of our concern. Julia's already taken three weeks off work to stay home with Ellie. She had the vacation coming, but she doesn't have an indefinite amount of time. Nor would I expect her to use it up babysitting even if she did."

Mark shook his head, at a loss for words. It wasn't his fault that Jana had left him in the lurch. At the same time, he wanted to kick himself for not considering the sacrifices John and Julia were making for her—for him, really.

Freddie brought their salads, but no one picked up a fork. When the server was out of earshot, Mark turned to Jana's father. "I don't know what to say, John. I—I just kept thinking Jana would—" He realized Ellie had slipped back into the booth beside him. He glanced over his shoulder at her, but she was jabbering to herself, head bent over the coloring book again.

He propped his elbows on the table and rested his chin in his hands. "I don't suppose there's any way we could get her in a day care there in Calypso? Just for a few weeks. Until I can figure something else out. I had a chef quit on me last week and you can see how crazy things are around here…" He spread his hands to encompass the filled-to-capacity dining room.

John looked to his wife. "Julia? Is that something you'd consider? You're the one who'd still get the brunt of—"

Mark jumped in. "I'm sorry if I put you on the spot, Julia. I just now thought of the possibility. I don't expect an answer right now. Maybe it's too much to ask…"

John put a protective hand on Julia's back, studying her, as if he was as curious as Mark about her response.

"I'll have to talk to my boss at Parkside. With the new wing opening, things are going to get a little crazy there, too, in the next few months. I'm probably looking at working some overtime myself."

"I understand." Mark looked at the table before meeting Julia's eyes again.

She studied him for a long minute and Mark could tell she was seriously considering his request.

She fingered the edge of her dinner napkin. "Would you be able to come and get Ellie on the weekends?"

"I—" Mark faltered, shaking his head. "I haven't found anyone to replace my chef yet. Even if I'm able to hire someone this week, they're going to need training. I just don't know how I can take this coming weekend off. That's our busiest time. But I'll figure out something by the following weekend. I promise you that. And if you can give me some names, I'll make some calls and try to get her into day care in Calypso—just temporarily, of course."

John and Julia exchanged glances and some silent communication passed between them. "Okay," John said finally. "But you'll have to have something worked out by next weekend, Mark. We can't go on like this indefinitely. It's not fair to Ellie, and it's not fair to Julia."

"Of course." Mark shook his head vigorously, even as he despaired inwardly. There was no way he'd have things squared away at McFarlane's in two weeks. Even if he hired two chefs. But how could he possibly tell that to Jana's parents? He was desperate.

The rest of the meal was a subdued affair and when John and Julia left with Ellie, nothing much had been settled. Ellie cried when he told her goodbye, and he felt like joining her.

When he finally crawled into bed at 1:00 a.m., even the dullness of two sleeping pills couldn't erase the realization that he'd barely spoken three dozen words to his daughter all evening.

Chapter Fifteen

"**I**'m coming. I'm coming." Julia dashed down the stairs while the phone kept ringing, then laughed at herself when she realized she was talking to an inanimate object. John always teased her about the habit. Just last night when she'd hollered at the buzzer on the clothes dryer to shut up, he'd laughingly told her, "I won't worry until you start expecting the dryer to talk back."

The phone jangled again. She'd turned off the answering machine several days ago. With Ellie here, she never could seem to get to the phone before the machine picked up, but she'd forgotten how annoying that insistent ringing could be—and how persistent some callers could be.

She reached the kitchen slightly out of breath and snatched up the receiver.

"Brightons. This is Julia."

"Oh, Julia. Good. I was just about to think you'd actually gone somewhere for your vacation."

Julia straightened, recognizing the voice of Don Overmueller, the administrator at Parkside. "Hi, Don. No, I'm here. We were just upstairs. Is everything going all right there?"

"Busy, but then you know that's nothing new." He paused for a moment. "Listen, Julia, I know you have your granddaughter there and all, but I wondered if you might be able to get away for a few minutes this afternoon to come in to the office."

"This afternoon?"

"I know it's short notice. If tomorrow would be better, I could probably make that work…" His hesitance told her that he didn't want to wait, but he offered no explanation as to why this seemed so urgent.

"Well, I'll have to find someone to watch Ellie, but I could probably work something out. What time were you thinking?"

"Could you be here by four?"

She glanced at the clock on the microwave and did some quick calculations. "I'll do my best. If you don't hear from me, just plan on me being there at four."

"Thanks, Julia. I appreciate it. I'm sorry to interrupt your vacation time."

She waited for him to offer an explanation, but when none was forthcoming, she hung up the phone, deeply curious about Don's reason for calling her in. After they'd talked to Mark at McFarlane's, she had put in for another week off from work. But she still had two weeks' vacation coming and the directors were encouraging employees to use up their accumulated time.

Don couldn't be upset about that. But it was odd he hadn't given her some hint of his purpose for calling. That wasn't like him.

But now what was she supposed to do with Ellie? John was in a meeting until five, but maybe he could slip away early. She rang his cell phone, but only got his voice mail. She left a brief message, but didn't hold out hope of hearing back from him.

Maybe Robbi could help. She dreaded imposing on her friend, especially to babysit, but she'd taken Robbi's turn volunteering at the Mom's Hour at church two weeks in a row last month, so she didn't feel too bad calling in a favor. She picked up the phone and dialed Robbi's number.

At ten till four, with Ellie happily ensconced at Robbi's, Julia's heels clicked on the tile floor of the hallway that led to the administrator's office.

She waved as she went by the accounting offices.

"Hey, you!" Heidi Streckler waved back from her desk. "I thought you were supposed to be on vacation."

Julia popped her head in the office to say hello, but she was careful not to stay long enough for anyone to ask why she was here. If she was about to lose her job, she didn't want to have to face her coworkers later, and if Don was calling her in about a private patient matter, she'd have to play dumb anyway. Best to keep moving.

It felt surprisingly good to be back in the building. She'd forgotten what energy the workplace held. John would have laughed at that. Okay, maybe the accounting department of a nursing home wasn't exactly a hotbed of vibrant activity. Still, there was something about the professional atmosphere that Julia had always thrived on.

But as she neared the door to Don's office, she was overcome with apprehension again. Whatever his reason, it had to be something major for him to ask her to come in on such short notice.

The door was open, but she knocked before entering anyway. Don's secretary glanced up from her computer, then smiled, apparently expecting her.

"Hi, Janice. Is Don in?"

"He's waiting for you. How's the vacation going?"

Julia forced a smile. "It's going fast. Very fast."

The door to Don's office was open. Julia went through and heard Janice close the door behind her. She couldn't remember the last time the administrator's door had been closed.

"Julia! Thanks for coming in on such short notice." Don sounded chipper. Not the voice of a man about to fire someone.

She relaxed a bit and took the chair he indicated.

"I'll get right to the point. You know the new wing is just about ready to open. The board has been doing some brainstorming and we think it's time we hired a full-time director of finance. We'd like you to consider taking the position, Julia." He smiled as if he'd just handed her a peach of an offer.

And oh, he had! Julia sat stunned and speechless.

Don leaned forward. "You have the education, the experience and the seniority we're looking for. I—along with the board— have full confidence you'd do a stellar job at the position."

She became aware that Don was studying her.

He chuckled. "This isn't a demotion, Julia. In fact, it's a rather substantial promotion. With a salary to match."

She responded with nervous laughter. "I'm sorry. I—I just wasn't expecting this. I'm flattered, Don. I really am. But I don't have a clue what this would entail."

"Well, to be honest, the board doesn't, either. We'll all be feeling our way as we go. But with the increase in staff and residents, we definitely need to make some changes." He steepled his hands over the desk. "Would you like some time to think about it?"

Her head was spinning. A substantial promotion, Don had said. She and John could finally make that trip to Europe they'd dreamed about. She could help the boys pay off their school loans. John wouldn't have to worry about retirement the way she knew he sometimes did.

It would be an adjustment. She wasn't naive enough to think she could just step into a job like that without facing a steep learning curve. But it was just the sort of challenge she'd always tackled with finesse. And frankly, after eight years, her accounting job had become a little routine. She loved the people she worked with and it would be tough telling them goodbye. Though of course she'd still see them every day. But it would be different. Even after she'd been made head of the accounting department, she was always just one of the girls. This would change things somewhat.

She wasn't sure why she was so stunned by Don's announcement. She certainly would have considered herself the logical choice for the promotion, had she known they were creating the position. She could hardly wait to tell John. What fun it would be to call Sam and Andy tonight and tell them their ol' mom was moving up in the world.

She left Don's office in a happy daze, her mind already buzzing with ideas for the new position they'd created.

She was halfway to Robbi's to pick up Ellie, when it hit her. What if they didn't have things ironed out with Ellie before Don wanted her to start the new job? He hadn't mentioned a specific time frame, but the new wing was scheduled to open after the first of the year and she assumed she'd start the job around the same time, if for no other reason than that's when they'd have the extra office space. She actually blushed to realize she'd already started mentally decorating an office in the new wing.

She'd have to insist that John call Mark tonight and see if he'd found out anything from the day care centers he'd supposedly called. Part of her was starting to wonder if Mark was as interested in getting his daughter back as he claimed.

Robbi and Ellie were sitting on the steps of Robbi's front porch when Julia drove up.

"Everything okay?" Robbi asked when Julia stepped from the car.

"I think so." She curbed a grin.

"You look like the cat who just ate the canary."

Julia affected a swagger. "Well, if you must know, you are looking at the new Director of Finance for Parkside."

"You're kidding?" Robbi squealed and jumped up to throw her arms around Julia. "He called you in to give you a promotion?"

"Well, I haven't exactly accepted the offer yet, but yes. That's what Don's call was all about."

"But of course, you'll say yes."

"Of course. It's an amazing offer. I never in my wildest dreams even imagined it. Parkside just created the position."

"That's wonderful, Julia!" Robbi put an arm around Ellie. "Your Go-Go is something else, sweetie!"

Ellie's face was a puzzle. "Somethin' else? Somethin' else besides what?"

Julia and Robbi exchanged looks and burst out laughing.

"And you don't necessarily need to answer that, Ms. Robbi," Julia teased, her spirits soaring as the reality of Don's offer soaked in.

"Something else besides a great Go-Go." Robbi hugged Ellie to her side before turning to Julia. "So what did John say?"

"I haven't told him yet." She checked her watch. "He's probably just now getting out of his meeting. We'd better get going, Ellie. Do you need to pick up toys inside?"

Robbi waved her off. "Don't worry about it. We spent most of the time outside anyway. You go on. Celebrate!"

"Hey, thanks, Rob." Julia bent to whisper in Ellie's ear. "Can you tell Robbi thanks for watching you?"

Ellie turned shy, but she mumbled something that sounded like thank you and Julia let it go.

She couldn't wait to get home and tell John the good news.

Chapter Sixteen

"Well, she's down for the count." John slid the screen door and came to join Julia on the deck. His shoulders sagged and his eyes drooped with weariness.

"Thanks for doing story duty. Here—I fixed you some tea." She handed him a tall glass of her famous sun tea.

"Thanks." John checked the clock. "I hate that we're just going to have to wake her up again when Mark gets here."

"I know, but at least he's coming."

He nodded his agreement. They sat for a few minutes, sipping the cold drinks and enjoying the last of the Indian summer day.

After a minute, John reached to touch her hand. "So what did you tell Don?"

She watched his face. His reaction to her announcement hadn't been ripe with the enthusiasm she'd expected. "You're not one hundred percent about this... Why?"

"Oh, no, honey, I am! It's just a surprise, that's all."

"So you're okay with me taking it?"

"When did you say you'd start?"

"Don didn't give me a date yet, but I'm guessing it won't be until after the first of the year."

A spark of something like relief came to his eyes. "Oh, that's good. That's good."

"But I'll have to let him know right away if I want the position. So they can find someone else if—"

"Sure. Of course." John grew quiet again.

Too quiet. She touched his arm and lowered her voice. "Tell me what you're thinking."

He seemed not to hear her, then focused again, as if coming out of a trance. "I'm sorry, babe. Forgive me. I'm preoccupied."

"Did something happen at work?" She tried to keep the irritation from her voice. Couldn't he just be happy for her?

"No, it's nothing like that." He reached for her hand. "I just can't quit thinking about Jana. Wondering where she is and what's going through her mind right now. I'm sorry. I didn't mean to put a damper on your news. I'm thrilled for you. I really am."

"Thanks." She gave a halfhearted smile.

"I'm proud of you, babe. It's an incredible honor that Don chose you for the position."

She squeezed his fingers, trying not to view John's compliments as too-little-too-late. That wasn't difficult. She understood his preoccupation. She was worried about Jana, too. If it had been Sam or Andy who'd disappeared, she would have been beside herself, and every bit as distracted.

Reluctantly, she disentangled her fingers from his and rose from the deck chair. "I'd better go check on Ellie."

But John pulled her back, and onto his lap. He wrapped his arms around her and planted a kiss on the top of her head, then tipped her chin to meet his gaze. "I am very proud to be your husband, Mrs. Brighton." He measured out the words, giving each one equal weight. The love and pride in his eyes was unmistakable.

"Well, now, *that's* more like it." She laughed into the curve of his shoulder, suddenly self-conscious, realizing she'd been fishing for his words of approval.

"Seriously, Julia. I'm excited for you. I know you'll do an incredible job."

Now she pulled back to bestow a smoldering come-hither look on him. She beckoned with one hand. "Keep it coming, keep it coming…"

He laughed, but his expression grew serious and he placed his hands on either side of her face and drew her close. There was a passion in his kiss that they hadn't shared for a while. And they were due. She took him by the hand and started to pull him up from his chair.

The jangle of the phone from inside the house brought groans from both of them.

"I'll get it. You check on Ellie." She winked. "I'll meet you in the bedroom."

On the way inside, Julia gathered their iced tea tumblers and snack plates from the patio table. She dumped everything into the kitchen sink and picked up the phone.

"Julia? Hi, it's Mark."

"Hey, Mark. How are you?"

"Oh…I'm okay, but. Well, I hate to do this, but I'm going to have to cancel on you this weekend."

"Mark—"

"I know I promised, but—" his words tumbled over each other as though he'd carefully rehearsed his list of excuses "—I have half my waitstaff out with some nasty virus, and I did hire a chef, but he's pretty green and nowhere near ready to be left on his own yet. But listen, I can take Monday off. Would it help if I came and got her then? I'd have to bring her back early Tuesday morning, but I could take her overnight so you guys can get away if you need to and—"

She bit the inside of her cheek, struggling to quell the anger and disappointment. Disappointment in Mark, disappointment that she and John weren't going to get the break she'd looked forward to all week.

"We already had plans for tomorrow." She sighed, not caring if Mark picked up on her frustration. "But I guess it's nothing we can't change. But Mark, I'm almost out of vacation days. Have you found out anything about a day care?"

"Oh, that. Yes, I meant to tell you. I made some calls and unfortunately, all the church day cares around there have waiting lists a mile long. But there is a spot in a day care downtown. I don't know how far out of the way that'd be for you or John. I wondered…would you be willing to check it out? Would you mind?"

In his sigh, Julia could almost hear the slump in his shoulders. She softened a bit. "If you'll give me the number, I can follow up for you. Maybe when you come to get Ellie on Monday, I could go with you…we could take Ellie, too. Just for a visit, to see if it would be a good fit."

"I'd sure appreciate it, Julia." The relief in his voice was palpable. "If you're sure it's not too much trouble."

"I don't mind. But you'll need to make the final decision, Mark. I don't want responsibility for that."

"Of course not. I'll take care of everything once we've seen the place and can make sure it'll work." He cleared his throat. "I suppose Ellie is already in bed?"

"She is."

"I'm sorry I missed her. I'll try to call and talk to her tomorrow night."

An awkward pause hung between them. "Well, I'd better go," Mark said finally.

"Just a minute. Let me see if John wants to talk to you. Hold on." She muted the phone and carried it back to their bedroom. "John?"

He answered from the master bath.

"Mark's on the phone. It's not going to work for him to come this weekend. Do you want to talk to him?"

John opened the door and popped his head out, toothbrush in hand. "What? He's not coming?" He held out his hand for the phone.

"What's up, Mark?"

Julia slipped into the bathroom to get ready for bed, but she listened to John's terse end of the conversation through the open door. Her spirits wilted as John's voice grew tighter by the minute.

It was a pretty good bet that Mark's phone call had ruined any chance of a much-needed romantic interlude with her husband.

Mark hung up the phone and strode back through the restaurant, a strange snippet of Scripture wending its way through his mind. "I do not understand what I do. For what I want to do I do not do, but what I hate I do... What a wretched man I am... Who will rescue me...?"

His defense to both Julia and John had sounded weak in his own ears. He *did* feel caught between the proverbial rock and hard place. He had grave obligations to the restaurant, to the investors who had trusted him with their money. And he truly could not just up and leave the place to run itself. With the skeleton staff and an overflow crowd, it wouldn't be long before the business would self-destruct.

But he had Ellie to think about, too. She needed him more than ever with Jana gone. And he was taking advantage of John and Julia's love and commitment to his daughter. He hated the things he'd heard coming out of his mouth when he spoke with them tonight. Lame excuses. And half-truths. *Be honest, McFarlane. At least be honest with yourself. They were lies.*

At the door to the kitchen, he felt a hand on his shoulder and whirled to come face-to-face with Denise Kelligan. "Hey, Denise. I thought you were off tonight."

"Rhonda asked me to fill in for her."

"Again?"

She nodded. "She's dealing with some personal issues. Listen, Mark..." She looked around as if making sure no one would overhear her. "I just wanted to let you know I've been thinking about you—after what you told me the other night, about your wife and all. I hope everything works out okay." She held his gaze, her eyes searching him in a way that made him feel vulnerable.

But hadn't he given her tacit permission to inquire by confiding in her the other night? In this, too, he owned responsibility. He scuffed a shoe on the carpet. "Thanks, Denise. I...appreciate that."

She looked away, blinking. He had the distinct impression her demure posture was feigned.

As he started to move on, she reached for his arm. "Mark, if you ever need to just...talk, well, I'm here."

He set his mouth in a tight line and nodded, desperate to get away. And strangely drawn to her at the same time.

"I mean it. I'm here for you." She moved closer. "I know what it's like to be where you are. It's not easy, but you'll make it through. I'm proof of that."

He didn't know what she was referring to, or why she claimed to know how he felt. Part of him was curious, and longed to talk things out with someone who understood what he was going through. But another part of his brain clanged a warning.

Two of the waitstaff pushed through the double doors from the kitchen. They eyed Mark and Denise as if aware something out of the ordinary was transpiring.

The last thing he needed was for rumors to start flying among his staff. Turning away from her, he stammered an excuse and hurried back to his office.

Sitting at his desk, he wondered if Denise had told anyone about Jana. Had he only imagined it, or was Denise coming on to him back there?

He wanted to feel flattered. What he felt instead was— He stopped, not even wanting to examine where his thoughts tried to take him.

Absently, he picked up the phone from his desk and dialed Jana's cell phone. He needed her so desperately right now. Where was she? Why was she doing this to him? To Ellie? He paced back and forth as the same message he'd heard over and over played one more time.

The mailbox is full. The simple, mechanical words had an ominous ring to them this time.

For the first time in a long time, a blaze of fury swept through him like an out-of-control forest fire—the way it had when Jana had first left. He wanted to take his wife by the shoulders and shake some sense into her. And he wanted her back in his arms, back in his bed, back in his life. He wanted their little family to be together again.

The ache inside him deepened, a pain so real, so physical, he feared he might be having a heart attack. He tried to slow his breathing, tried to redirect his thoughts to the mundane cares of his job. He'd managed to do it successfully for almost a month now. Why wasn't it working tonight?

He collapsed into his desk chair and put his head in his hands. "God, help me. Help Jana. Please, God. Bring her back. Where did we go wrong? Where did I go wrong?"

Nothing. No response. Not the peace he'd sometimes felt after praying. Not the inner assurance that the answer was just around the corner. Certainly not the confirmation he'd felt when he'd sought God about marrying Jana, about buying the restaurant.

Nothing.

It was as if the ceiling were concrete, his prayers rubber, ricocheting off to pelt him, taunt him. He was seized with a sudden urge for revenge. The thought was strong to march out to the hostess stand and take Denise up on her offer of comfort and a listening ear.

But he wouldn't do it. Not tonight. He knew a trap when he saw one. But, dear God, it was tempting.

Chapter Seventeen

Jana heard the telltale *ping* and looked down at the gas gauge. The Escape was low on gasoline. She doubted she put more than four or five miles on the car each time she drove back and forth to the market, but at the price of gas, she'd be better off stocking up on groceries and conserving what was left in the tank. She could walk down to the market if it came to that. Though today, just getting in the car and driving here had seemed to consume every ounce of energy she possessed.

She parked in front of the market and turned off the ignition. The minute she stepped from the car, the chill of winter penetrated her thin jacket and seeped into her bones. The aspens overhead had all shed their leaves. She'd missed it somehow and now the breathtaking beauty of autumn was gone and the mountains had a stark look to them. It was fitting somehow.

She put her hand on the door to the market, then pulled back to make a quick check of her wallet. She was down to less than four hundred and fifty dollars. But unless she had to pay to have propane delivered—she'd be fine for a while. It didn't cost much to squat on someone else's property.

She opened the door and went inside. As usual, the store was mostly empty. There was a new woman behind the counter today, and Jana relaxed a little. She wouldn't have to deal with the talkative proprietor. She grabbed a grocery cart and started down a narrow aisle, selecting items and mentally calculating the total in her head. At the tiny produce counter she tried to decide if she could keep fresh vegetables without them freezing or turning to mush in the cabin's on-again-off-again refrigerator.

"Well, good morning there! You're still here, I see."

She whirled to see the proprietor toting a basket of bagged lettuce.

"Oh… Good morning." She'd done her best not to encourage conversation with the man, while he'd done his best to talk her head off. "Yes. Um…do you have any russet potatoes?"

He grabbed a five-pound bag of potatoes from beneath the produce counter behind her and placed it on the bottom of her cart. "You're getting to be a regular around here. Where you stayin' anyway?" He extended a hand. "I'm Gus, by the way."

She pointed to his smudged name tag and forced a smile. "So I see… Nice to meet you." She started to walk away, but decided to take a risk. Maybe she could find out something about the cabin without revealing she was staying there. "I've been camping, doing some hiking up in this area."

He took in her jeans and thick sweatshirt as if trying to decide whether he believed her or not.

She plunged ahead, urged on by a sudden rush of adrenaline. "There's a cabin—a little A-frame—a couple miles up Alta Springs Road." She motioned toward the highway. "I wonder if you know who I'd talk to about renting that."

"Oh, you must mean the Gambles' place. Set back off the road quite a ways?"

"Yes. That's the one. I—I hope it was okay to hike up there. The trail wasn't marked but—"

He stroked his beard. "Well, it is private property, but I doubt they'd mind too much. 'Specially if it meant a rental. The Gambles, they don't get up here much anymore…ever since he had his heart attack. 'Course, their boys come up to fish now and again in the summer. They don't rent the place out anymore, but once in a blue moon. 'Course, ol' Shorty Hewitt was checkin' on the power lines up that way just a week or so ago and said he saw smoke from the chimney. I thought maybe that was you."

She held her breath and scrambled to come up with a nonanswer. "Do you have a number where I could reach them—the Gambles, was it?"

"I can get it for you if you're interested. Place is pretty rundown, though. Now, there's a couple other places not far from here that'd be a far sight nicer and probably not much more money."

"Thanks. I—I'll let you know if I decide to check them out. I'm kind of in a hurry today."

She rushed through the rest of the aisles and checked out as quickly as possible, managing to avoid Gus.

On the way back up the mountain, she replayed her conversation with the elderly man. She'd tried to play dumb, but what if he suspected she was the one staying in the Gambles' cabin? What if he called them to check it out? Where would she go if they evicted her? Probably to jail.

The sobering thought spun in cadence with her tires on the twisting mountain road. Half a mile from the turn onto Alta Springs road, she checked her rearview mirror and gasped. The reflected strobe of blue-and-red lights on the road behind her made her heart stop. Hands trembling, she turned down the radio. Sirens wailed in a distant crescendo that chilled her more than the frigid air.

Instinctively, she tapped the brakes and steered the car as close as she dared to the narrow mountain road's almost nonexistent shoulder.

She stopped the car, fighting the bizarre temptation to climb from behind the steering wheel and make a break for it into the woods. Had she said something that gave her away and made the owner of the market call the police?

The sirens grew louder, and in the mirror's reflection she watched the pulsing lights gain on her.

Frantic, she sifted through the contents of her purse for her wallet with her driver's license. She found it, then rifled through the glove compartment, praying the insurance card was there.

What if the card was expired? She didn't remember when the insurance premiums were due on this vehicle, but if the card she carried had expired she'd have to come up with proof of insurance. Had Mark even paid the premiums after she'd disappeared?

She closed her eyes, fighting for composure.

She raised up to check the mirror. Relief flooded her, as the officer eased around her, giving a brief wave as he went by. The patrol car picked up speed and disappeared around the curve ahead, sirens still blaring.

She put her forehead on the steering wheel, all at once over-whelmed and paralyzed by the barrage of threats that had ambushed her in a matter of seconds. She stayed that way for a moment wondering where the policeman was going, and why she suddenly felt such disappointment that it wasn't her they'd been looking for?

Chapter Eighteen

"Look, Go-Go, look!" Saucer-eyed, Ellie gasped. "It's a rhino-potomus! *Two* of 'em!" She let loose of Julia's hand and made a beeline for the fence. Julia caught John's eye and they doubled over laughing at Ellie's inventive name for the hippo lumbering toward the water's edge outside the pachyderm house at the Brookfield Zoo.

John parked the little wagon they'd rented—for no reason, as it turned out—and put an arm around Julia. He nuzzled her ear. "You having fun?"

"I'm having a blast." And she was. The zoo was a whole different experience through a toddler's eyes.

She leaned into her husband's embrace and arm in arm, they watched Ellie zip toward the hippos' pen, her ponytail kiting behind her.

The weekend was turning out to be a lovely one. Ellie had been a peach all day and with her rushing ahead of them to inspect each new exhibit, Julia and John had managed to capture a little much-needed couple time together. Not exactly the romantic candlelight-and-quiet-dinner-at-home Julia had hoped for before Mark called to cancel, but a surprisingly close second.

As Ellie moved farther from them, John grabbed the wagon

in one hand, grasped Julia's hand in the other and took off at a jog.

When they caught up to Ellie, she was clapping and cheering at the hippo's antics in the water. They stood together, more entranced with Ellie's glee than with the comical behemoth in the water.

After a few minutes, John knelt beside Ellie and pointed. "Do you want to go in?" He winked up at Julia. "Who knows, maybe they have a hipponoceros inside."

Julia cracked up, but Ellie's eyes widened and she tore through the Saturday crowd for the entrance to the pachyderm house.

Two hours later, Ellie showed no signs of slowing down, but Julia's energy was fading fast. She slumped against John. "I could not do this every day."

He laughed and put his hands on her shoulders, kneading out the knots.

She leaned into his caress. "Mmm, that's wonderful. Don't stop."

But he did stop, too soon. She turned, and recognized the faraway look that had come to his eyes. His gaze was on Ellie, giggling hysterically at the antics of a tiny spider monkey, but Julia could read his thoughts.

She touched his cheek. "You're thinking about Jana?"

He came back to her, nodding. "I can't imagine what's going through her mind right now. It breaks my heart that she's missing so much. Missing all this." He flung a limp hand in Ellie's direction. "There has to be some way to find her…"

Julia sighed and put her arm around his waist. "God knows where she is, John. He knows exactly what it will take to bring her back. We're doing exactly what we need to be doing right now…just loving Ellie."

John set his lips in a tight line, but his arm around Julia told her he appreciated her words.

He glanced at his watch. "We probably ought to get moving if we're going to make it to the restaurant before Mark's swamped with the rush hour." He hollered for Ellie.

"I hope he doesn't mind that we're coming today." Julia had

heard John leave a message on Mark's voice mail. "Did you ever hear back from him?"

John shook his head. "No, and I'm frankly not too concerned about whether he minds or not. This is his daughter. He ought to be moving heaven and earth for a chance to see her."

Julia had given up trying to defend Mark to John. She hated the animosity that Jana's disappearance had placed between them. Lately she tended to agree with John's assessment of his son-in-law. *Their* son-in-law. John had always tried to include her. He despised the "step" designation and never applied it to her or to himself where their kids were concerned. Once, when a discussion about where to spend the Memorial Day weekend threatened to turn into a your-kids-my-kids argument, John had finally declared, "They're all *our* kids, Julia. Yours, mine, ours, in-laws, outlaws—same difference."

She'd heard variations on the theme numerous times since. Although lately he seemed willing to distance himself from the in-law part of his comment where Mark was concerned. Now, not wanting to let anything spoil the perfect day they'd spent together, she didn't argue with him. Instead, she caught up with Ellie and prepared her for the fact that it was time to leave the zoo.

The little girl's brow wrinkled in what Julia was learning to recognize as a prelude to tears. "But we didn't even get to see the stripey zebras yet."

"We'll just have to come back another time, then, won't we? That'll be something to look forward to."

Ellie looked skeptical, but she didn't pitch a fit.

"Besides, if we're late, your daddy will be worried. He's probably watching out the window wondering where you are." Julia regretted the words as soon as they were out of her mouth, and they garnered exactly the disbelieving roll-of-the-eyes from John that she'd wanted to avoid.

She ignored him and started gathering their jackets and Ellie's bag from the bed of the wagon. On the way out, John diverted Ellie with a ridiculously expensive plush toy zebra from the gift shop, and they managed to make it to the parking lot without one tear.

When they arrived at the restaurant, Mark was in the lobby talking to the young assistant manager Julia recognized from their last visit. She was a beautiful girl. Julia had noticed her the last couple times they were here. Now, she watched as the young woman followed Mark's every move with wide doe eyes. She laughed too loud at something Mark said and warning bells went off in Julia's head. It didn't take a genius to figure out that this girl had a major league crush on her boss.

But to his credit, Mark didn't seem to notice—or else he pretended not to. When he spotted them, he scooped Ellie into his arms and had her giggling within a minute of their arrival. He turned to John and Julia. "I apologize again for messing up your weekend plans. And thanks for going to all this trouble...getting her here to see me, I mean."

"We're glad to do it," Julia said, before John had a chance to harrumph too loudly.

"I'm still planning on coming up Monday morning to check out that day care center with you, Julia."

She nodded, glad he'd been the one to bring it up. "I'll be ready."

Ellie tugged on Mark's pant leg. "Is it *my* day care, Daddy?"

When Mark glanced at Julia, she read his mind. He expected *her* to answer. She let her eyes roam the room, deflecting Ellie's question to him.

Mark knelt in front of Ellie. "It might be your *new* day care, sweetie. In Calypso."

"But what about Miss Betsy at *my* day care? She won't know where I am."

Again, Julia felt Mark looking to her for help. She pretended not to notice.

"We'll be sure and let Miss Betsy know. In fact, I already called her and told her you were staying with Grandpa and Go-Go for a while."

That seemed to satisfy Ellie. Mark straightened and tapped Denise on the shoulder. "Is our table ready?"

She brightened and included Mark's guests in her cheery response. "I'll go check. It should be ready."

She was back in less than a minute to lead them to the same corner booth where they'd eaten the last time.

Dinner went well and Mark only left the table once when the assistant manager interrupted him about some problem at the cash register. But he returned almost immediately, and seemed much more attentive to Ellie than he'd been last week. Julia hoped John noticed.

It was past Ellie's bedtime when they finally left. She fell asleep in her car seat on the way home and John and Julia spent the forty-five-minute drive home talking about everything but the McFarlanes. It felt good to finally have her husband all to herself—almost as if they'd gotten their date night after all.

Later, while John carried Ellie in the house and tucked her into bed, Julia went to shower and slip into her prettiest nightgown.

She couldn't help the smile that lifted the corners of her mouth. If she were lucky, the evening was just getting started.

Chapter Nineteen

With Ellie gripping her hand until it hurt, Julia walked through the playroom one more time. In the office behind her, she could overhear snippets of Mark's conversation with the director of Calypso Playcare Center. *Playcare.* It was a name Julia didn't find endearing in the least—especially not after touring the place. Mark couldn't seriously be thinking of leaving Ellie here, could he?

She patted Ellie's hand and panned the cavernous room one more time. In one corner a dingy sheet covered a mattress on the floor where two little girls napped. How they could sleep, she couldn't imagine since several rowdy boys in the adjoining room were making enough noise to wake the dead.

The entire place smelled of sour milk and cooked cabbage and something else she had no desire to identify. And over it all was a stifling chemical cloud of some industrial strength air freshener.

The one child care provider she could see didn't look a day over seventeen. She was a sweet kid, and appeared to be competent, but she had her hands full trying to keep twenty-some children corralled.

Ellie's thumb had shot into her mouth the minute they walked in the door and there it remained. Julia finished her walk-through as quickly as she could persuade Ellie to straggle after her. As they passed by the large, windowed office, she motioned to Mark that they'd wait for him outside.

On the sidewalk in front of the nondescript building, October had suddenly turned wintry. A gust of north wind nearly took her breath away. She pulled Ellie close. They'd come in Mark's car and it was locked, so the two of them huddled in the shallow entryway, waiting for Mark. Julia draped the tails of her coat over Ellie's shoulders. Still, out here was preferable to remaining inside the center another minute. Apparently Ellie felt the same since she'd followed Julia willingly and had finally taken her thumb out of her mouth.

Julia looked back through the smudged front window and a disquieting knowledge seeped into her soul.

There was no way they could leave Ellie here. Not even for one day.

Finally Mark appeared through the doorway. "Oh, you're locked out? Sorry! You should have asked me for the keys." He clicked the automatic entry twice and the car's lights flashed briefly.

Out of habit, Julia went around to buckle Ellie into her car seat, fighting the wind against the door the whole time. Mark seemed not to notice.

When they were on the road again, he turned to Julia. "Well? What did you think?"

She tried to read his expression, stalling for time. "What did *you* think?"

He lifted a shoulder. "Looked pretty good to me. I really don't know what to look for though."

"Do they have an opening?"

"Oh, yes. I thought you heard." He smiled as though he'd just handed her an unexpected gift. "I reserved it. Ellie can start tomorrow if you want." He frowned. "I told them it'd be Monday, though. You should probably call if you want to put her in sooner."

Julia didn't respond. She couldn't. She felt queasy at the mere thought of leaving Ellie in that place all day.

Mark leaned over the backseat. "Hey, squirt. What did you think of the day care? Pretty cool, huh?"

Julia turned, curious how Ellie would respond.

She turned her face from Mark and stuck her thumb back in her mouth.

"Mark…" Julia shot up a quick prayer. "I don't want to interfere, but I just didn't have a good feeling about the center."

He looked at her askance. "You didn't? But, why? Why didn't you say anything while we were there?"

She resisted the temptation to tell him she thought he had enough brains to see for himself how terribly unsuitable it was for his daughter's needs. Instead, she said, "Did you notice the smell?"

He shrugged again. "I just thought it smelled clean."

"That chemical was covering up a lot of other odors. Did you ask them about inspections and their accreditation? And what about the teacher-to-student ratio? While the director was in her office with you, there was only one person—she looked like a teenager—to watch all those kids. What if something had happened to one of them?"

"Julia—" Mark gripped the steering wheel until his knuckles turned white "—in case you hadn't noticed, I don't have the luxury of being picky. I don't have any other options."

"Have you looked into private day care? Some grandmotherly type who could keep Ellie in her home?"

A sheepish smile split his face. Then something like remorse replaced it. "Um…no offense, but that's sort of what I've had ever since Jana left."

What was he talking about? All at once, it hit her that he meant *her*. She laughed and the tension was broken. But inside her, somewhere in the region of her heart, something was happening. A profound knowledge seeped into her soul and she somehow knew her life was about to change. Drastically.

And possibly forever.

Chapter Twenty

The wind pushed hard against the cabin and Jana burrowed deeper into the musty sleeping bag. The fire had died down and she shivered with cold, but she didn't have the energy to get up and go out for another log from the dwindling pile below the deck.

She stared into the fading embers. The days were melting into one another. She had no idea whether this was Tuesday or Sunday. Whether she'd been here for two weeks or ten. With the skies overcast, she couldn't have told anyone whether it was ten o'clock in the morning or three in the afternoon.

She glanced toward the kitchen and spied the remnants of the last meal she'd eaten on the littered countertop. An open can, the lid jagged from the rusted manual can opener. She ought to drive down to the market and buy some more soup. But she hadn't felt hungry for a long time.

Did the Escape have any gas in it? She couldn't remember.

The wind moaned around the A-frame, reminding her that the water in the toilet had been slushy this morning. If the temperature continued to drop, the pipes would probably freeze and then she'd be in a fix. She couldn't remember when she'd last let the generator run long enough to heat the hot water tank. Each time she woke up, she boiled a kettle of water over the fire—to wash her face and fix a cup of hot chocolate. Those were her pleasures each day. A clean face, and something sweet and warm to drink. Beyond that, she was merely existing.

She'd been in this place—not the cabin, but this dark place inside her soul—one other time in her life. When Dad put Mom in the nursing home. Mark told her she'd stayed in that…that *stupor*…for almost a month. And then, somehow, without her doing anything about it, one day the cloud had just lifted.

It was like coming home from a long trip. She remembered being away for a long time, but she wasn't sure where she'd been. She'd never talked about it with anyone. Not even Mark. But of course he knew. He hadn't been able to do anything about it, though—except pray.

She had one memory from that time—a terrible memory— of her husband facedown on their bedroom floor, pleading with God. She couldn't remember the form his prayer had taken; she only remembered the agony on his face and the knowledge that she was the cause of it.

Ellie hadn't been born yet. Thank God.

She stared into the fireplace. A log shifted, stirring the embers. A smaller hunk of wood flared and flames shot up again. They mesmerized her, dancing and leaping as they consumed the forest's fuel.

Then something changed. She leaned forward on the sofa, not trusting her eyes. But then the image came into focus. A short gasp escaped her throat. It was Ellie! Right there, walking around in the fireplace. Stretching her hand out and smiling.

Jana threw off the sleeping bag and jumped off the couch. She cried out, reaching for her daughter, grasping again and again for Ellie's outstretched hands. Trying to get to the fireplace, Jana tripped on the pine coffee table that hulked in front of the couch. On her knees before the hearth, she looked up at the flames.

Ellie was gone.

A frantic, high-pitched sound filled the room and made Jana cower…until she realized it was the sound of her own laughter.

Trembling, she forced herself to look into the fire again. Nothing. The flames crackled innocently, nothing more than ordinary orange-and-yellow tongues of fire.

Well, Mark couldn't argue with her now. She was mad. Certifiably crazy.

Out of habit, she turned her wrist over to check the time, but she'd lost her watch somewhere. She tried to focus on the clock on the mantel. She'd synchronized it with her watch the second day after arriving. She could hear the clock ticking. Too loud. Marking off the seconds of her life.

It was ten minutes to six. Morning or evening, she didn't know. It didn't matter.

She pulled the sleeping bag over her head. As she drifted off again, she made a wish—squeezed her eyes tight and tensed up, the way she'd wished on stars when she was a little girl. She wished that when she woke up, her long trip would be over and she would be home.

Wherever home was.

Ten minutes to seven. John took off his glasses and rubbed the bridge of his nose. The computer screen blurred in front of him. He pushed the chair away from his desk, stretching his legs. He'd worked late every night last week and was on track to do the same this week if he didn't make some progress on this report. It was due to the state school board first thing tomorrow morning. But he couldn't seem to concentrate.

Jana.

She was all he could think about. It had been more than a month now since Mark had last heard from her. And longer since he'd spoken to her himself. It bothered him that he couldn't remember what they'd talked about the last time he'd talked to her on the phone before that ominous Saturday when Mark had called to tell them she was gone.

It was different with his sons. Since Brant and Kyle lived in their wives' hometowns in Indiana, it was more of a production calling them on the phone. It only happened once a month or so. In between, they exchanged brief e-mails, but John could have told anyone exactly what he'd conversed about with each of the boys the last time they'd called. With Jana not even an hour away in the city, it wasn't unusual for them to see her—or at least talk on the phone—as often as once a week. Their conversations usually centered around Ellie's latest antics. He'd gotten out of the habit of asking Jana how *she* was. Had he missed a hint in her voice that something was wrong? Had she tried to convey to him whatever had driven her to take such desperate measures and he'd missed it?

Having Ellie with them now almost seemed at times like having Jana back. Sometimes when he and Julia played with Ellie on the floor, he would look up and be shocked that it was Julia sitting across from him instead of Ellen. Instead of Jana's mother.

He smiled to himself, remembering Ellie's silly knock-knock joke at the dinner table last night. The image made him momentarily forget the frightening thoughts that had pulled him from the work he needed to be doing.

Ellie looked so much like Jana had as a child. The same dark curls—like Ellen's—and the same blue-gray eyes. And she was as precocious as Jana had been, though John granted it was more becoming in his sweet grandbaby than it had been in his daughter.

Oh, he and Ellen had laughed themselves silly—out of little Jana's hearing, of course—at some of the lines she came up with. Like the time she rejected her Sunday school teacher's offer of an oatmeal raisin cookie, saying she liked raisins, "but not with cookies in 'em." But it wasn't always "cute" to have a three-year-old popping off wisecracks. Jana had embarrassed them more times than he cared to remember.

Just like she was doing now. The thought stopped him cold. Was that what it came down to? His daughter was missing—maybe even dead—and he was worried about what people thought? No. He loved Jana. Loved her so much he could scarcely allow himself to think about what she might be going through right now.

He felt as if he should be doing something, but what could he do that he hadn't already done? Besides, if anyone should be concerned about taking action it was Mark. He was the one—

Pray for her. The words startled him, coming to his mind as clearly as if they'd been spoken aloud. But he knew their source. That quiet, gentle voice of the Holy Spirit that had so often corrected his thoughts and urged him to prayer.

Not caring whether he was alone in the building or not, John slipped from his chair and sank to his knees in one smooth motion. "Oh, Father," he whispered. "Please be with my daughter. Keep her safe. Bring her home to her family. Please God. I—I don't even know how to pray…whether she's even alive…"

But she must be. Why would God have impressed on him to pray if Jana were dead?

He went back to prayer with renewed fervency. When he looked up a few minutes later, he thought surely an hour had gone by. But the clock on his computer hadn't yet turned to seven o'clock.

Chapter Twenty-One

The supper dishes were only halfway done when giggles from the living room compelled Julia to move to the doorway of the kitchen to see what was going on.

John was crawling on the carpet on all fours—galloping actually—with Ellie astride his back like a horse. Ellie had apparently looped his necktie from work this morning around his collar for reins and she circled one hand in the air, shouting "Giddyup! Giddyup!"

Something about the scene raised a giant lump in Julia's throat. To see her dignified, professional husband playing on the floor with this little girl made her feel more tender toward him than she could ever remember. Because they'd married after each of their children were grown, she hadn't had the chance to see John in the role of daddy. It touched her deeply. Especially when she considered that he once was Daddy to Ellie's mother.

How it must break his heart to have Jana estranged from him. To not know even where she was or what was happening to her. Julia twisted the dish towel in her hands, deep in thought.

"Hey, Go-Go!" Ellie spotted her in the doorway and prodded her "horse" to trot Julia's way.

John crawled to the doorway and smiled up at her. "Hop on, Go-Go," he teased.

She laughed. "I don't think you really mean that."

"Okay. Maybe not. But you're missing out on all the fun. We were going to do some barrel racing. Maybe you could be a barrel."

She reached to smack the horse's rump. "Hey, watch it, buddy, or I might just run and grab my branding iron."

John threw his head back and laughed, bucking Ellie and causing her to grab onto the reins for dear life. Julia steadied her, ready to scoop her off her steed's back.

But Ellie let out another gleeful squeal. "Do it again, horsie! Buck me again! Come on, Grandpa!"

The "halter" tightened around John's neck and he feigned a choking sound.

Laughing, Julia wadded up the dish towel in her hand and tossed it back to the countertop. The dishes could wait. She went to curl up on the sofa and watch the little cowgirl put her horsie through his paces.

Later that night, when John and Julia were getting ready for bed, he sat on the bench at the end of their bed, head down, silent.

"Did she wear you out?"

John looked up and Julia could tell immediately that it was something more than that. He shook his head and opened his mouth to speak, but no words came forth.

"John? What is it?" She hurried to his side and knelt on the floor at his feet.

"I can't get Jana off my mind, more than usual today. I feel… impressed to pray for her. As if something bad is happening to her."

Julia's blood raced. She had always admired her husband's sensitivity where spiritual matters were concerned. She took his hand. "Let's pray then. Right now."

He touched her cheek, his voice a whisper. "Thanks, babe."

She and John had prayed together regularly right from the beginning of their marriage. And even before that. Because they'd come so close to letting their friendship slip into an affair during the difficult years of Ellen's illness, she and John had wanted to be sure they were within God's will when their lives intersected again after Ellen's death.

John was usually the one to instigate their prayer times, but now she reached for his other hand. He squeezed so tightly she winced. Sensing his deep emotion, she took the lead. "Dear God, please be with Jana. Wherever she is this very minute, Lord, wrap Your comforting arms around her and let her know that You still love her. Please keep her safe, strengthen her body, and especially her mind. Don't allow her to believe whatever lies she's been entertaining. Give her a sound mind, Lord Jesus, and most of all, please bring her back to her family."

Julia paused, feeling the tears close to the surface, but when John didn't take up the prayer, she continued. "God, our hearts are broken for Mark and Ellie. They need their wife and mother. And…we need our daughter."

Something like a sob escaped John's lips at that. At his tears, Julia's sprang unbidden. They wept together in each other's arms. After a long while, a gossamer veil of peace fell over Julia. She prayed John felt it, too.

In bed a few minutes later, Julia heard his deep, even breathing within seconds of turning out the lights. But she lay there staring at the ceiling, wide-awake. She watched the clock turn to midnight and then 1:00 a.m., and finally, afraid her restlessness would awaken John, she got up and went out to the living room.

She wrapped an afghan around her and curled in the same corner of the sofa where she'd watched John and Ellie cavort earlier that evening.

Ellie. What would happen to her if Jana didn't come to her senses and come home? Her heart sank with a knowledge she hadn't wanted to explore before. But in the quiet of the early morning, she couldn't ignore it any longer.

Something wasn't quite right with Jana. Maybe it was something as relatively simple as depression. But maybe it was something deeper. She'd never thought of Jana as unbalanced before now, but people were sometimes frighteningly adept at hiding mental illness.

But even if Jana did come home, there were obviously some serious issues to deal with. They all had to face the reality that

Mark and Jana's marriage might not survive. And where would that leave Ellie?

Julia's thoughts drifted to the incredible offer Don had made her at Parkside. She wanted that position so badly she could almost taste it. It would be a challenge, but one she was up for. It might mean some overlong hours for the first few months, and almost assuredly it would mean some training, maybe even college classes. The very idea energized her almost as much as it terrified her. She'd always loved the whole atmosphere of academia that made her feel young again—and alive with possibility.

She started, held her breath for a moment, thinking she'd heard Ellie cry out in the guest room. More than once, Ellie had awakened Julia and John after a nightmare she could never remember well enough to tell them. She leaned toward the hallway and craned her neck, listening. Only silence. She must have imagined it.

Julia's thoughts drifted back to the job offer at Parkside. Even if she didn't step into the position until after Christmas, there was so much to think about. She'd have to train someone to take over her management position in accounting. And some of the training Don had in mind might start as early as November.

Again, she heard a sound. This time, she recognized the sleepy, distressed moan from the guest room. She heard Ellie rustling in the bed, but before she could rise from the sofa, she heard the thump of little feet on the floor. Ellie appeared in the doorway, her long flannel nightie hugging her thin form. Whimpering, she started down the hall toward the master bedroom.

"Ellie?" Still draped in the afghan, Julia jumped up from the sofa and raced down the hall to catch up with Ellie before she woke John. "Ellie, come here, sweetie. Go-Go's right here."

Julia scooped her up and enveloped her in the afghan. Ellie snuggled in, sucking her thumb, still half-asleep.

The corner of the sofa was still warm and Julia settled back in, relishing the heaviness of the child in her lap. Poor baby. What kind of monsters must her dreams hold?

She grew drowsy herself, Ellie's rhythmic breathing lulling her. She tried to steer her thoughts back to Don's job offer, but the weight in her arms wouldn't let her go there.

How could she do any of the things she'd been dreaming of if she and John still had responsibility for this little girl? It wouldn't be fair to Don or to anyone at Parkside for her to accept the position and then end up doing a half-baked job—calling in sick every time Ellie ran a fever, taking off early if they wanted to get Ellie involved again in dance lessons or gymnastics, after canceling her lessons in Chicago.

The thought of Ellie in that awful day care center was enough to make her stomach churn.

But if she didn't take Don's offer, who would they hire in her place? She almost laughed at the question. There would be people lined up for the position the minute word got out that she'd turned it down.

But she was the only "Go-Go" Ellie had. And this was the time she was needed most desperately.

In that moment, Julia knew what she would do—what she had to do. She would call Don tomorrow and tell him that she couldn't take the job. Then she would go down to the HR office and investigate what it would take to get an immediate leave. If she remembered correctly, the Family Medical Leave Act allowed for her to take off twelve weeks and her old job would still be waiting for her at the end of the leave. Hopefully she'd still retain her benefits throughout the leave.

Deep disappointment, grief almost, filled her as she contemplated her decision. How had she gone in the blink of an eye from being eager to accept a lucrative and prestigious position at Parkside, to being ready to ask for a three-month leave from her regular job? To be a stay-at-home mom again at fifty-one? It was almost too much to digest.

Ellie stirred and snuggled deeper into the nest of Julia's arms. *Oh, Ellie. How can one little thirty-seven-pound girl change everything so quickly?*

* * *

"You're doing what?" John put the newspaper down and stared at Julia across the kitchen table. Surely he hadn't heard his wife correctly.

"I don't think I have a choice, John."

"You're not serious."

"I am serious. I've prayed about it. I've tried to think of every possible solution and there just isn't any other way."

"Oh, Julia." A heaviness settled over him. "I don't want you to do this because there aren't any other options. There are. There have to be." He racked his brain for even a short list. "Maybe I should take an early retirement."

"John, don't be ridiculous."

"Well, it makes as much sense as you taking this leave, turning down Don's offer. Frankly, with all the junk the board is dealing with on this building project, the prospect of retirement is rather appealing." He forced a smile.

"Yes, and this would be the worst possible time for you to bail out on them."

She had that right.

"Not to mention that if you retire we couldn't afford to take Ellie in."

He frowned. "Well, you have a point there. What about… foster care?"

"John! *No!*"

He held up a warning hand. "Just temporarily…until Jana comes back. Or at least until Mark has the restaurant up and running."

"No. Absolutely not. I can't believe you'd even consider it."

He *had* entertained that grim possibility for Ellie—had nightmares about it actually. "You're right. I wouldn't consider it." He *would* retire before he'd let her go to strangers.

Julia let out a relieved breath.

"What about Brant and Cynthia?" he said. "Or Kyle and Lisa? Maybe they'd consider it. Just for a while. It'd be easier for either of them to fit another child into their lives. I mean, what's one more, right?"

She studied him, one hand propped on her hip. "Other than the fact that Lisa's six months pregnant and Cynthia's just gone back to college, you mean? Besides, Mark would never agree to that. How would he ever see Ellie if she was half a day's drive away?"

"It's not like he sees her that often as it is," John grumbled.

"Well, no... But he'd never see her if she was in Indiana." Julia sighed. "John, please. I've thought this out. I'm doing it because..." She stopped and swallowed hard as if she were trying to decide if she could truly commit to her next words. "I'm doing it because it's the right thing to do. And because I want to. I really do."

"You'd tell Don no? You'd really do that, Julia? I've never seen you so happy, so excited about anything, since Don asked you to take that position."

"I was happy. It was a great honor to be given that offer. Even if I say no, it was still an honor. And who knows, the position might open up again in a few years. I might still have the opportunity. Someday."

"But what if you don't?" John hated with everything in him that she'd even had to deliberate this choice. He was terrified she'd ultimately resent it.

She shrugged. "If I don't, I don't."

He voiced his fears now, wanting to get everything out in the open before he even considered agreeing to the incredible solution she was suggesting. "If you're serious about this—and I'm not saying I'm convinced it's the only way—but..." He reached across the table for her hand. "I don't want you to look back on this and resent it. Resent me."

"John, I would never do that. Surely you know me better than that."

Oh, how he loved this woman! Loved her more than he had room to hold inside. "I'm sorry, Julia." He brushed a wisp of hair from her forehead. "I do know you better. And do you have any idea how much I love you for it?"

She wiggled her eyebrows. "Maybe you can show me later."

He laughed and patted her cheek. But he wasn't ready to

move away from the seriousness of what she was considering. He wanted her to be sure it was the right thing. Sure it was the best thing for Julia, for Ellie. For all of them.

Chapter Twenty-Two

"We should probably get started." Mark propped his elbows on the table and steepled his index fingers. The private banquet room was stuffy and he loosened his tie as he looked around the drink-littered table at the friendly faces of his investors. He hoped they'd remain as congenial after this meeting adjourned.

He opened the folder in front of him. The five men took his lead and opened identical folders Denise had placed in front of each of them after dessert had been cleared away.

He'd taken Denise up on her offer to help with the shareholders meeting, but he'd quietly dismissed her after reports had been distributed and the last round of coffee poured. He was disappointed he wouldn't have a chance to chat with her tonight. That admission—even to himself—filled him with guilt.

He cleared his throat, ready to launch into his report. But before he got a word out, Hank Lowery jumped in. "Mark, do you mind if I open us in prayer?"

He dipped his head, chagrined that he'd forgotten. "Please, Hank. Of course."

As the older man prayed, a strange compulsion came over Mark to share what had been going on with Jana. To tell them about her leaving him and his struggle to find care for Ellie while continuing to run the restaurant. The prayers of these men Mark admired and saw as mentors would have meant the world to him.

But he couldn't let them see that kind of vulnerability in the man who was supposed to be in charge of their investments. How could they ever trust him to manage their interests if they saw how weak he really was? If they saw that he couldn't even manage his own family.

By the time the chorus of amens closed Hank's prayer, Mark had talked himself out of unloading his troubles. When they lifted their heads and gave him their full attention, Mark made sure all they saw in front of them was a competent businessman who was handling their investments with wisdom and integrity.

He referred again to the stockholders' report. "As you can see, the news isn't all bad. Since the last quarter, we've managed to bring up the weekday take considerably, thanks mostly to the Tuesday night promotion. But overall we're still undergoing some first-year struggles." He sneaked a look at the investors' expressions as they perused the financial report.

Their faces were hard to read so he plunged in with his report. "As you'll see from the spreadsheet on page four, our operating income increased about thirteen percent—that's slightly less than our revenue increase."

A murmur of mild concern filtered around the table.

William Weirmeyer raised a hand.

Mark grinned. "Go ahead, Bill. This isn't school. You don't need permission to speak."

That broke the ice a bit.

"I just wonder where this falls with your projections."

Mark shook his head. "It's actually off a little more than I expected. And like you, I'm not happy with that result. But our operating costs—mainly the cost of foodstuffs—were considerably higher than we budgeted for this quarter. Fortunately, we did a good job of keeping general and administrative expenses down, with only a one-and-a-half percent increase for the quarter."

He panned the room, trying to gauge the response. Five sober-but-polite faces stared back at him. "One other piece of good news to report—I was finally able to hire a full-time chef to replace Frank Wiley. She's still in training, but Tanner seems to think she's working out well. That has helped take a lot of the pressure off." He didn't tell them that he thought Tanner had a thing for the beautiful new sous-chef. With the luck he'd been having lately, the two of them would probably quit to start their own restaurant and take half his staff with them.

He struggled through the rest of the meeting, and two hours later, when the men had dispersed, he walked back through the closed restaurant. At the abandoned hostess stand, the clock on the guest pager transmitter flipped to eleven o'clock. He did one last walk-through of the building before going back to straighten and lock up his office.

He stood in the main dining room for a minute. The room was always at its best this time of night. Clean tablecloths, floors mopped to a shine and all the glasses and bottles sparkling in the decorative racks. He tried to see the place with objective eyes, wishing Jana were waiting at home for him so he could bounce the details of the meeting off her, get her perspective on things. Would he ever stop missing her? It was a mixed blessing that lately his anger had given way to longing for his wife…for a chance to start over with her.

He went to the back door and let himself out. In spite of having to give the shareholders less than triumphant news, Mark was proud of his restaurant. No one expected him to be raking in the dough the first year in business. He'd worked his tail off and he was making a go of it. It hadn't been easy, and he fully expected to have another few years of long hours for little return. But eventually it would all pay off and he'd have a steady income, security for the future, and a little free time to enjoy the fruits of his labors.

And for what? The question haunted him as he locked up and walked through the back parking lot. He looked up to see a few crystal flakes of snow swirling in the glow of the parking lot lights. He hadn't heard there was snow in the forecast.

With his overcoat slung across one arm, he fished in the pocket for his keys, then slipped the coat on and buttoned it up against the chill November air. The headlights flashed twice with a press of the automatic entry keypad.

He glanced up and did a double take. The car's headlamps silhouetted a female figure standing beside the passenger side door.

For a minute her stance, the vulnerable way she wrapped her arms around herself against the chill night made him think of Jana. *Was* it her? Had she come home to him? His throat went dry.

He quickened his steps. As he came closer, the light from the parking lot's streetlamps fell across the feminine profile.

His breath caught. "Denise. What are you doing here?"

The clock on the mantel clicked to eleven o'clock and Jana stood, barefoot, looking up into the blackness of the A-frame's loft. She set a tentative foot on the first rung of the ladder-steep stairway and started the long climb.

At the top, she picked her way across the planked floor to the far side of the loft. It was the first time she'd braved the space since arriving at the cabin. She and Mark had slept here together, but she'd forgotten how low the ceiling was. The loft was only intended for sleeping and she had to duck to keep from hitting her head on the rafters. At the back wall, she knelt to look out the triangular window tucked beneath the pitched roof. Her spirits lifted at the scene beyond the soot-smudged glass.

A half-moon illumined wet snowflakes, as big as her thumbnails, floating down from the sky. They sifted through the dark one by one, faster and faster.

This was what she'd been waiting for. Her way out. If this flurry kept up, by morning, there would be enough snow to accomplish her intention.

Ironically, she felt alive and invigorated with her mission. There was a sense of resolution to this moment. She'd thought of little else these last days as the wind howled around the cabin and the last of the purpling leaves evacuated the sparse deciduous trees surrounding the cabin.

As soon as the idea had entered her mind she'd prayed for the snow to come quickly. She remembered reading somewhere that freezing to death was painless. She would simply fall asleep. And never wake up. If they ever found her, no one would suspect it had been intentional.

It was an easy answer to everyone's problem. An answer to her prayers.

She pinned her stare beyond the window where snowflakes tumbled from the sky and meshed together, knitting a lacy blanket over the pines behind the cabin.

Chapter Twenty-Three

Mark slowed his steps, peering into the dimly lit parking lot, his thoughts in chaos. "Denise? Is everything all right? I thought you'd gone home."

She tipped her head and flashed a coy smile. "No. I thought you might want to talk, you know, after the meeting."

"That was…thoughtful of you. But…" But *what?* She was right. Hadn't he just been thinking how nice it would be to have someone to talk to right now? Someone to help him be objective about his doubts and fears. Denise knew the restaurant—probably better than Jana did. She had an idea of his struggles, the obstacles he faced. He thought she understood how this place had been the fulfillment of his dreams. And he'd already told Denise about Jana.

"Where's your car?"

She looked toward the Pier 1 parking lot next door.

A tree-lined median separated the two parking lots. Why had she parked way out there?

She dipped her head. "Do you want to…get some coffee or something?"

"Sure, if you want to." As soon as he heard the words come out of his mouth, he knew exactly why she'd left her car so far from the restaurant. And he'd fallen for it, hook, line and two-ton sinker.

She brightened. "I'd love to."

He couldn't very well retract his acceptance now without appearing rude. But he was wise to her. He'd let her know it, too. Gently, though. After all, she knew he was going through a rough time. She was only trying to be nice.

"The Starbucks over on North and Wells is open twenty-four hours," she offered.

"Okay. Hop in."

He started around to open her door, but she held up a hand and let herself in before he could get there.

"So how'd your meeting go?" she asked, when they were on the road.

"It went okay. I wish I'd had better news for them, but I think they understand that it takes a few years to get started."

"Well, they surely understand that with everything you've been going through—with your wife and all—things are going to be shaky for a while."

He glanced at her from the corner of his vision. "The shareholders don't know anything about that, Denise. There's no reason for them to."

"Oh. I just assumed… Sorry." She put her head down, as if she'd been scolded.

"You didn't know. It's no big deal." But it *was* a big deal. He knew full well he should have asked for the prayers of the godly men who'd believed in him and trusted him with their livelihood. Why had he let his pride keep him from sharing his heart with them? Well, he wouldn't make that mistake with Denise. He needed to talk to someone. It couldn't be good to keep all his fears bottled up inside.

He pulled into the Starbucks parking lot, surprised to find it crowded this late at night. While he ordered their coffees, Denise staked out a leather sofa in a relatively quiet corner of the coffee shop.

He was relieved to see an overstuffed chair adjacent to the sofa open up by the time their order was ready. He handed her the warm cappuccino and took the chair.

She curled up in the corner of the sofa closest to him and took up the conversation where they'd left off in the car. "Have you heard from her again? Jana?"

He took a sip of steaming coffee and shook his head. "I'm starting to think I may not."

"Ever? But what about your daughter? Wouldn't your wife have to contact you if…" She shook her head.

"What?"

"I just meant, if she wanted a divorce."

The word took him aback. *Divorce.* He hadn't allowed himself to entertain that thought. It wasn't something he wanted. *So why are you here?* He brushed the thought away as if it were a sticky cobweb he'd inadvertently walked into. "I don't know. I think Jana might be—I don't know—cracking up or something. Her mom died of Alzheimer's when she was only in her fifties. Early-onset, they called it. But it's hereditary, so Jana thinks—"

"You think your wife has Alzheimer's?"

"I don't think so, but she really let the whole thing with her mom mess with her mind. Maybe she's just depressed or something. I'm no psychiatrist, but apparently she couldn't handle being a wife and mom anymore."

"Well, she has to be pretty messed up to not want that darling little girl of yours."

Mark forced a smile. "Yeah, she's really something. I don't know what's going to happen with Ellie. There's no way I can spend any kind of quality time with her and still keep the restaurant running."

"I'm sorry, Mark, that's got to hurt. Is she still staying with your in-laws?"

He nodded. "She's happy there. They're good people and they love her. But they're out in Calypso, so it's not like I can see her any time I want. And I don't know how long they'll be able to keep her. They both have careers."

Denise set her coffee cup on the low table in front of the sofa and reached to put a hand on Mark's arm. "I can't even imagine what you're going through. I wish there was something I could do."

He feigned a cough, a flimsy excuse to slip his arm out from under her touch. What was he doing, spilling his guts to a thirty-something assistant manager? But if Jana were here, he wouldn't need anyone else to talk to. He would be home in bed. Holding his wife's hand across the chasm of the king-size mattress. What comfort he'd always gotten from holding Jana's hand, prolonging the afterglow of their lovemaking.

He'd teased her that if he had to choose between a hug and holding her hand, he'd choose holding hands.

"No way," she'd said. "Seriously? You'd choose holding hands?" He could almost see her incredulous expression. And the way it had turned to laughter when he'd answered, "Hands down!" He felt the corners of his mouth turn up at the memory.

Oh, dear God, I miss her so much.

Warm fingers entwined with his, squeezing, speaking a language all their own. He dragged himself from the memory, so real it left him shaken and longing for Jana's touch. Looking down at his hands, he understood. Denise had knit her fingers with his. And she spoke the language he was so homesick for. Fluently.

He didn't dare meet her gaze, for he knew he would see the same hunger in her eyes. And it terrified him.

Chapter Twenty-Four

Jana swept the last of the ashes from the hearth and took the ash can out to the deck. She dumped the contents over the railing, watching as the gray ash pocked the snowy blanket below.

She brushed off her hands and set the pail by the door. The sun had popped through a breach in the clouds, but a few flakes still drifted through the morning air. Inside, she packed the few items she'd brought to the cabin into her bag. She checked the side pocket. Good. The letter was there. Her brain was working better today. She hadn't forgotten. She hauled the bag, along with a plastic grocery sack full of trash, down to the Escape. At least she would leave the cabin in better condition than she'd found it. Maybe that would justify her trespassing.

She ran back up the stairs and locked the front door, sliding the security gates over the door and securing them with the padlock. Below the deck, she turned off the generator and padlocked it. Breathing hard, she stopped to lean on the rail and rest a minute before going back up to put the keys in their hiding place above the door frame.

She knelt beside the Escape to tie a loose shoestring, then straightened to take in one last view of the place that had sheltered her for, well, she wasn't sure how long. But weeks—many weeks—she felt sure.

She climbed behind the wheel and turned the key. It had been a long time since she'd gone to the market for groceries, but the engine turned over the first time. *Thank you, God.* Slowly, she backed around the side of the A-frame, shifting into second gear and pointing her vehicle up the mountain. The engine revved and the Escape skidded on the snow as it climbed the rocky terrain. Snowflakes lit on the windshield and stuck. Jana didn't turn on the wipers, but let the curtain of white shadow the car's interior.

The trail ended only a few hundred yards from the cabin, but Jana forged her own path, prodding the car farther up the mountain into uncharted terrain. The top of the A-frame was still visible in her rearview mirror when she reached a point where the Escape wouldn't fit between two aspens.

This was the end of the trail for her. Hopefully the vehicle would be hidden among the trees. She checked the sky. It wouldn't be long until the white paint would blend in with the snow.

She put the gearshift in Park and cut the engine. Leaving her jacket on the seat, she scrambled out of the front seat and closed the door. The mountain rocks were slippery underfoot and she faltered, catching herself with her bare hands. The snow bit at her fingers and sent a chill all the way through her. She shivered and regained her balance, climbing on past where the Escape hadn't been able to go. Her hands tingled with the cold and her teeth chattered violently. This wasn't supposed to be painful.

She'd been walking for probably ten minutes when the sun broke through the clouds. Its warmth penetrated her black sweatshirt and seeped into her skin. It felt good. But Jana was dismayed to see how quickly the sun's rays melted the thin blanket of snow.

Powdered branches glistened for an instant before shedding their coats. The mountain did the same. Within a few minutes, the traces of snow dissolved into tiny rivulets, leaving the rocks shining in the sunlight.

She climbed on for what seemed like an hour. But when she turned to look where she'd been, her hopes sank. The paint on her vehicle was the only spot of white in sight. Shoulders sagging, she half slid, half hiked back to the Escape and got in. She threw it in Reverse and started backing down the mountain. The steering wheel didn't want to cooperate and it was slow going.

She maneuvered between two close-set firs, only to feel the back tire slip. She gunned the engine. The vehicle roared and the wheels spun, but nothing happened. She shifted back and forth from first gear to Reverse, rocking the car. It seemed to be high-centered on a rock. On the verge of giving up, she gunned it one last time.

The Escape lurched backward and started rolling. Fir branches scrubbed the windows like brushes in a car wash. Jana slammed on the brakes, but nothing happened. She gripped the wheel and rode the brakes. That horrible, dreamlike sensation of falling overtook her. Then everything seemed to be happening in slow motion. She felt shaken like a rag doll. A loud *bang* made her gasp and clap her hands over her ears. She sat behind the wheel, dazed for a minute. Finally, she checked the rearview mirror.

A veritable forest was pressed against her back windshield. She climbed out of the car and picked her way over unstable rocks to the rear of the Escape. It was welded against a thick, gnarled tree trunk. An ominous hissing sound emanated from somewhere under the car.

The river roared somewhere below her. For a moment she wondered if the icy waters might serve the same purpose as the traitorous snow. But she didn't have the courage to consider it for long.

Shivering, she grabbed the bag with her clothes and toiletries in it and slung it over her shoulder. She started back the way she'd come, picking her way down the slopes.

The cabin was nowhere in sight. But soon, she rounded a curve in the trail and the pitched roof of the A-frame appeared, poking through the trees like a church steeple. She pressed on, keeping the cabin in her sights and reassuring herself. Winter came early to Colorado. It would snow again. Tomorrow might be the blizzard of the century.

She would wait for it.

Chapter Twenty-Five

"You're crazy, Julia." Robbi Tobias adjusted the sweatband on her forehead and slowed to a walk.

Julia was grateful for the breather. Her friend always pushed her harder than she liked when they went jogging.

"I admire what you're doing—don't think I don't." Robbi's smile held a spark of mischief. "But I still think you're crazier than a loon to take this on."

"Maybe I am." Julia sighed and stopped in the middle of the jogging trail, breathing hard. "But what else am I supposed to do?"

"You have other options." Robbi jogged in place, hands at her waist. "This is exactly the kind of thing government programs exist for, Julia. It doesn't have to be permanent. Mark could surely get Ellie in foster care or at the very least some sort of extended day care until he gets on his feet." She eyed Julia, sympathy coming to her expression. "Still no word from Jana?"

Julia shook her head.

"Where do you think she is?"

"I don't know. I truly thought she'd have come to her senses by now. Unless she squirreled away some money Mark didn't know about, I can't imagine how she's managed to get by this long. John thinks she probably sold her vehicle and is living off that money."

"Can't they trace her through the car? If she sold it, there'd be a record of that, wouldn't there?"

"That's what John thought. The car is in both of their names, but Mark still has the title, so if she sold it, it probably wasn't on the up-and-up."

"You don't think…?" An apologetic tone crept into Robbi's voice. "Is there a chance Mark knows something he isn't telling?"

Julia hesitated. "No. I think John was a little suspicious at first—not that Mark had done anything terrible, he's a great guy—but just that maybe there was more going on in their marriage than he was letting on. But if Mark's bluffing, he's a consummate actor. I think he's just under a ton of pressure with the restaurant. And a little bewildered that Jana would actually leave him."

"How long has she been missing now?"

Julia did some quick math and the answer jolted her. "It's been six weeks." Had Ellie really been with them that long? At first, they'd counted every day, hope dwindling the longer Jana went without contacting anyone. But now, in some ways it seemed as though Ellie had been part of their lives all along.

Robbi took off at a slow jog. "How long does it have to be before the police will get involved?"

Julia shook her head. "Unless something comes up that could be construed as suspicious, they won't get involved. Mark went to the police right away, but just to double-check, John talked to a guy from our church who's a policeman. He confirmed everything Mark was told."

"Wow. That's almost scary that a person can choose to just disappear if they want to."

They jogged together in silence before Robbi spoke again. "It must be strange not knowing where she is."

"It is. Mark has called every one of her friends he can think of and it seems like she never confided in anyone. Either that, or they're keeping secrets for Jana. John admits that she was always pretty private, but now he's decided he's going to 'interview' Jana's friends and see if maybe they'll tell him something they wouldn't tell Mark."

"That's probably a good idea."

Julia sighed. "I guess. But I doubt he's going to find out anything Mark didn't already know. My guess is she's holed up in an apartment somewhere just trying to figure out what to do next. But John has nightmares about the alternative. And if it weren't for the note, and that one phone call Mark had with her I'd honestly wonder if she was—" She couldn't finish the sentence. For John's sake, she refused to believe that Jana would have actually done anything to harm herself.

But in her mind, she had sorted back through every memorable conversation she and Jana had ever had for hints of where she might have gone. And she came up with a blank every time.

Robbi looked thoughtful. "Have you ever thought about where *you'd* go if you needed to escape?"

Julia pointed at herself. "Me? I guess I've never needed to escape." She grinned, remembering a few nights with Ellie that she wouldn't have minded avoiding. "Well, at least not until recently. But with John, I still feel like a newlywed, and with Martin, well, maybe if he'd lived, we would have come to a point where I needed a break. I don't know…I just can't imagine that. What about you?"

Robbi laughed. "Paul has me spoiled. Why would I want to escape from a man who cooks me gourmet dinners and gives the world's best massages?"

Julia rolled her eyes. "Good point." She slowed her stride, already winded again. "Maybe your husband needs to have a talk with my husband."

Chapter Twenty-Six

John stared at the school calendar on his desk blotter. November 25. His hopes for having Jana home by Christmas were waning fast.

The district office was quiet on this Saturday morning of Thanksgiving weekend. It didn't feel much like a holiday. How had Jana celebrated the day? He ached to think of her alone on a day that was supposed to be for family. It had been a quiet day for him and Julia, too. Brant and Kyle had both spent the holiday with their wives' families in Indiana. Julia's boys hadn't come home, preferring to wait and come for Christmas instead. Oh how he hoped his family would have something to celebrate by then.

Mark had come and had dinner with them and Ellie on Thursday since, for once, the restaurant was closed. But it had been a subdued affair and Mark's presence only emphasized Jana's absence.

He'd felt guilty leaving Julia home alone with Ellie today, but he hadn't wanted his granddaughter to overhear the conversations he hoped to have if he could catch anyone at home.

He stared at the notepad with the list of phone numbers on it. Mark's list. He wasn't sure even what he would say if someone answered. Taking a deep breath, he dialed the first number on the list.

A squeaky-voiced child—probably not much older than Ellie—answered. "Hello. This is Theresa Maria Abriano."

He smiled into the phone, thinking of Ellie. "May I speak to your mommy, please?"

A long minute later, Jana's friend was on the line.

"Laura, this is John Brighton. I'm Jana McFarlane's father. I don't think we've met, but I'm sure you know the situation with Jana."

"Yes… The last time her husband called me, he said they still don't know where she is."

"No. We don't. That's why I'm calling. I wondered if you might have heard from her."

"No. I'm sorry." Another long hesitation. "I told Jana's husband everything I know. I wish I could be more helpful."

"And you don't have any idea where she might have gone? There wasn't a place she talked about—or a friend, someone she might have gone to stay with?"

"I'm sorry. I really don't know anything. Jana was pretty quiet. We mostly just talked about work when we got together."

"I understand. You didn't notice anything the last few weeks before she left, did you? Did she seem depressed or confused?"

"Not that I noticed. She was maybe a little stressed—work was pretty hectic and she talked about how her husband was putting in some long hours. But I wouldn't say she was depressed exactly. It just seemed like the normal complaints."

"Listen, Mark mentioned that you and Jana had lunch the day before she left him. He said Jana ran into someone there. You don't happen to know who it was, do you?"

"Oh my, that seems like so long ago. We were at Buca di Beppo, I remember that."

"We're just trying to follow every lead."

"Of course. Well…I remember Jana seemed really happy to see the woman. I got the impression she was a family friend or something. Maybe someone she hadn't seen in a while?"

"Do you remember what she looked like? Anything?"

"Oh, dear. I'd make a terrible witness." Nervous laughter

came over the line. "Let's see… She was middle-aged. Maybe fifty-five or sixty? I don't know. It's so hard to tell people's ages these days. She was petite…with really short hair. Almost like she'd had cancer or something. But that's just a guess."

John racked his brain to think who Jana might know that matched that vague description. Petite, short hair… "It wasn't Sandra Brenner, was it?" He hadn't seen Ellen's friend since shortly after the funeral, but that sounded like her. Sandra had always worn her hair shorter than most of the men John knew.

"Jana didn't introduce us. I'm sorry. I don't think I ever knew the woman's name."

"Well, it does sound like her. Sandra was a friend of Jana's mother. Did she have kind of a low voice?"

"I'm sorry. I really don't remember." Laura sounded increasingly uncomfortable with John's interrogation.

"Well, thank you, Laura. Thank you for taking the time to talk to me. If you think of anything else, I'd sure appreciate it if you'd give me a call." He gave her his cell phone number.

"Of course. I sure hope you find her."

He hung up, looked up Sandra's number and dialed it.

Her voice came on the line.

"Sandra, hey, it's John Brighton."

"John! My goodness, I haven't talked to you in ages. How are you?"

"Well, not too good, actually. That's why I'm calling, Sandra. We don't know where Jana is."

"I…I don't understand."

"She left her husband."

"Oh, my goodness! I just saw her in the city a few weeks ago. She didn't say anything…"

So it was Sandra.

"Actually, we think she left the day after you talked to her."

John could almost picture Sandra's mouth hanging open in shock. "I had no idea. She seemed—well, I didn't know her that well—but she seemed fine. We had a lovely visit."

"She didn't mention anything about where she was going?"

Sandra breathed a heavy sigh into the phone. "Nothing that I can remember, John. Oh, I'm so sorry."

"Do you remember what you talked about? Did she seem upset?"

"No. Not at all. I asked about her little girl. She told me she's three now." Sandra laughed. "I was still picturing—Ellie, isn't it?—as an infant. Let's see… We talked about Ellen…how it didn't seem possible she could have been gone four years now. I asked how *you* were doing, of course. I told her how happy I was when I heard that you and Julia had gotten together again."

"Again?" John held his breath. What in the world had Sandra said to Jana about him and Julia?

"I *am* happy for you, John. Like I told Jana, I'm so grateful you had Julia in your life after…after Ellen didn't know you anymore. I can only imagine how excruciatingly difficult that must have been. I just met Julia that one time, of course, but I'm glad you can finally share your lives. And I know Ellen would agree."

A pang of nausea gripped him. "Sandra… Did you tell Jana that Julia and I…that we knew each other…before Ellen?"

He and Julia had decided long ago that their friendship—their relationship—before Ellen's death was something their children didn't need to deal with. When they met again, after Ellen's death, they had no doubt that God's blessing was on their union.

Julia's boys were still in college then, at a vulnerable and formative stage of their lives. Brant was a newlywed and Kyle engaged. Mark and Jana had just had Ellie. There had just seemed no reason to complicate their marriage by dragging out that old history.

But he hadn't considered Sandra. In the final years of Ellen's illness, Sandra had actually encouraged his friendship with Julia. An image from years ago startled him. He'd run into Sandra while he and Julia jogged in the park. Flustered, he'd introduced the two women, but he was chagrined when Sandra later came to him, aiming to ease his "guilt" and telling him she was happy for him. She had assumed he and Julia were having an affair.

He couldn't blame her. Most people would have guessed the same. But it wasn't true.

"I'm so sorry. I just assumed your kids knew that you and Julia—"

"That we what, Sandra? There was nothing—" He'd been going to say there was nothing between him and Julia back then, but that wasn't exactly accurate. There had been something between them. Something frightening and wonderful. *And wrong.* But he and Julia had ended their friendship before it turned into an affair. They had ultimately done the right thing. He tried again. "Julia and I did *not* have an affair, but our children aren't aware that we knew each other before. Maybe you should stop assuming where my family is concerned."

"John. I'm sorry. Truly I am." Her voice seemed to hold genuine dismay. "I never dreamed your kids didn't know. Please, I'll be happy to call Jana and apologize…set the record straight."

Venom boiled in his throat. "That would be a lovely gesture, Sandra, if we had a clue where Jana is." He hung up the phone, trembling.

He pushed back from his desk and put his head in his hands. He'd taken his anger and frustration out on Sandra. But the truth was, he had only himself to blame.

Chapter Twenty-Seven

Julia heard the back door open and John's briefcase hit the floor in the mudroom. She dropped the lid back on the spaghetti sauce and went to greet him. "Hey, you. How did it go? Were you able to find out anything?" Standing on tiptoe to kiss him, she noted the sag of his shoulders. "You look tired."

He sighed. "I'm weary." He gave her a look she couldn't quite read.

"Is everything okay?" She studied his face. "Bad news?"

He looked past her to the kitchen. "Where's Ellie?"

"She's watching a video. What's wrong, John?"

"We need to talk."

"That doesn't sound good."

She followed him to the kitchen where he filled a drinking glass with tap water and downed it all at once. He set the glass in the sink and reached for her.

She went willingly into his arms. "John, what happened?"

"I spoke with Laura Abriano today." He replayed his conversation with Jana's friend, and how it had led to him calling Sandra Brenner.

The implication of what he'd learned from Sandra made her blanch. "She told Jana about us?" She pulled away slightly from his embrace to look into his eyes. What she saw there sent a terrible sinking sensation through her. She leaned back into the curve of her husband's body. "Oh, John. Surely that's not why Jana left? Because of us?"

John blew out a frustrated breath, but he put his arms around her and pulled her close. "I don't know. But it sure couldn't have helped matters any."

"Sandra actually thought we—" She couldn't make herself finish the thought.

John rubbed soft circles on her back. "I told her the truth."

Julia looked up at him. "What is the truth, John? What we did…what we had together back then wasn't right."

He pulled away and tipped her chin, forcing her gaze to meet his. "No. It wasn't. But we acknowledged that a long time ago. We asked forgiveness. And it was given. This—" He pointed back and forth between them. "This is God's blessing. This is the best thing that ever happened to me. And I hope to you. Don't you ever think otherwise."

Tears sprang to Julia's eyes. She nodded her agreement. "But what if Jana said something to Mark?" A new thought struck her and she put a hand to her mouth. "Oh, John, what if she told Sam and Andy. Or your boys?"

"Oh, no." He seemed to consider the possibilities. "Don't you think they would have said something when we called about Jana? If they knew?"

"I don't know." A sick feeling washed over her.

"Do you think we should—"

"Grandpa!" Ellie burst into the kitchen.

Julia moved out of John's embrace and Ellie quickly took her place in John's arms.

"Are you gonna stay home now?"

Ellie had pouted this morning when John told her he had to go into the office. Julia had pouted a little, too. And now she felt like crying. And they couldn't even talk things out with little ears perking up to every word they said.

John set Ellie back on the floor and rumpled her hair. "Why don't you go finish your video so Go-Go and I can talk."

"It's already finished. I wanna play with you, Grandpa. You promised."

"We'll play after a while. Right now, you need to go on and find something to do. Go-Go and I were having a conversation."

"I wanna have a conversation, too."

"No, this is just for grown-ups."

"I won't inner-up. I promise."

"Ellie." John used the stern voice that he'd had to use too often of late. "Do as I say."

Ellie actually stomped her foot. "I don't wanna find somethin' to do."

"Ellie, I'm going to count to three and you'd better be moving by the time I get to two."

Julia cringed. John was pushing too hard and experience told her that Ellie would only push back. She had a lot of her grandfather in her.

"Are you gonna play with me then, Grandpa?"

"We'll talk about it later. Right now the clock is running and I mean what I said. One… Two…"

Ellie started jumping up and down, turning in circles and flapping her little elbows like a demented duckling.

"Ellen Marie, did you hear me?"

"I'm movin', Grandpa!"

"What?" John looked to Julia as if she might come to his rescue.

Ellie managed to glare at John while jumping higher and flapping faster. "You said I'd better get movin' by the time you counted! I'm movin' as fast as I can!"

"That is enough, young lady." As he knelt before Ellie, he caught Julia's eye. She shot him a look that said "and just how are you going to argue *that* one, Grandpa?" She finally had to turn away and smother her snickering.

She could hear in his voice that her laughter was tempting his own. She quelled her emotions and turned to see how he would handle the situation.

Composed, he gripped Ellie's shoulders until she stilled, then tipped her chin so she was forced to meet his eyes. "All right,

Ellie. Maybe you didn't understand what Grandpa meant. You listen carefully. Understand?"

She nodded soberly.

John's voice took a gentler edge. "Go-Go and I need to talk in private and we need for you to go play in your room or in the family room. You need to go right now. I'll let you know when we're finished so you can come out and have lunch with us."

"I'm hungry now."

"Well, it's not quite lunchtime yet."

"Soon?"

"Yes, soon. Now this time when I say 'get moving' you know what I mean, right?"

She nodded.

"Okay. Then get moving."

She shuffled in the direction of her room about as slowly as Julia had ever seen the child move, obeying the letter if not the intent of John's order. He waited patiently until she disappeared into her room.

"Close the door, please, Ellie," he shouted after her.

The door slammed.

John slumped into a chair at the kitchen table and put his head in his hands. "I'm too old for this."

Julia came to sit beside him, grateful they could laugh together, yet aware that Ellie's escapades weren't going to change the fact that she and John still had to face the issue Sandra's gaffe had presented.

She put her hand over his. "So where were we? Do you think we need to call the kids?"

"And come clean?"

She nodded, feeling fresh shame at this part of her history with this man she loved so deeply.

He sighed, nodding slowly. "I suppose it might be best."

"Do you want to go first or shall I?" Now that their decision was a reality, the prospect of calling her sons and confessing this failure of her past made her queasy.

"I'll make the calls, Julia. I'm the one who bears most of the blame. If I hadn't let you go on thinking I was available for so long we wouldn't be having to make this confession."

"John…" She wanted to argue, but her relief at his offer tempted her to keep silent.

John shushed her before she could muster a genuine protest. "I'll call. But I want you at my side."

It seemed her love for her husband grew new boundaries every day, and now they expanded again. She put her arms around him and willed her embrace to express what words seemed utterly inadequate for. "I'm already there, sweetheart. I'm already there."

Chapter Twenty-Eight

"You busy?" Denise Kelligan appeared in the doorway to Mark's office. She wore that tilted-head smile she seemed to always have on when she knew he was watching.

He shrugged. "No busier than usual. What's up?"

"There's someone on the phone for you. A John Brighton. He says it's important."

"Oh, sure. I'll take it."

"Line two." She leaned against the doorjamb, making no move to leave.

"Thanks." He waved, hoping she'd get the hint. The last thing he needed was for John to overhear Denise's flirtatious voice in the background.

Finally, he picked up the phone, then covering the receiver, he aimed a pointed glance at the door. "Would you close the door on your way out, please?"

Her grin changed to a pout, but she slipped through the door and closed it behind her.

"John, are you there? Is everything okay?"

"Everything's fine, Mark. Ellie's doing great. I didn't mean to scare you."

"Oh, no. I just—"

"I'm sorry to bother you at work, but you're pretty hard to reach anywhere else."

Mark gave a polite laugh, trying not to analyze whether John meant that as a jab.

"Before I get to what I called about... Well, you probably get tired of me asking, but have you had any word from Jana?"

"No, John. I'm sorry. You know you'll be the first one I call if...when I hear from her."

John cleared his throat. "Listen, the reason I called..." There was a long pause, filled only by a sigh that made Mark wonder what was up. "Did Jana mention who it was she ran into that last day before she left?"

"With Laura? No. She never said anything. The only way I even knew she went out to lunch that day is because Laura told me."

"Well, I talked to Laura, too, and I figured out who it was Jana ran into that day."

"Oh? Who was it?" A tiny alarm sounded in his brain as he remembered Julia's early suspicions that Jana had run off with another man.

"It was a good friend of Ellen's. Sandra Brenner."

Mark let out a relieved breath as John went on. "I don't think you ever met her—except maybe at the funeral. It seems that Sandra told Jana something that was probably very upsetting to her."

Mark reached to tilt the blinds that covered his office window. A striped pattern of light fell across his desk. What was John getting at? He had no idea where this was going. Unless Ellen's friend had said something that convinced Jana she did indeed have Alzheimer's disease. But surely no one would be that insensitive...

"Sandra was under the impression that Julia and I had an affair. While Ellen was still living."

Mark straightened in his chair, every fiber in him suddenly alert.

"That's not true," John added quickly. "But we *were* friends—during Ellen's illness. Closer friends than we should have been under the circumstances. But I'm fairly certain Sandra left Jana with the impression that I was unfaithful to her mother."

"Whoa. I had no idea. If that's really what she told Jana—"

His mind spun in fifty different directions. "That would have been tough on her."

"Yes, I know." John's voice was shaky. "We kept it from all our kids because, well, we stopped seeing each other when we realized the…temptation we faced. We asked forgiveness and we didn't feel it was necessary to bring all that up when we met again. That wasn't until years later. After Ellen had died."

"Oh, man." Mark's brain went into overdrive. If this Sandra woman had told Jana that her father had an affair, it would definitely have messed with her mind. Especially if she thought she had Alzheimer's herself. She must have despaired that if her own father couldn't stay faithful to her mom through this illness, how could he, Mark, remain committed? But Jana hadn't known the whole truth. Had she deserted him and Ellie based on one false piece of information? Somehow, he had to find Jana. Make her aware of the truth.

"Mark…" John's voice pierced his thoughts. "Julia and I want to ask your forgiveness. We thank God that He showed us before it was too late how close we were to falling into serious sin. But it seems that even the feelings we flirted with have had repercussions now. It breaks my heart that this might have put Jana… over the edge."

Mark nodded against the hard plastic of the phone. The resemblance to what was threatening to happen in his own life came into hard focus. He was flirting with a mighty temptation himself and he knew it. He tried to push the image of Denise Kelligan from his mind.

"I just pray—" John's voice broke. "I pray that I'll have a chance to explain it to her. To let her know that Sandra was mistaken. And that Julia and I made things right before God."

"I pray the same." Mark hurt for his father-in-law, and he ached to think Jana might still believe the rumor her mother's friend had circulated. His own guilt muddled his thoughts. He rose and paced the tiled floor of his office, phone in hand.

"We're planning to call each of our kids. We just want to get things out in the open, so no one else will be hurt by this—and so we can be up-front about our past together. We'd appreciate it if you wouldn't say anything until we've had a chance to talk to all our boys."

"Of course. I won't say anything. And John, I appreciate you letting me know. Please tell Julia the same."

"Thanks. I will."

Mark hung up and paced the floor. John's call unsettled him. Made him examine his own actions. The other night at Starbucks, he'd pleaded exhaustion and taken Denise back to her car in the restaurant's parking lot shortly after they finished their coffee. But he'd fantasized other scenarios ever since.

Denise had made it crystal clear that she was available. Mark got the impression she merely thought he was playing hard to get. He had allowed his anger at Jana to let him entertain thoughts he had no business entertaining.

But John Brighton had been down this same road. Funny, Mark had never once considered such a possibility during the years Ellen was dying. He did some quick math. John must have barely been in his fifties when Ellen began her slow agonizing decline into dementia. Fifty seemed a lot younger now than it had back when he and Jana were happy newlyweds. He'd never contemplated the temptations his father-in-law must have faced during the years Ellen was ill. Even now, John was a good-looking guy. He'd probably had a few Denises in his life, offering everything Ellen could no longer give him.

Apparently Julia had been one of those temptations, though she'd never struck Mark as that type. John said they'd been "friends." But what, exactly, did that mean? John denied they'd had an affair. Strangely enough, Mark believed him. He'd been part of the Brighton family long enough to know that John was a man of his word—a man who'd always lived by *the* Word—even before Jana's mom got sick.

Mark had seen himself that way, too. He was a follower of Christ. He ran an honest business. His employees, his vendors, his board—they all knew that he could be trusted. That he operated on a higher principle than most of the world.

But when he examined the way things really were, he knew he was fooling himself. He'd changed. Lately, he didn't feel quite so principled. When he was with Denise, when he was thinking about her, his thoughts weren't anything he wanted a spotlight shone on. The sad thing was, he didn't even really like the woman. He'd spent enough time with Denise to discover that she was rather shallow and self-centered.

And she seemed to be under the impression that he was loaded. Where she got that idea he hadn't a clue. He was barely keeping his head above water and that was with a house where the electricity was rarely in use and there were zero mouths to feed. He ate—when he ate—at the restaurant. The insurance premium was due on the Escape again and he'd decided not to pay it. Unless Jana had a bank account somewhere that he didn't know about—or unless someone else was supporting her—she had to have sold the Escape for cash to live on.

He'd watched the credit card statements carefully and she hadn't put one thing on their card since she'd filled up with gas the day she left. She'd cashed her paycheck from the museum and had taken a two-hundred-dollar cash advance on the credit card at an ATM in a Wal-Mart store the morning she disappeared. Still, in total it wasn't enough to live on for very long.

The Jana who could have done that, who could have left him and Ellie and just disappeared, was someone he didn't know. But he missed the woman he'd fallen in love with, the woman who had given him his daughter.

He drew stark geometric shapes on the vendor notepad on his desk, tracing the sharp lines over and over again until the lead sliced through the thin paper. He missed his family. He missed the man he had been when he was with them.

Chapter Twenty-Nine

Jana headed up the trail, walking stick in hand. The sky was clear today. There had been a light dusting of snow nearly every day since she'd first made this hike two weeks ago, but none of it had amounted to anything. By now, hiking every morning had become a habit.

At first, she'd kept a constant eye on the sky, praying for signs of a storm. But lately she'd discovered other things to observe—the incredible beauty of the rock formations, the ever-changing landscape of the clouds, the fascinating trail of paw prints and bird tracks that traced the landscape, and the family of cardinals nesting in the towering pine just north of where the Escape was "parked."

The odd thought made her smile. Stranded was more like it. And yet, up here, with no one to answer to, it didn't seem like such a catastrophe that she'd dinged up the car. Okay, it was worse than a mere "ding." The engine would still start, but she couldn't get the stupid vehicle to budge. She ran the ignition's accessory only long enough to listen to the weather report each morning. She'd located a Denver station that came in fairly clear and reported the weather every ten minutes.

Yesterday she'd made the trek down to the little market. She'd bundled up in layers of clothes and pulled on a hat and some mittens she found in a crate in the loft. But with the wind biting her face all the way down the mountain road, she was grateful for the sun on her back. Returning to the cabin, with two grocery bags and the wind at her back she stayed warm enough, and her mouth had watered at the thought of the food in her sacks. For ten days, she'd existed on a few crackers and a can of soup or a package of tuna each day. She felt sure she'd lost ten or twelve pounds since she arrived here. But her daily hike had ramped up her appetite. She touched the waist of her jeans. They didn't hang as loose on her as they had only a few days ago.

Halfway down the mountain, she came around a curve in the trail—a spot where she had a clear view of the cabin. From here, it looked like a child's Lincoln Logs creation, though she could make out some details. The wide front window caught the sun's reflection like a mirror and winked at her.

She eyed the white bullet-shaped propane tanks under the A-frame's deck and a tinge of worry crept in.

She didn't have any clue how long they would last before the propane ran out. She'd been heating water for a shower nearly every day now. How long would she have to stay up here before a deep enough snow fell?

She'd gathered fallen branches on her hikes and brought them down the mountain to supplement the fast-dwindling stack of firewood. It crossed her mind that she may well freeze to death— or die of starvation—whether a big snow came or not. But she didn't relish the thought of starving.

Her trail of thoughts startled her. She'd once obsessed about such things day after day, but recently these thoughts had mostly been forgotten. Until now.

It had been agonizing to walk back to the cabin that day after she'd wrecked the Escape. To open the cabin back up and start all over again the next day was almost more than she could stomach.

Only planning her "getaway" had kept her somewhat sane. Now, the thought of what she'd planned to do was the very thing that made her feel insane.

No. Insane wasn't the right word. Her thoughts had been more lucid these past few days than they had in a long time.

Ever since she'd come back down from the mountain, she'd been sleeping like a log. But it was a good sleep, a restorative sleep. Not the awful sleep of the dead that she knew those first weeks in the cabin. Still, sometimes she was tempted to go back to the days she'd spent in a stupor on the sofa in front of the fireplace. That wouldn't be good. She knew that much.

The places her thoughts had taken her lately were painful. She'd done a terrible thing. To Mark. And to Ellie. And her poor father. Dad must be worried sick. Maybe they'd all given up on her by now. Maybe they thought she was dead and had done their grieving and moved on.

She'd have to decide what to do about that.

"Be with them, God. Please be with Ellie and Mark, and Daddy." She'd started talking to God again. Just a little. Mostly to thank Him for the beauty she saw around her. And to pray for Ellie and for her husband. She could at least do that. Surely God would listen to those prayers. Prayers for people who didn't deserve what she'd inflicted on them.

What she'd done—leaving her family the way she had—was too terrible to face yet. She locked the fact away in a little compartment in her mind. Eventually she'd have to take it out and examine it. Before the snow came, she'd have to deal with it. Decide what to do.

"Please, God." She spoke the words aloud and they startled her. She couldn't even say for sure what she meant, what she was pleading for.

In spite of the biting cold, a rush of warmth laved over her. No, *within* her, as if an extraordinary heat coursed through her very veins. Peace. If she hadn't been so far from God, she might have considered it to be that elusive "peace that passes understanding." But she knew better. That couldn't be for her. Not after what she'd done.

She'd been so selfish. So thoughtless. Thinking of no one but herself. It made her feel sick.

Visions of Ellie danced in her mind. Her little girl crying herself to sleep with pitiful sobs. Jana could see Ellie's heart literally breaking. And there was Mark, wearing a bewildered expression, not understanding why his wife had left them without even explaining what was going on in her befuddled brain.

Why did she see things so clearly now, when everything had been so foggy before?

The crack of a branch made her jump. She stopped to listen. She heard it again, softer this time. She'd learned that the mountains, the trees, had their own language. It was never really silent up here. But this was different. Unlike anything she'd heard before.

A shiver rolled up her back as she remembered a conversation she'd overheard in the market yesterday. There'd been more cougar sightings. The flier, warning campers to beware, was still posted.

Jana quickened her steps and started back down the mountain. Being mauled to death by a cougar wasn't how she wanted to go, either.

Chapter Thirty

December first. Julia sat at the kitchen table and stared at the calendar. She hadn't bought one Christmas gift yet. How could it be that she wasn't working, yet she was further behind in every aspect of her life than she'd ever been before.

The house was a disaster—she hadn't dusted once since Ellie had come to stay, and the only time she ran the vacuum was to clean up toddler-size messes—which, she was discovering were bigger than any adult mess she'd ever encountered. It was a good thing God gave babies to young people.

Ellie seemed to be doing okay. She was happy most of the time and she'd adjusted to their rules. Julia had buckled down on the potty training and after a few rough days, Ellie was doing remarkably well. She was still in diapers at night and still had a few accidents at naptime, but it was bearable. Still, Julia was exhausted from doing laundry and bedding twice a week, trying to cook three nutritious meals a day, and trying to keep up with an active little girl.

John was going to have to pitch in if he expected her to get caught up on—

"Hey, babe." As if her thoughts had summoned him, John appeared in the doorway. "Trying to get the week lined out?"

"Try the rest of the year."

He peered over her shoulder. "Christmas is just around the corner, isn't it?"

"Funny you should mention that." She turned, ready to tell him what she'd just been thinking, but she was startled to see the hunch of his shoulders, the dejection on his face. And he was thin. She hadn't realized what a toll this ordeal had taken on his physical appearance.

"It's not going to be the same this year."

She slid from her chair and went to wrap her arms around him. "Maybe Jana will be home by then. Christmas always seems like such a hopeful time. Maybe she'll come to her senses and realize what she has waiting for her at home."

John tightened his arms around her and she felt his body shudder with silent sobs. "Oh, John. Honey… She'll be back. God's watching over her."

He straightened, caressing her hair, kissing the top of her head, as if he could somehow draw strength from their love. When he spoke next, his voice was steady. "I thought she'd be back long before now. I wonder…I wonder if something's happened to her."

Since that first day they'd gone to pick up Ellie, they hadn't spoken of Mark's fear that Jana may have intended to harm herself. But Julia knew it was constantly in the back of John's mind. She'd had similar fears, but wouldn't have dared voice them until now.

"John…" She placed her hands on either side of his face and welded her gaze to his. "Jana knows better. You raised her well and she knows where to turn with her problems. God will keep His hand on her. I know He will." It was hard not to look away, for fear John would sense the tiniest bit of skepticism that crept in.

He gave her a frail smile and placed his hands over hers on his face. "I couldn't have borne this if I didn't believe that. For a long time I blamed Mark. He's not perfect, and he does work too much, but I think Jana bears more of the blame than I thought. I don't understand how she got so mixed-up. It doesn't make sense. She has so much to live for. So many people who love her and need her…"

"I know. I wish we could talk to her. She's a smart woman. I feel like if we could just see her, we could make her understand. But where would we even start…to look for her?"

He shrugged. "I don't know. I've racked my brain trying to think where in the world she could be. Trying to think the way she might think. And all I come up with is that if I were her, I'd be thinking it was about time I got my pathetic self home." He looked at her, a spark of panic in his eyes. "You don't think she really could be in the early stages of Alzheimer's, do you?"

"Oh, surely not. From what Mark said, I think she might have had some sort of emotional breakdown. She might be suffering from depression, but I can't imagine it has anything to do with Alzheimer's. Or dementia of any kind. She couldn't have held down her job if that were the case. Could she?"

He shrugged.

Her mind raced, trying to think what to say that would comfort him. "You know… Jana and Mark were married—was it almost ten years?—before Ellie came along. They had it pretty easy. And for the first couple of years, she had Mark's help with Ellie. I think maybe she was just overwhelmed with the whole motherhood scene." Laughing softly, she pointed down the hall toward Ellie's room. "Tell me, don't *you* feel a little over-whelmed at times?"

That coaxed a smile from him, but he quickly sobered again. "That may be true, but what does it say about Jana? At the first bit of difficulty, she runs away? Stays away for weeks? Maybe it's wrong of me, but I'm ashamed of her."

She held him again, praying for the right words. Finally, she drew back and looked at him. "I understand, but…let's wait until we hear Jana's side of the story before we form any judgments."

He let out a ragged sigh. "I'm sorry. I don't know what I'm saying. I'm her father. I should have known there was something wrong. I just wish this was over. This whole stupid thing."

She put a finger to his lips. "Shh. Don't. Don't do that to yourself. Let's just pray for her. That's one thing she desperately needs."

He caressed her cheek with the back of his hand. "I married

a wise woman." Pulling her to him again, he clung to her as if he were drowning.

Julia summoned strength and willed her voice to steady. "Lord, we love Jana, but we know You love her even more. Please, God. Bring her home quickly. We want everything to happen in Your perfect timing, but, Lord…I'd love to have her home for Christmas."

Immediately, she regretted voicing her wish aloud. What if Jana wasn't home by Christmas? Not that she'd planted any hope in John's mind that wasn't already there.

But he took up the prayer in her stead. "Father God, forgive my lack of faith. I'm so weary and so worried about my daughter. Please be with Jana, Lord. Keep her safe, Father. Put Your angels around her and keep her from every kind of harm. Oh, God, I love her so much…I—" He broke down again.

"Amen," Julia whispered.

"Go-Go?"

John and Julia turned as one. Ellie stood in the hallway in her nightgown. Julia unraveled herself from John's arms and went to her. "What's the matter, honey?"

"I had a bad dream."

"Oh, I'm sorry. Do you want me to tuck you back in?"

Ellie sniffed. "Could you and Grandpa *both* tuck me in?"

Julia looked to John. "Grandpa?"

"Okay. Just this once."

She lifted Ellie into her arms and John followed them down the hall.

They went through the nightly ritual of tucking, good-night kisses and hugs all around for the plush rabbit Ellie called Stuff-Bunny.

John gave her one last tuck for good measure and stood, turning out the lamp beside her bed. He put his hand on Julia's back to usher her out of the room, but before they reached the door, Ellie started to whimper.

"I'm scared! Please don't go, Grandpa. Go-Go, please stay with me!"

This was something different than her usual bedtime excuses. They looked at each other and together, went back to her bedside.

Julia felt Ellie's forehead, thinking maybe she was coming down with something. She felt warm, but Julia didn't think feverish. "What are you afraid of, sweetie?"

"I'm scared my dream'll turn on again."

Too bad there wasn't a remote control for dreamland. "What did you dream about? Can you tell Go-Go?"

Without warning, Ellie started to sob. Julia threw John a worried glance and scooped Ellie into her arms, holding her close. "It's okay, sweetie, it's okay. You don't have to talk about—"

But the nightmare poured out before Julia could finish her sentence.

"There was a bad, bad man and he told my mommy to go away and…and—"

"Ellie." John knelt beside her bed, forming a circle with Julia. "There's no bad man. You're safe in Grandpa and Go-Go's house."

"I know, but I want my mommy." Her breath came in ragged gasps. "I want to go see my mommy. I want my daddy to take me and go get my mommy back."

Her cries tore Julia apart. A sense of utter helplessness weighted her down. How could she offer an ounce of comfort to this little girl, when the only thing she wanted was her mother's arms? And for her father to be her hero. Julia's own tears were close to the surface, and from John's iron grip on her arm, she knew his heart was breaking, too.

She stretched out on the quilt beside Ellie, stroking her cheek. John slipped off his shoes and joined her on the other side of the bed. The three of them lay there, gathering comfort from one another until finally Ellie's even breaths told them she'd fallen asleep.

John finally eased off the bed and crept toward the door.

"I'll be right there," Julia mouthed.

He was sitting on the edge of their bed staring at the clock when she came into the bedroom a few minutes later. "It breaks my heart," she said.

"Why do you suppose she dreamed about a bad man?"

Julia studied him. "What do you mean?"

"Ellie said a bad man told her mommy to go away."

"I think that was simply a little girl's way of dealing with her grief. You think it was something else? Something more?"

"I don't know. I don't know what to think. I have never felt so powerless in my entire life. I have to do something, Julia! I don't care if Jana is an adult. She's my daughter. I can't just sit here and do nothing."

Julia sat beside him. "What would you do, John? What could you possibly do that you haven't already done. Where would you start looking?"

"I don't know…" He released a ragged sigh. "But this is going to kill me."

Julia was beginning to fear that very thing.

Chapter Thirty-One

"Mark, I need to talk to you."

Denise Kelligan stood in the doorway to his office and Mark realized she was becoming a familiar sight there. Her excuses for seeking him out had gone from mostly believable to nonexistent.

It was his own fault. He pushed away the thought. "What is it, Denise?"

She stepped into his office and bent to move the chair that sat in front of the door propping it open. "Do you mind if we talk privately?"

She had his attention now. "Uh…sure. Have a seat."

She nudged the door shut and came to sit on the edge of his desk.

"Mark. I've wanted to talk to you for a long time now." She wet her lips and inspected a pearly pink fingernail before meeting his eyes. "I've tried to say this a hundred times, and I always chicken out, but something you said the other day made me realize that it's time I was just open and honest with you."

He drew back. Where was this going? "What did I say?" He'd never seen her so serious.

"It was last week when I stayed to help you clean up after that party, remember?"

He remembered the night, but he didn't remember saying

anything that would have necessitated a private consultation with him. "I'm not sure," he said finally.

"It's like this, Mark." Her self-confident demeanor seemed to dissipate and she turned shy, hesitant. "I have so much respect for you. You're the best boss a woman could ever want. I admire everything you've accomplished—the restaurant, I mean. I know how hard you've worked to make this dream come true. But more than that, Mark."

Her words gathered steam and she scooted a few inches closer to him across the top of his desk. "So much more. I admire the kind of man you are. I feel like we've really become close over the last few months and…well, I know you probably have some reservations about—about dating your employees, but I just want you to know that—"

"Whoa. Whoa…" He pushed his chair back and scrambled to his feet. "Denise. I'm not sure you want to say what I think you're going to say."

"Yes. I do." She held up a hand, her eyes sparking with unmistakable passion. "I've thought about this long and hard and I finally realized that I will regret it for the rest of my life if I don't tell you how I feel about you. I love you, Mark. And I want you to know that I'd do anything to make you—"

"Denise… Stop. Please." He came from behind the desk and put a hand on the doorknob, desperate for air. "We're both going to regret it if you continue."

All at once, as if it were chalked out on one of Trevor's advertising boards, he saw the stark truth of what had happened here. He had led Denise on, flirting, encouraging her thinly veiled offers. Yes, she'd been the one to pursue him first, but he'd been flattered by the attention. He'd been so vulnerable after Jana's rejection. It had stroked his injured ego to know that someone found him attractive, someone wanted him, even if his wife didn't.

But he'd never felt anything for Denise but affection— *No.* The word came from somewhere outside of himself. He recognized the voice that, until recently, had guided his life in times of trouble. He'd shut that voice out again and again in the past weeks, angry that God had allowed Jana to leave him. That he'd found himself trapped in what was supposed to be his dream. This stupid restaurant. But now he knew God was asking him to be honest before his Maker. And to be honest with himself.

Denise stood there, waiting for him to explain himself. What could he tell her that was true, and that set things right with her. As if scales had slipped from his eyes, he saw the selfishness of how he'd treated Denise. What he'd felt for her was nothing more, nothing less than lust. Shame burned through him. If it wasn't bad enough that he'd entertained thoughts of violating the sacred vows he'd made to his wife, he'd also allowed this poor woman to think that she had a chance of gaining his affection.

"Denise, I'm sorry. You...you've misunderstood my intentions." He buried his face in his hands and rubbed it, as if he could somehow wash away his culpability. But when he looked up, Denise's tears were all the reminder he needed. *Be honest.* "It's not your fault. I should have been more clear." He held up his left hand, twisted it until his wedding ring caught the light. "I'm still married. I don't know what will happen with Jana, but I'm—" He swallowed hard. Did he mean the words he was about to speak? Could he say them with integrity?

He met her watery gaze. "I'm committed to my wife, Denise. I love her."

Denise looked as though she was going to say something. Instead, she slid from the desk and bolted past him out of the room.

Mark dreamed about Jana that night. He awoke still thinking of her. Warm thoughts. Missing her more than he'd allowed himself to in many weeks. He fought against the blare of the alarm clock and the neighbor's dog barking, wanting to drift back to sleep. Resume the dream. Hold on to the feelings it evoked.

They'd been someplace vaguely familiar in his dream. Somewhere in the mountains he thought. Yes, he remembered. Camped out on blankets in front of a massive stone fireplace.

Jana looked so beautiful in the firelight. Her skin luminous, her smile only for him.

He struggled to remember. He knew that place. It was something from a long time ago. In his mind, he started to pull back from Jana's face, wanting to figure out their surroundings. But he squinched his eyelids tighter, afraid if he let her vision fade, he'd forget what she looked like. And he'd lose her all over again.

He drifted, dreaming again. He watched her as she slept in the bed up in the loft of that cabin where they'd stayed on their honeymoon. That was it. It was the fireplace from the cabin they'd rented in Colorado. That first morning after their wedding day, he'd watched her sleep in the canted light of early morning, hardly believing he was waking up beside this amazing, beautiful woman.

He'd thought he loved Jana before that—and certainly he had. But that morning, for the first time, he had this extraordinary, warm feeling inside. Something he'd never felt before that didn't have anything to do with making love for the first time— though that had been incredible. He hadn't understood that elusive feeling. And then all at once, it had come to him: this was what it felt like to have a home. A place to belong. Someone to belong to. And looking down on her innocent, sleeping form, he'd realized that for him, it was Jana. *She* was home for him.

A dog howled somewhere. Mark stirred, opened his eyes, realizing too late that he'd ruined the dream. A deep sadness overwhelmed him.

But he remembered enough. He remembered how Jana had come to mean home for him. She still did.

A compelling need to see her face overwhelmed him. He'd never carried photographs in his wallet, but there had to be pictures somewhere in the house.

He crawled out of bed and padded to the kitchen. There. On the refrigerator was the family photo gallery. He'd grown so accustomed to the montage of images plastered on the side-by-side doors that he'd ceased to see them. But now, he perused them with new eyes.

Jana stared back at him from a glossy snapshot, smiling. A

two-year-old Ellie sat on her lap, and John had his arms around both of them. It was a photo Mark had shot at the Brighton Thanksgiving last year. Not even a year ago.

He searched Jana's eyes, trying to find some hint of the angst she must have been feeling then. He saw nothing. It had been him she was smiling at in that instant the camera had captured. Her smile seemed genuine. He'd been the reason for her happiness. Hadn't he?

Or was it merely the camera she'd graced with her smile? That wasn't even a year ago. How could she have changed so much in such a short time?

What had he missed?

Chapter Thirty-Two

Leaving Julia sleeping, John tiptoed from their room and crept down the hallway in the gray light of the December morning. He stopped and stood in Ellie's doorway, watching the slow rise and fall of the mound of covers she was buried under. One skinny leg stuck out from the tangle of quilts.

He went to her bedside and covered her leg, tucking the quilts around her. Maybe she'd sleep another hour or two. For Julia's sake, he hoped so.

Ellie had been up again last night, the fourth time in as many days, crying and shivering from the aftereffects of another nightmare. He and Julia were both worn-out from getting up with her in the wee hours of the night.

At least Julia could catch up on her sleep when Ellie went down for her nap in the afternoon. He was frazzled to the bone, and it was starting to show at work. Yesterday he'd snapped at the district secretary over a stupid little mistake. He apologized, of course, but how long would his staff's patience hold out? Or how soon would it be before he was the one making mistakes in his work?

Surely there had been times like this when his own kids were little, but he didn't remember this weary-to-the-bone exhaustion. It made him feel ancient.

And yet, hadn't he and Julia said only a couple of nights ago, as they sat cross-legged on the living room floor roughhousing with Ellie, that she made them feel young again.

He felt guilty for his earlier whining thoughts. Ellie was a precious blessing. No doubt about it. He reached to brush an errant curl off her cheek.

Her face felt warm. Too warm. He pressed the palm of his hand against her cheek, then her forehead. She was burning up! Alarmed, he switched on the lamp on the nightstand. Ellie stirred and rolled over on her back. Her face was flushed, her lips parched.

John flew back to the master bedroom, his heart racing as fast as his feet. He croaked out Julia's name.

She sat straight up in bed, looking groggy-eyed and confused. "What's wrong?"

"Ellie's burning up with fever."

With the calm of a seasoned mother, Julia eased out from under the blankets, slipped on the robe that hung on the bedpost, and followed him to Ellie's room.

Julia knelt by the bed and felt the little girl's forehead with the back of her hand. Ellie stirred and changed positions, but didn't wake up. "She does feel warm. Let me go get a thermometer."

She came back a minute later with a plastic strip that she pressed to Ellie's forehead. After a few seconds, she frowned. "Her temperature is almost a hundred and three." Even in a whisper, John detected the quiver in her voice.

"What should we do?" Caring for sick kids had never been his strong suit. Ellen had been the one to play nurse any time their children were sick.

Julia put a finger to her lips and motioned for John to follow her out of the room. When they were in the hall again, she turned to him with a worried frown. "Probably the best thing right now is to let her sleep. I probably should take her temp with a more reliable thermometer, but I don't think I even have one in the house."

"Do you want me to run to the pharmacy?"

"What time is it? They won't open until at least nine."

"Don't they have an emergency number?"

She smiled. "I don't think this is an emergency yet. But Harrison's opens at eight. They'll probably have a thermometer. Would you mind going?"

"No. I'll go. I can call in to the office on my way." He was thankful to have an assignment. "What kind do I get?"

"I'll make a list. You probably ought to get some pain reliever, too. But not aspirin."

"Write it down. I don't have a clue about these things."

She made him a list that included Popsicle frozen treats and 7-Up. He laughed, feeling much relieved that Julia was taking charge. "Who knew it could be so much fun to get sick?"

She set down her pencil and grinned up at him. "Maybe you'll be lucky enough to catch whatever it is she has."

But when he came back from the store two hours later, Julia wasn't smiling. She met him at the door, still in her robe, a lethargic Ellie in her arms. "I think we need to take her to the—" She mouthed the word *doctor* silently.

Fear shot through him. "Why? Is she worse?"

"Her temperature is spiking even higher and her glands feel swollen to me. I tried to call Dr. Morton, but he's on vacation until next week. His nurse suggested we bring her in. The PA can squeeze her in. They don't like to see a fever that high in a three-year-old."

John looked at his watch. He was already an hour late for work. "Can you handle it or do I need to come with you?"

She sighed. "If you'll hold her for a few minutes while I throw some clothes on."

He held out his arms. Julia transferred Ellie, who was awake, but her eyes were drowsy-looking and she seemed to be barely aware of her surroundings.

John didn't like it one bit. "I'll go with you. Hurry up and get dressed." He hadn't meant it to come out so gruff, but Julia didn't seem to notice. She practically ran back to the bedroom.

On the way to the hospital Julia sat in the backseat keeping an eye on Ellie, while John dialed Mark's number on his cell phone.

"Stupid voice mail." He left a terse message, then punched the phone off. "Do you have the number for the restaurant?"

She shook her head. "He wouldn't answer there anyway."

In the rearview mirror he watched Julia pull the medical permission note Mark had written for them from her purse.

"I just hope they'll accept this and go ahead and see her even if we can't get a hold of Mark. We should have had him send copies of his insurance card."

In the waiting room, Ellie fussed and clutched at her neck. "My froat hurts, Go-Go. It hurts."

"I know, sweetie. We're going to have the doctor take a look at it. Maybe he'll have some medicine that will make you feel better."

John prayed that medicine wouldn't come in needle form.

They finally got in to an examination room after half an hour in the waiting room crowded with coughing, sneezing patients. John imagined Ellie—and himself—picking up far worse diseases than whatever she was suffering from now.

The physician's assistant—a young man who looked barely old enough to be a college student—checked Ellie over and took a throat culture. He wrote out a prescription for an antibiotic, telling them they could wait to fill it until they got the lab results later that afternoon.

Mark finally returned their call moments after Dr. Morton's nurse phoned with the lab results.

John relayed the lab's news to Mark. "Ellie has strep throat. They prescribed an antibiotic and think she'll be fine in a few days, but I think you need to come."

"You mean…come and get her?"

"No. Not necessarily. But she needs her dad."

Julia coached John from the kitchen table. "Tell him about the nightmares."

"She needs to see you, Mark. She's been having nightmares and now this. She's a pretty sick little girl. She needs to know that you haven't abandoned her, too."

There was a long pause and John regretted his choice of words. But not enough to take them back.

"I've told her how things are," Mark said finally.

"But she's too young to understand. All she knows is that the two people she trusted and loved aren't there anymore. I'm asking you—please come. Surely there is someone who can cover for you for a day or two."

Julia narrowed her eyes. "Tell him to close the stupid restaurant down for a week if he has to."

John started to relay Julia's message, but Mark saved him the trouble. "I heard what she said. I can't close the restaurant, but I'll see what I can do about getting away. Give Ellie my love."

John hung up without replying.

Chapter Thirty-Three

Traffic was horrendous on I-55 out of Chicago. Mark had half a notion to turn around and go back. Call John and Julia and tell them he couldn't come.

What is wrong with you, McFarlane? Two voices warred within him. He missed Ellie terribly. And the news that she was sick made him ache for her. Even worse, that she'd been having nightmares. What had Jana done to their daughter? He stopped short, knowing that Jana couldn't take all the blame.

Ever since the night Denise had come into his office, he'd been forced to take a good look at himself. He was trying to be honest about what he saw when he looked in the mirror each morning. But the truth was painful. What he'd discovered was that Mark McFarlane had a long history of deceiving himself, of not looking at the truth when it was staring him in the face.

He pulled into the left lane to pass a sluggish semi. Why was he so eager to get out of this trip to Calypso? He'd only been to see Ellie one time in the weeks she'd been with John and Julia. He counted back to the end of September. Almost nine weeks since Jana had left, and John and Julia had come and taken Ellie home with them. And he'd made the effort to see her once. Pathetic.

Sure he'd seen her almost weekly, thanks to John and Julia bringing her to the city. But… *Be honest.* He forced himself to seek the truth. When it came clear, he would have hung his head if he hadn't needed to keep a close eye on the traffic. Even when they'd brought his daughter to him, he had been preoccupied and inattentive, cutting the visits as short as possible, and making excuses to escape into his work.

Why? Why had he done that? It didn't even make sense. McFarlane's was a demanding company to run. No one was disputing that, but it wasn't going to curl up and fold while Mark spent a couple days in Calypso.

Why was he so reluctant to be the father Ellie needed now in Jana's absence?

The answer hit him with as much power as if the semi he'd just passed had run him over. He couldn't face Ellie—or John or Julia—because it was *his* fault that Jana had left. He was the one who should have noticed how desperate Jana was, how she was struggling. He should have done whatever it took to make sure Jana felt secure. He should have insisted Jana go to the doctor and get relief from her fears that she'd inherited Alzheimer's. Any husband worth his salt would have done that for his wife.

But he'd been too busy. Too wrapped up in creating his mighty kingdom, making his dream come true. When all the while, Jana's dream was shriveling and dying before her eyes.

Oh, Jana. He longed to look over in the passenger seat and see her there, beautiful and vulnerable. He had the words that just might begin her healing. He could take her hand, wrap her in his arms and reassure her that he would always be there for her. Why hadn't he done that? While there was still time?

"Do you want me to take her and put her to bed?" Julia stood over Mark with her arms out.

Ellie was heavy on his lap—and too warm, the fever still burning inside her. But Mark relished the feel of her weight in his arms. "It's okay. I'll just hold her for a little while."

Julia seemed pleased by his response, and for the first time, he comprehended that she and John must have worried that *both* of Ellie's parents had bailed on her. Well? And hadn't they? The revelation pained him. Because it was true. Whether that had been his intention or not, he had abandoned his daughter at the very time in her short life when she'd needed him most.

He looked down on her sleeping form, her eyelashes feathered against round cheeks. She was so beautiful. And she looked so much like Jana right now it jolted him. And sent a knife of conviction straight through him.

The truth hurts. Never had he understood the old adage so clearly.

"How long did the doctor say it would take her to get over this?"

"They said she'd start feeling better after being on the antibiotic for about forty-eight hours, but she has to take it for ten days."

"That long?"

"Just to make sure it doesn't come back."

"Oh." How long did they expect him to stay? He'd made arrangements at work to be off two days. And even at that, he fully expected to come back to a mess that would take him a week of double overtime to straighten out.

Tanner was already working long hours, still trying to train the new chef—and woo her at the same time, it appeared.

After his run-in with Denise Monday night, he hadn't felt comfortable asking her to pick up the slack. He'd half expected her to quit after she ran out of his office, but she'd shown up at work the next night wearing a long face, and trying to pretend nothing had happened. He'd wanted to explain himself, apologize again for leading her on, but when he finally got a minute alone with her in the empty lobby, she brushed him off before he could say two words. "I got the message, Mark. Believe me, I got it loud and clear. You don't need to say anything else."

So he hadn't. But it wouldn't surprise him if her days at McFarlane's were numbered, and then he'd be training a new part-time assistant manager, too.

Why did everything have to be so complicated? He didn't want to stir up trouble so soon, but the Brightons needed to know he couldn't stay for long. He cleared his throat. "Julia, I appreciate you guys putting me up for a couple nights. I—I'll need to head back early Friday morning."

Julia perched on the edge of the sofa beside him. She reached to stroke one of Ellie's legs, and Mark watched her, touched by the expression of deep compassion veiling her face. Ellie was much loved here. That was a comfort.

"Mark, what are your plans? Have you thought about what you're going to do…for the long term?" She looked down, keeping her eyes on Ellie. "This has been hard on her. As much as we love her, this isn't home. I think she needs to know what's going to happen to her. She needs a sense of security that she doesn't have right now. I think that's why she's having the nightmares."

Mark closed his eyes. "I don't know what to say. *I* don't know what's going to happen, Julia. How can I begin to tell Ellie?"

"You can tell her that you'll always be there for her. You can let her know when you'll be back to see her next—and then keep that appointment."

He couldn't meet her eyes. There was this huge elephant in the room every time they were together: the question of what was going to happen to Ellie if Jana didn't come back. He had to make some decisions. "I know," he said finally. "We need to talk."

She nodded. "John will be home around six. Let's have dinner and then we can talk after Ellie is in bed tonight. I haven't decided what to fix for dinner." She grinned. "I'm always a little nervous cooking for you."

He waved her comment away, grateful to move on to a more pleasant topic. "I've eaten your cooking often enough to know you're a wonderful cook. But hey, why don't you let me cook tonight. I have a couple of new dishes I've been wanting to add to the menu at McFarlane's. You could be my guinea pigs."

"That's the best offer I've had yet." Julia clapped her hands, then winced when Ellie stirred at the noise. But Ellie settled back in on Mark's lap.

"You make me a grocery list and I'll run to the store while you spend time with Ellie. Thanks, Mark."

"It's no big deal." He looked Julia in the eye. "Seriously, Julia… I hope you and John know how much I appreciate everything you've done for Ellie. For me. I don't know how I would have survived if I hadn't known Ellie was with you."

She gave his knee a motherly pat. "It's our privilege. I hope very soon this will all be a distant memory. We're praying every day that will be so, Mark."

"Yeah…me too."

Mark's own mother had been gone for over eight years, but suddenly he missed her desperately. And yet, he was glad Mom wasn't here to see how messed up his life had become.

Chapter Thirty-Four

Mark watched their faces around the round oak dining table as they took their first bites of the entrée he'd made.

Julia closed her eyes and made all the right noises. "Scrumptious!"

John swallowed and licked his lips. "This is delicious. A keeper for sure. Now what did you call it?"

"Spicy Basil Chicken. Jana and I had something like it the last time we went to expo in New York. This is my version of it anyway." He'd forgotten how much fun this part of his job was. He hadn't had time to experiment in the kitchen for months.

Ellie grimaced and spit a bite of chicken out on her plate. "I don't like it, Daddy. It's stinging!"

Except for the fact that her curls were still a tangled mass after her nap, Ellie looked much better than she had even this afternoon. The medication must have finally kicked in. And the two-hour nap she'd taken on his lap probably hadn't hurt, either.

"Here, let Go-Go cut off some of the 'hot' part. This sauce might be a little too spicy for you." Julia leaned over and cut a few hunks of white meat out of the center of Ellie's serving and put them over to the side of her plate. "There. Try that."

Ellie clamped her mouth shut and shook her head. "I don't

want it." She pushed her plate away, folded her arms across her chest and scowled.

John reached across the table to scoot her plate back in front of her. "You need to eat a few bites, Ellie. Go-Go cut it all up for you. Now you try it again."

"No. I don't wanna." She started to whimper.

"Ellie. Stop that." John's voice was stern.

Mark was taken aback. John had always been a softy when it came to his granddaughter. Why was he being so short with her, especially when she wasn't feeling well?

Feeling protective, he took Ellie's fork and threaded a small bite onto the tines. "Here, try this bite. See, there's no sauce on it."

She leaned as far back in her chair as was physically possible and welded her lips together. "Uh-uh."

Mark put the fork down, keenly aware that John and Julia were watching how he would handle this. "Okay, Ellie. You may be excused, but I don't want to hear about it later tonight when you get hungry. Do you understand?"

She glared at him. He ignored her and turned his attention to his own plate.

A few minutes later, the adults were in the middle of a conversation when, from the periphery of his vision, he saw Ellie slip from her chair and slink off toward the family room. He ignored her.

But Julia apparently had been waiting for the cue. "Are you guys ready for dessert?" she asked. "It's nothing fancy—just ice cream…"

Ellie flew back to the table, and climbed onto her chair. "I'm ready!"

Mark reached out to stop her, opened his mouth to remind her that she hadn't eaten her dinner. But her eager face made him decide to let it slide this once. It wasn't worth making an issue over. He was only here for a short time, and he hated to spoil the moment making a big scene over nothing. Besides, she probably needed something in her tummy with the medicine she was on. He pulled her chair out and helped her get situated.

Before pushing back his chair, John gave Ellie a look Mark couldn't quite interpret, but it wasn't adoration.

"I'll help you dish up." John followed Julia into the kitchen.

Mark cleared away the dishes and carried them in to the sink. As he was scraping the scraps from Ellie's plate into the garbage disposal, John eyed the plate. "Are you sure you want to throw that out?"

"Believe me, she's not going to eat it."

John shrugged and Mark went back to the dining room. A minute later, Julia brought the coffeepot to the table and John came behind her balancing a tray with three bowls of ice cream. He set one in front of each of the adults.

"Hey!" Ellie clambered to her knees in her chair and put her hands on her hips, surveying the table. "Where's mine, Grandpa?"

"Your daddy said you couldn't have anything else if you didn't eat your dinner. Remember?"

Ellie turned to Mark. "Daddy?"

Mark gave John a look he hoped begged leniency. "We'll see," he told Ellie.

John turned away, but Mark could read in the set of his jaw that he didn't approve.

Well, tough. Who was the father here, after all? Mark took his empty coffee cup and spooned in a dollop of ice cream from his bowl. "Here, you can have a little of Daddy's." He handed Ellie his spoon and went to the kitchen for another one.

Ellie polished off her small serving in three bites and held out her cup. "More." She gave him an irresistible smile. It was a little game they'd often played. Mark gave her another bite.

She ate it and held out the cup again. "More."

He laughed. "No way, José. That's all."

"More in the freezerator?"

Mark turned to Julia. "Is there more?"

She nodded, but by her pinched expression, Mark got the impression she didn't think Ellie should have had any ice cream, either. Or maybe it was that he'd put her in the position of going against John's wishes.

He excused himself and went to the kitchen to dish up another small bowl. The more he thought about John and Julia's reaction, the more he fumed. He was Ellie's father and if he changed his mind and decided she could have ice cream, who were they to say otherwise? He dug out another king-size scoop and plopped it in the bowl just for spite.

He started back to the dining room, but John passed him in the doorway between the two rooms. In his hand was the coffee cup Ellie had been eating from.

Mark stared at it. "What—?"

John's voice was cold. "You know, you told her she was done eating for the night. She'll never learn to respect what you say if you go back on your threats."

Mark tensed his jaw. "In the first place, I never made a threat to my daughter, and—"

"I'm just saying, if you don't abide by the rules you set, she won't—"

"I do abide by the rules. But I haven't had a chance to spend time with my daughter in weeks. I'm not going to waste what little time I do have making a huge issue over something this ridiculous. Besides, Ellie's been sick. I doubt it's good for her to take that medicine on an empty stomach. I had my reasons for handling this the way I did. I'm not a complete idiot, you know."

John set the cup down on the counter and motioned for Mark to move into the kitchen. "Listen, Mark, I don't mean to overrule you here, but what you're not taking into account is that when you leave here, Julia and I are the ones who are going to have to suffer a spoiled little girl who doesn't respect the wishes of the adults in her life."

"Are you calling Ellie spoiled?" His blood had reached the boiling point now.

John looked at the floor before meeting Mark's eyes. "Maybe that wasn't the best choice of words. But she does know how to work you—and us. And that's my point. We are trying to teach her to obey, and if she's allowed to get away with disobedience from you, then we're the ones who pay for it later."

Mark could hardly believe what he was hearing. "Well, excuse me for having compassion for my little girl and letting her have a few bites of ice cream for her sore throat." He hadn't meant his comments to come out quite so acerbic, and he was fully aware that he had considerably plumped up his reasons for not backing up his rule.

"You're missing my point," John said evenly. "I understand why you let her go against your rule. What I'm saying is that you should have thought about that before you took her plate away."

Mark held up a hand, wrestling with a strong desire to punch his father-in-law square in the nose. Okay, now he was being juvenile. Still, John had overstepped his bounds. He took a deep breath. "I don't want to turn this into an argument. This whole thing has been tough on all of us. I'm sorry if you felt I didn't handle Ellie well, but I've gotten to see so little of her these past weeks. I didn't want her memories of me to be of an ogre."

John reached out and put a hand on Mark's arm. "I'm sorry. I—I wasn't seeing it from your point of view. But I don't think you were seeing it from mine, either."

"Let's just forget it right now. I came to spend time with my daughter." Mark pushed past him, not quite ready to give up his irritation yet.

By the time he got to the table with the ice cream, it was a moot point. Ellie had slipped away to play quietly in the family room.

He ate the extra bowl of ice cream himself. For the rest of the evening he nursed a bellyache, along with the knowledge that— one day at a time—he was losing his right to be Ellie's father.

Mark backed out of the driveway and waved to Ellie one last time. She was being brave, but it killed him to leave her again. Still, he was determined that this time would be different.

It sobered him to see how quickly John and Julia had become the parent figures in Ellie's eyes. He felt helpless and defensive, standing by while they usurped his authority. He knew it wasn't intentional. And in spite of the tension that pitted him and John against each other, he did understand his father-in-law's point. If John was going to have the responsibility for Ellie most of the time, he had to know she would obey him.

And that was exactly why Mark had resolved to make some changes. As soon as he was back on the freeway, he picked up his cell phone and dialed Hank Lowery. If any of his investors would back him, Hank would.

Hank's secretary put him through immediately. "Mark! How's it going?"

"Is this a good time, Hank? I need to talk to you."

"Sure. What's up?"

"I need to hire a full-time assistant manager for the restaurant as soon as possible."

The line was silent a second too long. "In addition to your part-time assistant? I didn't think the budget would support that quite yet, Mark."

"It's not enough, Hank. I need more help. I can't keep up these long hours. It's killing me. It's killing my family. I'll take a cut in my salary if I have to. I know that's not going to make up the difference, but I don't feel I have a choice."

"Is there a problem?"

He swallowed hard. "There's a big problem. My wife…Jana has left me."

"Mark." He could almost hear Hank trying to get his bearings. "I'm so sorry. I had no idea…"

"She's been gone for two months now. I should have let you—and all the shareholders—know before now, but I thought we'd work things out."

"Would you like Marcia and me to talk with you and Jana? We've done some lay counseling and it might help to—"

"I don't know where she is, Hank. I haven't seen her since September."

Mark interrupted the stunned silence on the line, explaining what had happened, begging Hank's understanding. "I suppose we'll need to call a special meeting, but I wanted to speak to each of the stockholders first."

"I'll support you, Mark. We'll do what we have to do. I'm sorry to hear about Jana."

"Thanks, Hank."

He called each of the other stockholders and explained the situation all over again. It killed him to hear the disappointment in their voices when he told them what had happened and about his plans. And yet each phone call cemented his convictions deeper. He was doing the right thing.

Still, he was painfully aware that this setback struck a real blow to men who had trusted him with considerable investments. Yet, one by one, each of them expressed even deeper concern over Mark's marriage and his family.

That is, until he reached Bill Weirmeyer.

"I don't think that's a workable idea at all, Mark. Not at this stage of the game." Bill's voice boomed over the road noise and Mark held the phone an inch from his ear. "You assured us when we started out that you'd handle the management yourself for the first two years. We've already allowed you a part-time assistant manager."

"I realize that, Bill. And it *was* my intention to do it myself, I promise you. I misjudged the workload. And I had no way of knowing I'd be dealing with a family crisis before that time was up."

"It's barely been one year," Bill said again. "And family crises are part of life. I assumed you counted that possible cost before you presented us with your proposal. This is unacceptable. I trusted you with my life savings. I don't care what it takes, you make this work."

"Bill, my family has to come first. I'm sorry. I'll sell out my stock if I have to. I'll give up my dividends."

"Have you called the rest of the guys? There won't be any dividends to give up at the rate you're going."

"I'm sorry, but if I lose my family over this, none of that will matter."

"Maybe not to you, but what about *my* family?" Bill was yelling now. "I've got kids to put through college and a mortgage—"

"Bill, I promise you, I'll do everything possible to minimize the loss. I really think we're going to see some gains in the next year that will offset the cost of a full-time assistant manager."

Bill seemed to soften a bit at that, but Mark hung up dreading the next meeting when he'd have to come face-to-face with Bill. Terror welled in him as he thought of the financial setback he would incur. If he hired another assistant manager full-time, it would take that much longer to pay off the loans he'd taken out to start up the restaurant. And his paltry retirement fund would most likely take the brunt of the decision.

Still, he kept coming back to something Hank had said. "What good is all the money in the world if you don't have your family to share it with you?"

He held tight to Hank's assertion as he dialed the *Sun-Times* to discuss placing an ad for an assistant manager.

Chapter Thirty-Five

"What do you think, Robbi?" Julia pulled another blouse off the rack at Nordstrom, and held it in front of her.

Robbi didn't hesitate. "It's you. Very young, very hip."

Julia wrinkled her nose. "Are you sure? I don't want to be one of those desperate grandmas trying to dress like a teenager."

"Don't worry. You're far from that. Besides, Ellie's keeping you young. Run with it."

Julia shrugged and added the blouse to the sheaf of clothes lopped over her left arm. "Okay, I'll try it on."

But she couldn't hide a wry smile, remembering the other night when Ellie had been running a fever. "Um…in the interest of full disclosure, there've been plenty of days when I *feel* every bit the grandma."

"Well, believe me, you don't look it." Head tilted, Robbi studied her. "In case I haven't said so recently, I admire what you're doing. I don't know if I could do it, Jules."

"You could if you had to."

Robbi clutched her chest dramatically. "Please, God, no!"

Julia laughed, then sobered. "I didn't think I could do it in the beginning, either. It was tough. You know how much I dreaded it—and what a huge adjustment it's been." She held up a gorgeous peach-colored silk suit, had a quick vision of Ellie's colored markers and Play-Doh, and immediately returned the outfit to the rack. "But now Ellie's become so much a part of our lives. It's almost like John and I had a baby together. That's something I never thought we'd have together, you know? It's been really special, seeing him with her. They're so sweet together." She shrugged, feeling vulnerable revealing these intimate emotions to Robbi. "I don't know… It does something to me. I've fallen in love with John all over again."

Robbi studied her. "And you don't regret turning down Don's job offer?"

Julia thought for a minute before answering, wanting to be honest with her friend—and with herself. "I guess I wish there was some way I could have it all. Isn't that what we women always want—to have it all, all at the same time?"

Robbi shook her head. "Oh, but it just doesn't work that way."

"No. It doesn't. But Robbi, I honestly don't have any regrets. I'd make the same decision all over again. I may not be twenty-five, but I'm not ninety-five, either. I figure even if we end up raising Ellie—permanently—she'll start school in a couple of years and then I'll be able to get back on track with my career. I mean, it's not like I have a Ph.D. that I'm wasting."

"Still, you invested a lot of years at Parkside." With the intuition of longtime shopping buddies, they eyed each other's try-on pile and headed toward the dressing room without needing to speak a word.

"They were good years, too. I loved my job at Parkside. But this is a new season in my life. And I'm grateful. It's been a good one. A time when I've grown a lot. Emotionally, spiritually, God has taught me so much. And he's made our marriage even stronger."

"Well, I'm happy for you. Except—" a twinkle came to Robbi's eye and she looked heavenward "—please, please, Lord, I'd really rather not learn and grow the way Julia has, okay?" She flashed a smile and disappeared into a dressing room.

Julia chose the room beside Robbi's. "Well, sweetie," she called over the thin wall that separated them. "You know what they say. Be careful what you pray for."

* * *

Jana came down the trail, singing. Somewhere along the way, trying to learn how to pray again, snippets of praise songs from her childhood Sunday school classes had begun to spring to her mind. She'd started singing them on her hikes, finding deep comfort in the melodies, and deeper meaning in the lyrics. Scripture songs. Straight from the Bible. Except she'd never really understood their meaning when she was a little girl.

At a ledge along the rough trail, she stopped to take in the incredible sight of a thousand aspens, their autumn coats long shed. Yet even the remnants of leaves and pine needles remaining seemed to whisper a song of praise as she crushed them beneath her feet.

She breathed her own prayer of thanksgiving. For God's creation, and for the Sunday school teachers and music directors who'd helped her learn these songs. Songs that had taught her how to worship again. Helped her find sanity again.

The river roared below her and she thought she detected the call of a bird. One she hadn't heard in these woods before. She cocked an ear in the direction of the sound. It came again. Only this time it caused her heart to skip a beat. It wasn't a bird at all. It was the sound of human voices.

She'd seen hikers on the main road into the village occasionally, but there'd never been anyone up here past the narrow lane that led to her cabin. In spite of her disquiet at the voices, she smiled at the slip of her thoughts. *Her* cabin. But she *had* come to think of the cabin as hers. Even as she'd grown to accept that the time had come for her to leave this place. It was time to face whatever consequences she'd made for herself.

The voices came closer now and she froze in her tracks. She wasn't frightened exactly. In fact, she was tempted to walk toward the voices. It had been so long since she'd talked to anyone. Even when she went to the market, she was always on her guard, not wanting anyone to ask questions she couldn't answer.

Now, as the voices below her continued, she moved off the rough trail and crouched by a brush-covered outcropping. She didn't want to risk having to explain why she was here.

She listened again. It sounded as if they were below her. A man and a woman. Though she couldn't make out their words, they seemed to be carrying on a normal conversation. Probably just a couple getting in a last hike before the weather turned frigid again. She felt a little foolish hiding like this. Not to mention it was too cold not to keep moving. She rubbed her hands together and watched her breath form a vapor in the chill air.

She kept listening and eventually could tell the voices were moving away. She hiked back down the trail and let herself into the cabin.

She fixed a plate of peanut butter crackers and a cup of tea. In spite of her growing sense of isolation, she'd come to treasure many things about her quiet life here in the mountains. She'd discovered a treasure trove of books packed away in boxes in the loft. Reading had made the days almost enjoyable, and she sensed that her mind had become sharper as a result. Up here, with no distractions, there'd been time to organize her thoughts, to sort things out. To set some order to her days.

But what would happen if she went back? Would the confusion overwhelm her again as soon as she had to deal with a job and a toddler and her marriage and a husband who was hardly ever home? Would she even *have* a family if she went home? She couldn't think too long about the answer to that question.

She looked down the trail to the A-frame's roof jutting through the pines. In spite of its wide front windows, the cabin grew dark early these days. She dreaded going back to the emptiness of that shadowed space. But it wasn't just the cabin that was empty these days. There was a cavern of emptiness inside her that echoed with loneliness, begged to be filled.

Oh, God, show me what it is I need. Lord, please… I want to be whole again.

Chapter Thirty-Six

Mark smiled to himself as he left the Calypso city limits. His daughter was such a little clown. She'd kept them all in stitches this weekend. It was good to see her happy and light-hearted. In some ways, he felt as if he was getting to know her for the first time in his life. And he loved the little person she was becoming.

He'd made a commitment to go see Ellie twice a week and he'd kept to it, even though the restaurant continued to present one challenge after another. The shareholders had reluctantly agreed to him hiring a full-time assistant manager. Brian Levy was a college dropout who was willing to take a little less than Mark had expected to pay, and that helped mollify the shareholders and had allowed him to fill the position almost immediately. Brian was doing a great job. The kid had caught on quickly and so far, every crisis that occurred while he was in Calypso, Mark had been able to handle over the telephone.

Best of all, Brian was willing to work every Saturday and Sunday, leaving Mark free to spend weekends in Calypso. He was eager to start bringing Ellie to Chicago for short trips, in preparation for when he could bring her home for good.

For now, he'd enjoyed spending time with her at the Brightons'. This weekend, John and Julia had gone to St. Louis for a couple of days so Mark could spend time alone with Ellie. Slow steps. But soon she'd be home and he would feel like a real father again.

He'd taken Ellie to Sunday school at the Brightons' church the last two Sundays, and she was all excited about being in the church Christmas program next week. If only Jana could be there to see her.

God, be with her. Wherever she is, Lord, comfort Jana. Let her know how much You love her and let her know that her husband wants her home. I need her home, Father. And Ellie needs her. Thank You, God, that I'm getting to know my daughter again. I'm so grateful that You—

His cell phone's chime disrupted his prayer. Probably Brian calling from the restaurant with another question. He flipped the phone open. "This is Mark."

"Hi, Mr. McFarlane? Um…a woman at your restaurant gave me this number to call. I hope that's okay, but I thought I should call. This is Laura Abriano. I'm—a friend of your wife's…"

He straightened in the seat. "Yes, of course. Laura. I remember." A tiny flame of hope flared inside him.

Laura cleared her throat. "You haven't heard anything from Jana, have you?"

He deflated. "No. I'm afraid not. I still haven't heard from her." He waited out an awkward pause, not knowing what else to say.

"Well, I don't know if this means anything at all, but I got a really weird phone call yesterday."

"What do you mean?"

"Someone called me from Jana's cell phone."

His heart began a fast *thud thud thud* in his ears. He slowed the car. "What do you mean *someone?* It wasn't Jana? I don't understand."

"Apparently this guy was out hiking and he found a cell phone. He was trying to find the owner and I guess my number was the first one in Jana's contact list." She gave a short laugh. "My name always gets me first on every…"

Her voice blanked to a dull drone for a minute as he tried

to process her news. "Did—did this guy say where he found her phone?"

"He was out hiking. I think he said his girlfriend found it."

"But where? Where were they hiking?"

"Somewhere up around Denver."

"*Denver?* Colorado?" He shook his head, trying to clear the confusion.

"That's what he said. He told me the phone was in pretty bad shape, like maybe it had been there awhile. He was shocked they were actually able to get it charged. I don't know whether he—"

"When did you say he called?" Adrenaline pulsed through his veins. He didn't know whether to be elated or terrified at this incredible news.

"It was yesterday afternoon. I took down the guy's number. Told him I'd have you call him. His name is Larry Harvison."

Mark pulled over to the side of the road. He dug a pen out of his shirt pocket and pulled a vendor's notepad from the glove compartment. His hands were trembling like leaves. "Give me the number."

Laura read a phone number to him and he wrote it down, reading it back for her twice. "I can't thank you enough, Laura. I'll be back in touch."

He hung up and punched in the number. Cars hurtled by on the highway, but he was barely aware of their presence. Why would Jana be in Colorado? They didn't know anyone in that state. Other than an occasional layover at the Denver airport, they hadn't even been through the state since their honeymoon.

The phone rang four times and kicked over to voice mail. Mark slammed the heel of his hand against the steering wheel. Traffic whizzed past his car and he had to strain to hear the recording. Finally the tone prompted him to leave his message. "Yes. This is Mark McFarlane. I believe you found my wife's cell phone. Please give me a call as soon as you can."

He recited his cell phone number and repeated it, fearing his voice was shaking too badly to be understood the first time. "My wife—" He started to say that Jana had been missing for weeks, that this was the first clue to her whereabouts. But a horrible thought came to him. What if this guy was somehow connected to Jana's disappearance? "This is urgent," he finally managed to choke out.

He hung up and gripped the steering wheel, trying to come up with a scenario that made sense. What if this guy wasn't on the level? Maybe he knew something about Jana, might even know where she was now. Had Jana put someone up to this?

A new thought chilled him. What if the guy was some psycho, playing games with him. Oh, dear God, what if all this time he'd assumed Jana had willfully stayed away, and instead she'd been trying to get home and someone was keeping her from it?

He must have sat there for a full five minutes, reeling under the weight of the possibilities, trying to decide what he should do now. Like an automaton, he put the car in gear and checked his mirrors. He was just about to ease back into traffic when his phone rang again. He threw the gearshift back in Park and flipped open his phone.

"This is Larry Harvison returning your call."

"Yes. Yes… Thank you for calling." He willed his voice to stop wavering. "My wife's friend said you'd found her cell phone?"

"Yeah. I sure did. Have you guys been looking for it?"

"Listen, this is extremely important. I need to know where you found that phone."

There was a pause on the other end. "We were out hiking. Um…is there a problem?"

"But *where* were you hiking? I need to know exactly where the cell phone was when you found it. And when was it?"

An awkward pause. "We just found it yesterday. But from the looks of it, the phone had been there awhile. We were up on Alta Springs Road, just off of 40 there. You familiar with that area?"

"No. Not at all. I'm in Chicago."

"Chicago? Wow. A long way from home."

"Laura—my wife's friend said you called from the Denver area."

"Yeah, I'm in Denver, but it was up near Alta Springs where we found the phone. That's maybe forty, fifty miles from here. Uh, listen, you want to give me an address where I can send the phone?"

"No. I'll pick it up."

"Here? In Denver?"

"Yes. As soon as possible. And I need your help."

"What's that?"

"My wife…I've been trying to locate her…"

"Oh, well… I don't know anything about your wife, but apparently this is her phone. We found it not too far from the road. My girlfriend and I were hiking. We were just coming back to the car, sat down to change our shoes and it must have been under this log we were sitting on. Misty kicked it out from under when she stood up. It was caked with mud. We didn't even think it would work but her kid's got one of those universal charger things that fit it and once we got it charged, the thing fired right up."

Mark didn't care about any of that. "Tell me the address again…where you were hiking." He pulled the pen from his pocket again, his hands shaking violently now.

"Up around Alta Springs. We were probably a mile-and-a-half off 40 on Alta Springs Road. There's a trail up there." A note of hesitance had crept into his voice. "Private property, actually."

Mark scribbled the name down. Something about it rang a distant bell. Maybe it was a well-known recreation area. He couldn't remember.

"There's not a marked trail." Larry said. "There's an old cabin on the place. The guy that told me about the place said they rented it out for years, but I don't think it's been used for a while now. When did you say she lost her phone?"

Mark tapped his fingers on the steering wheel. He needed to play it cool. Just in case this guy knew something. He needed to find out everything he could before the guy got jittery and hung up on him. He took a deep breath and poised his pen over the notepad he'd written the phone number on. "Actually, she's missing."

"Missing? Your wife? You mean, as in…disappeared?"

Mark hesitated, still not sure whether to trust this stranger. "Something like that."

"Well, I sure don't know anything about that. I just found the phone." Now Harvison sounded defensive. Or nervous? "Are the police involved?"

He sighed. "No. They won't get involved. But my wife has been gone for over two months and this is the first time I've had any lead at all on where she might be."

A long pause. "Whoa… She's been missing for two months?"

"Yes. Since September." Mark wasn't eager to divulge too many details to this guy. Not until he had a chance to meet him, find out what he really knew.

"Hey, I don't mean to pry into something that's none of my business but I could—" Larry cleared his throat.

Another pause followed and Mark predicted that any minute the guy would name an exorbitant price for his "trail guide" services.

"You know… I'm not sure I'm comfortable returning the phone to you…I mean if your wife's been missing that long. I don't want to be tampering with evidence or something…"

"Oh, no…" Mark backpedaled madly, terrified he'd scared the guy off. "It's not like that. I just want to find her. Make sure she's safe."

"Maybe you should talk to the police."

"You don't understand. I *have* talked to the police. They won't do anything."

Harvison's tone became businesslike. "I think what I'd better do is turn the phone in to the police. I'll take it to the Denver Police Department. You can contact them about it."

"No! Wait. Please don't hang up. Please…"

"I'm sorry, but I really think I'd feel more comfortable handling it that way."

"Wait! Wait…I'll pay you. Please. Just name your price."

"No, no… I definitely wouldn't be comfortable with that. I'll take the phone to the police. You can take it up with them."

The phone went dead.

For the second time in an hour, Mark slammed his palm on the steering wheel in frustration. His mind raced. Jana had been in Colorado? Why on earth had she gone there?

A dull ache started behind his eyes. He remembered John and Julia, that day Jana had first disappeared, intimating that she might be having an affair. He'd never believed that. But was it possible?

"Please, God. No. Please don't let that be true."

But surely if that were the case, one of Jana's friends would have known. Would have spoken up. And even if her friends had agreed to cover for her, Laura Abriano wouldn't have called him about the phone now if something fishy were going on. Laura would have called Jana. Or just left it be. Wouldn't she?

Chapter Thirty-Seven

"**Y**ou must have *something*." Mark stood at the ticket counter, tapping his fingers, his nerves a frazzled knot. The airport was swarming with Christmas travelers and tensions were running high.

The ticket agent clicked the mouse and scrolled down her computer screen. "Weather permitting, sir, I can get you on standby for a 6:10 flight in the morning. That would arrive at DIA at 7:35 a.m."

He let out a low growl. Judging by the lines at the counters stretching out on either side of him, his chances of getting on standby were worse than zero. "Isn't there anything else? A nearby airport maybe?"

She checked the screen again. "Again, sir, assuming the weather doesn't shut us down, I could have you in Colorado Springs around nine in the morning. Or I could put you on standby for the—"

"No. I can't take that risk." No way was he going to wait until morning and risk finding out he couldn't get on a flight anyway. He rubbed his temples, trying to think what to do.

A man in line behind him cleared his throat loudly.

"Sorry." Reluctantly, Mark stepped aside. It was a thousand miles to Denver. He checked the time. If he took off driving right now, he wouldn't get there until at least four tomorrow afternoon.

He'd have an hour of daylight, tops. If he took the Colorado Springs flight, he could rent a car and be in Denver before noon. He'd make phone calls on the road. What choice did he have?

As he stepped back in line, his cell phone rang. He checked the number and his blood pressure surged.

It was Larry Harvison.

"Ellie, hold still." Julia folded another tuck into the oversize angel costume and pinned it in place. "Come on now, I'm almost finished." She spoke around the lineup of straight pins she held between her lips.

Ellie fidgeted and squirmed. "But it's itchy, Go-Go."

"I know…I know. We'll give it a good washing when it's done and then it won't feel so scratchy. But I need you to hold still for one more minute, okay?" Julia threaded another pin through the crisp muslin fabric.

The phone rang. "Saved by the bell, girlie. I guess that'll have to do." Julia sighed and slipped the gown over the tangle of auburn curls.

Ellie cheered and scurried off to play in her room.

Julia struggled to her feet and ran for the phone.

"Hi, Julia. I hope I didn't catch you in the middle of dinner."

"Mark. Hi. No, not at all. You had a safe trip home?"

"Yes. Fine."

"Good. We were just finishing up an angel costume for your little angel."

He gave a short laugh. "Now *that* I'll have to see."

"The last rehearsal is Wednesday night and Ellie is—"

"Listen, Julia—" Mark seemed not to hear her. "I'm heading to Denver first thing in the morning. I've got…some things to take care of."

"Oh? I didn't realize you were going out of town. Tomorrow?"

"I didn't know, either. That's why I'm calling. I'll have my cell if you need to get hold of me, but I just wanted to let you know where I'd be."

"Did you say Denver? Are you flying?" Hadn't she just

heard on the news that Colorado was expecting a major winter storm?

"Yes. Actually I couldn't get a flight straight into Denver. I'm flying in to Colorado Springs. Then I'll drive on up to Denver."

"Have you checked the weather there?"

"Yes. That's one reason I couldn't get a flight. Everybody's trying to beat the storm…get home in time for Christmas. Well… I won't keep you."

"Wait, Mark…" Something in his voice made her hesitate. "Is everything okay? You sound—"

"Everything's fine. I've got to run. I'll talk to you when I get back."

Julia was left with a dead connection humming in her ear. And a sense of unease. Maybe she was imagining things, but Mark had seemed…evasive.

She shot up a little prayer. Things had been going so well, and she and John were pleased with his commitment to spend more time with Ellie. They'd felt so optimistic.

She hoped he wasn't reneging already.

Mark hung up the phone and flipped the television on. The evening newscast was just starting. He watched for a few minutes but didn't comprehend a word of it. Instead, he thought about tomorrow, tried to think what he should do first. He replayed the last phone call from Larry Harvison in his mind.

Seems the man had experienced a change of heart after his girlfriend read the text messages on Jana's phone. Messages from him. Mark didn't even remember what he'd written.

"I feel bad about being so suspicious, but well…you just never know these days. And I apologize… It was an invasion of your privacy—your wife's privacy to read those texts, but, well, I just hope you understand. We didn't know what to do. We finally decided it would be best for everyone if we went ahead and turned the phone in to the police, but I thought it would save you some time if I let you know where you can claim it."

Mark had been too grateful to be angry.

"The police said you could pick up the phone at the district station on Cherokee. It's at I-25 and South University Boulevard. They said you might need a notarized note of permission from your wife to claim her property, but I explained the situation and they said they'd work with you."

He didn't know what he would do if the police wouldn't give him that phone. His only hope was that the phone might convince the police there was the possibility of foul play. How else could he explain Jana's phone showing up on some mountainside in Denver.

His hopes sank as half-a-dozen scenarios came to mind. The phone could have been stolen in Chicago and made its way across the country with the thief. Jana could have sold it for cash. Perhaps she did come to Colorado, but she lost the phone along the way, left it at a gas station or in a restaurant. He knew the police would have other ideas, few of which indicated foul play.

What would he do if this proved to be a dead end? He stretched in the recliner, his nerves taut. He ought to just go to bed. It was early, but he'd have to get up before 4:00 a.m. to make his flight. He was so wired he'd never sleep.

A weather map appeared on the TV screen. It reminded him he needed to pack the atlas for his trip tomorrow and check for directions online. He didn't have a clue where to find this police station Harvison had talked about.

He reached for the remote and started to turn the TV off, but the national weather report caught his attention. A perky weather girl motioned in front of the map. "It looks like parts of the U.S. could enjoy a very white Christmas as a band of major winter storms sweeps across the Northern Rockies. These storms currently extend from Northern Alberta to the Canadian border and are expected to move into Montana and Wyoming sometime tonight, blanketing much of the Northwest with up to a foot of snow, and continuing to move south into the early part of the week..."

Great. Mark sighed and bowed his head. *Lord, please don't let that storm hit Denver before I get there.*

He turned off the TV and went back to get ready for bed. Washing his face at the bathroom sink, he looked in the mirror.

He wasn't sure he even knew the man staring back at him. When he thought about his life with Jana, and how things had been between them just a year ago, he was shocked at the changes twelve months had wrought.

They'd been through some rough times, but they'd always made things work. Jana had taken her mother's death hard, and it had been difficult for her to adjust to the idea of her father's remarriage and her relationship with Julia. But he thought they'd made it through. Ellie had been such a gift at a rough time in their lives. At least he'd thought so. It had been difficult for Jana, not having her mother to consult as she went through her first pregnancy and to rejoice with her at Ellie's birth. But Mark had thought she was handling it all.

Apparently he'd been wrong about a lot of things. He hadn't bothered to take time to communicate with his wife. To ask how she was doing. To spend time with her, help her out with Ellie's care. He'd barely taken the time to pray for her, let alone pray *with* her.

As he had that day John and Julia had driven away with Ellie, Mark felt compelled to drop to his knees. He dried his face on a sour-smelling towel and stumbled to the bed, kneeling, face in his hands.

He poured out his fears to God. And in that moment, their marriage bed became an altar on which he relinquished his rights to his wife, placing her in the hands of a heavenly Father Who loved her far more than Mark could ever hope to.

Chapter Thirty-Eight

Mark sat up straight in bed, all of a sudden wide-awake. The clock on the nightstand showed eleven-fifteen. He'd only been asleep for an hour. His alarm would go off in four more. He needed to get some sleep.

But the dream was still vivid in his mind. Disturbingly so. The same dream from before. He and Jana on a pallet of blankets in front of a fireplace. On their honeymoon.

Was that cabin still there? Maybe if God answered his prayers and he found Jana, he could surprise her with a second honeymoon. Maybe even rent the same cabin.

He tried to picture Jana's face, the sound of her voice. And failed. He looked around the room. The walls were bare. They'd never hung their paintings and photographs after they'd moved here from the apartment. Too busy with their jobs—both of them—to make their house a real home. And why. They were rarely home anyway.

He wouldn't let that happen again. Not if he found her. Not if she was willing to come back to him. He had to convince her. Whatever it took, he would do it.

He eased out of bed and wandered through the house, room by room. The dream still played through his thoughts. It bothered him that he couldn't see Jana this time. The first time he'd dreamed of that place, he'd seen her so clearly. Her luminous eyes. The way she looked at him with such love. Had his apathy thrown away the privilege of even recalling her face?

In the dining room, he saw a stack of photo albums on the hutch in the corner. Ellie's baby book was there. He leafed through it. During her pregnancy, Jana had taken one of those scrapbooking classes that were all the rage. She'd filled the pages with fancy designs and neat lettering. But the pages after "baby's first photo" were sparse. A few photographs tucked between pages, a folded clipping from Calypso's little newspaper announcing the birth of Ellen Marie McFarlane.

He set the baby book aside and opened the next album. His hand stilled over the first page. There it was. The little cabin where they'd spent their honeymoon. Set back in the woods, it appeared smaller than he remembered. Far smaller than it had been in his dream. There were side-by-side photos: him standing on the deck waving, then Jana standing on the deck waving. They'd run back and forth taking pictures of each other, Jana bemoaning that they couldn't figure out how to work the camera's timer and there was no one to take a shot of the two of them together.

He turned the page. Ah. There they were at some little sidewalk snack shop. Together. Eating ice cream cones. Jana must have coerced some poor tourist to snap the shot or more likely she finally figured out the timer. He didn't remember it. Jana had labeled the photo Lovebirds.

For some reason, that tore him up.

He stood at the hutch, bent over the album, a giant lump in his throat. He leafed through the pages one by one, finally allowing himself to be lost in the memories.

There were a few mementos tucked in the back of the book. A menu from a BBQ joint where they'd eaten, and brochures from various tourist attractions. A photo of their white-water rafting excursion, most of the image a frothy spray of water. He could barely make out Jana with him at the back of the orange raft. Laughing, carefree. Eager to get back to the cabin to make love again. He remembered that part.

He started to close the album. It was too hard to look back from where they were today. He tamped the loose items on the dining table and tucked them back inside. A wrinkled brochure stuck out at an odd angle. He pulled it out and smoothed the creases. It was a homemade job, hand-designed and obviously printed on a cheap copy machine.

A name across the top caught his eye. Alta Springs. He turned the brochure over, staring at the words, the connection slowly registering. Alta Springs Road. The road they took to get to the cabin. The name of a little tourist town nearby where they'd gotten groceries and gas.

The place where Larry Harvison had found Jana's cell phone.

His knees buckled and he reached behind him for a chair. How could he not have put this together before? It had been right in front of him— She was at the cabin! Jana had gone back to their honeymoon cabin.

Or at least tried to. A chill went through him as he examined reasons her phone would have been found in the woods there.

He grabbed the brochure, flipped it over, looking for a phone number. He found it, below the owners' names. Ron and Edie Gamble. The dining room clock ticked toward midnight. But it was an hour earlier in Denver. Maybe they'd still be up. He had to risk it.

A mechanical recording started. "The number you have reached is no longer in service. Please check—" He hung up and went to the computer in the spare bedroom. He entered the Gambles' name in the browser search field.

A number appeared. The same one he'd dialed, but with a different area code. He dialed the new number and waited through half-a-dozen rings before a groggy voice answered.

"I'm terribly sorry to call so late, but I need some information. Is this the Gamble residence?"

"Yes, this is Edie Gamble. I'm sorry. You'll have to speak up. Who did you say this was?"

"My name is Mark McFarlane. My wife and I stayed in your

cabin in Colorado for our honeymoon a few years ago…thirteen years ago actually. Do you still own that cabin?"

"Oh, yes, we certainly do. We haven't rented it in a while, though. My husband's been ill and we haven't been able to keep it up, and Ron doesn't have the heart to list it with a Realtor."

"But it's not being rented right now?"

"Oh, no. It's been empty for ages, except when our boys get up there to fish every once in a while."

"Are you sure there's no one staying there now?" He hesitated for a moment. Should he risk telling her everything? "I have reason to believe my wife may be there."

"At the cabin? Oh, no. It's not rented now."

Mark's hopes plummeted. "You're sure someone didn't rent it…maybe as far back as September? Her name is Jana McFarlane."

"No, honey. I'm sorry, it's probably been at least two years since we had a lodger."

But Jana had been there. Didn't Larry Harvison finding her phone near there prove that? That couldn't be a coincidence.

"Would you mind if I went to the cabin? Took a look around? Can I get onto the property?"

"Oh, the property never has been gated. The cabin's locked, of course. But with this storm coming in, that road may not be passable."

"Do you live nearby? Is there any way I could get a key from you?"

"Are you here in Denver?"

"Oh, no. I'm…we're from Chicago."

"Oh, my. You say you think your wife is in Alta Springs?"

"I hope she is. I desperately need to talk to her."

There was a short pause. "Do you remember where you got the keys when you stayed there?"

Mark searched his memory and came up blank. "It's been a long time. Thirteen years. I'm sorry. I don't remember."

"You sound like a nice young man…Mark, was it? I'm guessing your wife would very much like to talk to you, too. I'm going to trust you. How tall are you?"

"Um…I'm about six-one." Mark was starting to wonder if the woman were senile. "Why?"

"Then you'll have no trouble. The key is where it's always been…on the—"

"—the ledge over that sliding security door." The image had appeared with her words, as clearly as if it were yesterday.

Mrs. Gamble chuckled. "That's right. Just lock everything up when you leave. I hope you find her."

Mark hung up, his nerves strung taut as guitar strings. He pulled back the curtains at the dining room window and peered out into the night.

Flurries of white powder swirled in the sky over the Windy City. He'd always liked the way a good snow cleaned things up, painting over the grime and soot of winter, leaving everything pristine.

So why was it that this snow brought with it such a rising sense of dread?

Chapter Thirty-Nine

The snow had started sometime in the middle of the night. Now, at 6:00 a.m., it shadowed the mountain in a diaphanous white veil. Jana pulled the last two logs from the pile beside the hearth and threw them on the glowing embers. She'd become a pretty decent fire builder, but she worried about how quickly the woodpile below the deck had dwindled now that the weather was colder.

She'd seen firewood for sale outside the market in the village but her cash was dwindling as fast as the woodpile.

She bundled up, layering her jacket over multiple sweaters, and pulling on the hat and mittens she'd borrowed from the cabin. Under the deck, she powered on the generator before filling her arms with split logs. She banged each log on the ground, checking for the black widow spiders she'd seen scurrying out of the woodpile until a few weeks ago. The cold weather seemed to have scared them off. She only hoped they hadn't found a way to get inside the cabin. What would she do if she needed medical attention?

After she replenished the stack of logs by the fireplace, she went to turn on the hot water heater. Her days had taken on a comfortable cadence since the morning she'd wrecked the Escape. She hiked every day while she waited for the water to heat for her shower. If she needed food, she hiked down to the market. She'd figured out that the proprietor took Mondays off, so that's when she went. He'd made her too nervous, asking questions about where she was staying and inquiring about her family. He was probably just being friendly, but she didn't want to raise his suspicions.

After reading every word of every page of the stash of old hunting and fishing magazines in the cabin, she'd gladly relegated them to the kindling box when she discovered the boxes of books in the loft.

She'd read *A Tree Grows in Brooklyn,* and plowed through *Great Expectations* and *A Tale of Two Cities*—novels she'd only skimmed the Cliff's Notes for in high school. In spite of their formal, rather stilted language, she enjoyed the stories. But more than that, they allowed her to escape into a world where she didn't have to ponder the reality of the mess she'd made of her own life

This week, she was working her way through Daniel Defoe's *Robinson Crusoe.* With this morning's snow, it was difficult not to make the comparisons of Defoe's adventures to her situation. If this snow kept falling, she would be as surely marooned in the cabin, as Crusoe and Friday were on their island.

She heated water over the fire and took her morning cup of hot chocolate in a chair near the window, keeping an eye on the weather. The snow fell like rain now over the mountainside, painting the gray decking a milky white, along with everything else in sight.

By ten, the snow had reached the bottom of the little built-in bench that ran the length of the deck, and she started to be concerned. She could always melt snow for water and she had enough food and wood for several days, maybe a week if she was conservative. But she remembered reading in an ad in one of the hunting magazines that some cabins in the Denver area weren't rented over the winter because they were too often snowed in.

Maybe she should walk down to the market. She could get a few more supplies and find out what the weather service was saying about this storm. She'd tried to start the Escape yesterday morning, to listen to the weather, but apparently she'd run the battery down playing the radio. Or maybe it was too cold for the engine to start.

One more look at the snow piling up on the deck convinced her trying to walk anywhere would be foolish. If she attempted a trek down the mountain, they'd surely be finding her body in the spring thaw.

The thought jolted her as if she'd grabbed hold of a fallen power line. That was exactly what she'd hoped for, *planned* for, the day she drove the Escape up the mountain. She'd had every intention of lying down and letting the snow bury her.

Her hands started shaking. Had she really intended to…*kill* herself? What was wrong with her? She didn't want to die. Not anymore. She hadn't thought that way for a long time. What had changed?

She remembered back to that day, the befuddled thoughts that had muddied her brain. But she'd changed. Somewhere along the way, without her even realizing it, the fog had lifted. Her thinking had straightened out, and she didn't feel so weighted down.

Oh, but there was Mark. And Ellie. She found herself back-pedaling, purposefully trying not to think about them.

But they were her family. A terrible longing swept over her. She missed them. Right now, she would give just about anything for her family to walk into the cabin. She would give her very life to be able to tell them how wrong she'd been. How sorry she was.

Oh, dear Lord… What have I done?

Was it too late to make things right? She had to talk to them. Had to at least let Mark know where she was. Even if he wouldn't take her back, even if she could never lay claim to her daughter again, she had to somehow make things right.

Oh, God, please let me get out of here. Please let me have a chance to tell them how sorry I am. To tell Ellie that I love her. And Mark.

Robinson Crusoe's story came instantly to her mind. She had just read the part where, upon leaving the island where he'd spent more than twenty-eight years, Crusoe wrote letters to his trustees and his partners. Letters of thanks for their loyalty and honesty.

She jumped up and hurried to the kitchen. The cabin was dim, but she remembered seeing a tablet in one of the drawers and she had several pens in her purse. In case something happened and she couldn't express to Mark and Ellie how much she loved them, how sorry she was, at least they might someday have her words.

She whispered a desperate prayer. "Lord, I'm so sorry. Forgive me for being so selfish. Please be with my family. And please, God, I beg You to let me do this one thing. Please don't let anything happen until I have a chance to make things right."

Outside the snow fell harder. It drifted beneath the door and by noon, it was almost a foot deep on the porch. Jana braved the stairs and brought in enough wood for two nights.

She kept the fire going, huddling close to its warmth. She heated soup and water for tea over the grate. And in between, she wrote love letters to the man she'd promised her life to, and to the little girl God had blessed them with.

Chapter Forty

The queue of passengers filed like cattle into the Colorado Springs terminal while the airport signs herded them in the direction of the baggage claim.

The faces Mark looked into held a mixture of relief and anxiety. They'd made it this far, but there was still the parking lot to brave. For some, like him, Colorado Springs was merely the first leg of a longer journey. And like him, everybody wanted to be home before the storm socked them in.

Home. That was what Jana was to him. He knew that with certainty now. And all he wanted was to take her in his arms and hold her forever. If she would still have him.

He hadn't checked any bags, so bypassed baggage claim and found the Hertz counter. Ten minutes later, with keys secured, he made his way out to the parking lot to pick up the rental car. As he walked across the slippery lot, the snow was still coming down, though he didn't think it was falling quite as hard as it had been when they'd first touched down a few minutes ago. But it was cold. He stopped to put his down coat on over his lighter jacket, and pulled on his gloves.

Behind the wheel of the SUV, he fidgeted, crawling at a turtle's pace behind airport traffic. He rummaged in his briefcase and pulled out the crude brochure from Jana's scrapbook. Spreading it out on the steering wheel, he tried to decipher the rough map on the back. Would Jana have remembered how to get to the cabin without a map? He didn't think he would have.

As the off-ramp dumped him onto I-25, snow started to fall in earnest. Huge, papery flakes floated down and pasted themselves across the landscape like leaflets dropped from an airplane.

He checked his cell phone and returned four calls from the restaurant. It seemed Chicago was getting its own snow. Not enough to close the restaurant, but enough that they were getting by with a skeleton staff. Unfortunately, they were also having to make do with a relatively bare pantry. He made a few calls to set up some deliveries, only to find that Brian Levy had already taken care of it.

The restaurant was in good hands. Mark was impressed. But more than that, it showed him that he wasn't as indispensable as he thought.

Except to Jana and Ellie. The revelation spurred him on. He had to get to Jana.

An hour and a half later, he was reduced to traveling forty miles an hour on the four-lane interstate. The windshield wipers were on full speed and still couldn't keep up with the wet snow. Many of the signs along the roadway were obliterated by clinging snow and ice, and he passed too many cars stuck or stalled on the roadside to make him risk driving faster.

He'd never prayed harder in his life, except maybe when Jana had been in labor with Ellie and he'd irrationally feared he might lose her.

It wasn't comforting to realize that his fear of losing her was entirely rational now.

The exit at the junction of Highway 40 loomed ahead and he tapped the brakes, veering sharply to the left. He got the SUV back under control and merged onto 40. Within a few minutes, in spite of the snow, things started to look vaguely familiar. He saw a sign with the word *Springs* in the middle, but a thick mantle of snow hid the first word as well as the part he assumed told how many miles it was.

He glanced at the map. He should be getting close. The world around him was eerily quiet, his tires nearly silent atop the snow. White drifts had formed along the sides of the road, blocking the driveways to many of the campgrounds and tourist shops along the way. But the wind had died down, at least on this stretch of the road.

The map on the brochure showed only a few landmarks along the way. He tried to read the names in the shop windows for some clue as to where he was. He passed a small grocery store, and up the hill from that, a coffee shop and a couple of souvenir places on the left. Everything seemed to be closed down, with windows darkened and parking lots mostly empty.

Looking to the right again, he was jolted by the sight of a tall figure in a white coat looming at the side of the road. He laughed at himself when he realized it was only a statue. The carved face of a black bear peered out from under a shawl of snow. The bear was posed in front of a small shed—or what was left of it anyway—and stood maybe eight or ten feet tall. He was holding some sort of sign, but the snow obscured its message.

He rolled down the passenger window of the SUV to clear it of snow, then powered it back up and studied the scene through the glass. He'd seen that bear somewhere before.

With Jana. That was it. He and Jana had used the cartoonish figure to mark their turnoff each time they came back to the cabin from the day's excursion. He knew Jana would have remembered it, too. His heart started working overtime.

He was close. He could almost feel her presence. *Oh, God, please let her be there. Please let me find her. Let the road be open. Get me through.*

"Go-Go, when's my daddy comin' next time?"

Julia looked up from the Christmas cookie dough they were mixing. "He'll be here next weekend, remember? For your Christmas program. And then he'll stay until after Christmas. Won't that be nice?" Julia tried to inject the excitement of the holiday season into her voice.

But Ellie must have sensed her trepidation. She nodded agreement, but instead of smiling, her thumb went straight into her mouth.

She hadn't done that for a while. It worried Julia. Gently, she pried the little hand away from Ellie's face. "Don't do that, sweetie. You'll need to wash your hands again before you help me bake."

She ushered Ellie to the sink and helped her with the soap. Ellie didn't protest, but she was too quiet.

They'd been glad when Mark started making an effort to see Ellie more frequently, but in some ways, it had created new problems.

In spite of having recovered from her strep throat, Ellie had been cranky lately, and recently the nightmares had gotten worse. Mark's weekend visits seemed to remind Ellie that she wasn't home…and Mommy wasn't home. She had quit asking when Jana would be back from her "trip." For a while now, she hadn't mentioned Jana at all.

Julia and John had agreed with Mark that until they knew what was going to happen with Jana and made some long-term decisions, it was best to let Ellie take the lead in how much to talk about her mother.

But Julia could always tell when Ellie's thoughts were troubled. Whenever she saw the faraway, doleful look come to those liquid blue eyes, she was tempted to take Ellie into her arms and squeeze the sadness out of her. Oh, if only it were so easy to relieve a child's grief.

And that's what it was. Ellie was grieving. They all were. Jana's disappearance had left them all in a limbo that was, in many ways, more difficult to handle than if she had died.

At some point, they would have to tell Ellie something other than "Mommy is on a trip." And Julia dreaded thinking how that might affect a fragile three-year-old.

The phone rang and Julia quickly dried her hands. She looked at the caller ID. "Oh, look there. That's your daddy calling right now."

Ellie's face brightened. "Can I talk?"

"If Daddy has time. Let me talk to him first." She put a finger to her lips and picked up the phone. "Hello."

"It's Mark, Julia. Is it snowing there?"

"Just a dusting. Are you in Denver?"

"Near there. And pretty much snowed in."

"Oh, dear. I wondered about that. I heard on the radio that—"

"I have some news."

Something in Mark's voice stilled her. "News?"

"I didn't want to get your hopes up. That's why I didn't say anything before. And I could still be wrong, but…I think I might know where Jana is."

Her breath caught. "Oh, Mark, that's wonderful!" She glanced at Ellie, aware she needed to temper her response. "In Denver?"

"Nearby, I think. I could be wrong, but…I don't think so. I'll tell you all about it as soon as I know anything. I just wanted to ask you to pray. Please pray hard."

"Is she okay?"

He was quiet for a few seconds before he finally responded. "I don't know. I hope so. Please just pray."

"I will. Oh, I will, Mark."

"I need to get off the phone. Give Ellie my love."

"Of course. Keep us posted, okay?"

But he'd already hung up. Julia looked down to see Ellie standing there, hand out for the phone, her eyes eager.

"Oh, sweetie. I'm sorry. Your daddy was in a hurry. You'll have to talk to him next time he calls."

Ellie's face fell and Julia picked her up, trying to distract her. "Your daddy sends you his love. And he said there's lots of snow in Denver."

Ellie's eyes grew wide. "'Nuf for a snowman?"

"What's that, sweetie? Oh… Probably a whole army of snowmen." Mark thought he'd found Jana! Julia's thoughts raced as she tried to keep Ellie engaged. Was that why he'd gone to Colorado? He'd implied—or maybe she'd just assumed—that he was going on business. How on earth had he tracked Jana there?

She couldn't wait to tell John. He was going to have a million questions and she didn't have any answers. "Oh, please don't let this be a wild-goose chase."

"Is my daddy chasin' a goose in Denver?" Ellie looked up at her, her brow a map of wrinkles.

Julia hadn't realized she'd spoken aloud. Smiling, she pulled Ellie into her arms, nuzzled the warm crown of her head. "You're a silly goose."

Ellie giggled. "I'm not a goose! Hows come we're talkin' about so many gooses?"

Julia burst out laughing. But as realization washed over her, her laughter turned to bittersweet tears.

If Mark really had found Jana, it was soon going to be awfully quiet around this house.

Chapter Forty-One

Mark stood beside the SUV, shading his eyes from the stark white glare. The scene on the road in front of him was like something from a black-and-white photograph. Only a few exposed evergreen branches offered splotches of color to relieve the endless vista of snow and tree limbs.

The drifts were at least three feet high across the road. But this was the right one. He'd cleared snow off the sign to make sure. Alta Springs Road.

He got back in and drove a hundred yards up the narrow path, dodging fallen branches and drifted snow. He couldn't remember how far up this road the turnoff to the cabin was. The deeper in he went, the more constricted the roadway became.

He stopped and got out again to assess the situation. The snow was powdery and blowing clear of the road in some places. The SUV might make it through. He was sorely tempted to just go for it…plow his way through the drifts. But if the wind started blowing again and the road drifted completely shut, or if he got himself stuck, it could be deadly in a storm like this.

And he didn't know for sure Jana was even there. Something deep within him told him she was. Or at the very least, that the cabin held a clue to her whereabouts.

Stomping off the wet snow that clung to his shoes, he climbed back into the vehicle. He'd go back to the little group of shops he'd seen a mile or so down the mountain. Maybe someone here would know if there was another way up to the cabin.

He backed out to the main road, turned around and drove back to the little tourist center he'd passed. There were only two vehicles in the parking lot now. A pickup was parked in front of the food market.

He pulled his collar up around his ears and got out. The snow had insulated the world, muffling every sound. He slipped and slid to the door only to find that it was locked. Great. Now what? He cupped his hands and peered through the glass.

There was a light on somewhere in the back. Probably just a security light, but it was worth a try. He banged on the door with his fist and waited. Nothing. He banged again.

A crunching sound made him turn to the left. A man appeared around the side of the building, bundled from top to toe in snow gear. Head bent against the storm, his salt-and-pepper beard nevertheless collected snowflakes as he trudged through a foot of white powder.

He jumped when Mark shouted a greeting, then chuckled. "Didn't see you there. I'm sorry but we're closed. Not gonna be much business on a day like this. You'll have to go on up to San Angelo." He pointed west. "But I wouldn't bet on them being open, either."

"No... No, I wasn't needing groceries. I'm trying to find a cabin up around this area."

The elderly man scratched his beard. "You have a reservation already?"

"Oh, no, I don't mean a place to stay. I'm looking for the Gamble cabin."

"Oh, sure. Didn't know they were renting again. You got the place for the holidays?"

"Not exactly. I stayed there once several years ago." He shuffled his feet in the snow, impatient. "It's a ways up Alta Springs Road, if I remember right, but I was afraid I'd get stuck. Is there a back way in?"

"That road comes out about eight miles yonder." The man gestured broadly. "But you'd have a whale of a time coming through that way. The cabin's only about a mile and a half up the road this way. You say you tried to get through?"

Mark shook his head. "The road's drifted pretty bad. I wasn't sure I should risk it."

The man rubbed his hands together. "You might be able to get up to the driveway. It's a mile or so up to the entrance. The cabin's another half mile maybe. But I doubt the lane is passable. It's pretty rugged. You say you've been there before?"

"A long time ago."

"I'm surprised they'd rent the place out this time of year. It'll be tough going opening up the place in this storm."

Mark met the man's steely gaze. "I talked to Mrs. Gamble—Edie—last night. She gave me permission go up there. I think my wife might be there."

"You think?" The man's grizzled face wore a frown.

It hit Mark that if Jana *was* at the cabin, she'd probably have come down to the village for supplies. This guy might know her. He took a risk. "Her name is Jana McFarlane. I think she's been…staying around here. You wouldn't know her, would you?"

"Jana McFarlane?" Again, he rubbed at his beard. "Can't say the name rings a bell. How long's she been here?"

"I really don't know for sure."

"I see a lot of people in a week. Most folks through here are summer people, tourists. I'm pretty good with faces, but it don't do me no good to memorize names on account of soon as I do they're gone and there's a new one to memorize."

"My wife—Jana—is thirty-four, about five-six, light brown hair, real pretty."

"Well, now, that could be a lot of people. And beauty is in the eye of the beholder." He winked.

Mark reached for his wallet. "Here… I have a picture." The cloudy plastic sleeve obscured the photo. It was an old one. A head-and-shoulders shot Jana had taken for her résumé when she applied for the job at the museum. Mark fished it out and thrust it toward the man, shielding it from the falling snow. He should have thought to bring a more recent shot.

The man looked at the photo. Looked at Mark, then back at the photo. "I believe I have seen her. Hair's a little shorter in this picture and she's gussied up here, but it looks like the same girl."

"You've seen her?" A flame of hope kindled inside him. "When?"

"She apparently hiked around here. Asked about a rental cabin once. Same one you're asking about as I recall. She wasn't a real talkative sort, though. Used to come in for groceries."

"Used to?" He could scarcely breathe.

"Haven't seen her around for a while…been three or four weeks maybe since she was in last. Nice girl, though. That's your wife?"

"Yes. Where was she staying? Do you know?"

He shook his head. "Like I said, she was pretty quiet. Didn't say much."

"Was it the Gambles' cabin?"

"She never said that I recall. But it could have been. They haven't rented it out for a few years, but somebody said they saw the chimney smokin' a few weeks ago. Guess it could have been her." He stepped back and eyed Mark as if he were just meeting him. "You and her have a falling-out?"

"You might say that. I need to find her." He shaded his eyes and looked up at the sky. Snow was still falling but the visibility was decent. "I'm going to check out the Gambles' cabin."

"Now?"

"I can't risk getting snowed out."

The man looked up at the sky. "It might be too late."

"You said it's a mile and a half. I'll go in on foot if I have to."

"You'll probably have to. But if this snow keeps falling you don't want to stay up there too long. You might get to spend the winter there."

Mark studied his expression. He didn't appear to be joking.

"You got shoes?" The man asked.

Mark looked down at his hiking boots. "Excuse me?"

"Snowshoes. You might need 'em up there."

"No. I don't."

"Come with me." He turned and started toward the front door, then did an about-face, his right hand extended. "I'm Gus Alberts."

Mark shook his hand. "Mark McFarlane. I appreciate your help."

"Don't mention it."

He followed Gus inside. The man disappeared into a room behind the cash register and returned with a pair of snowshoes. "Here you go."

Mark took the unwieldy contraptions and turned them over, inspecting the straps. "Um…I've never worn snowshoes before."

Gus showed him how to strap them over his boots. "The trick to walking in these things is to keep your legs wide. It helps to be an old cowboy—a little bowlegged." He demonstrated, chuckling, then handed the shoes back to Mark, and slipped a business card from a holder on the counter. You have a phone on you?"

Mark nodded.

"You have any problems up there, you call this number." He tapped the bottom of the card. "That's my home number. I just live a couple miles down on 40." He pointed out to the road. "Do you have food and water?"

"I'll be okay."

"You better stock up in case we get snowed in. May not be another chance."

Mark waved him off, eager to get going. "I'm fine. Thanks for everything." He felt a little guilty. He probably should give the guy some business for all his trouble. But he didn't have time to waste. He held up the snowshoes. "I'll bring these back as soon as possible."

"Good luck. You be careful up there." Gus clucked his tongue and studied the sky. "Looks like the sun's tryin' to come out, but you never know with these storms. This could turn into a bad one. I'm serious… Don't stay up there so long you get stuck."

Chapter Forty-Two

Mark put the SUV in low gear and sent up a prayer as he plowed through the snow on the far edge of the road, staying as far from the drifts as he could. They seemed to have gotten deeper even in the short time he'd been talking to Gus Alberts.

He should have taken the man up on his offer of some food. He had bottled water, but his food supply consisted of half a large muffin he'd grabbed at a kiosk in the airport and a couple of candy bars he'd brought with him from home. He hoped he didn't get stranded in this storm. He felt in his pocket for the card with Gus's phone number on it.

He plowed through almost a mile of snowdrifts. Frequent curves in the road kept him from seeing more than a few feet ahead, but surely it couldn't be much farther to the entrance of the cabin's lane. Gus had said a mile and a half.

Rounding a curve the SUV hit a drift that must have been four feet tall. The tires ground and crunched the snow, rocking the vehicle. Inch by inch, he eased forward. When the car groaned in protest, Mark backed up and took a run at it. It was like hitting a wall, jolting him off the seat.

By rocking back and forth, he was able to push through a few more feet, but finally he'd reached the end of the navigable road.

He'd have to go in on foot from here. There was a narrow path along one side of the road where the snow was only a few inches deep. He got out and surveyed his surroundings. Trees towered over him on all sides, making the roadway hard to discern. The map had shown the drive on the left. He supposed it would be too much to hope for a sign marking the driveway.

He turned around to look behind him. More of the same. It was three-thirty and there was plenty of light, but the sky had turned gray with no hint of where the sun was. It would be easy to get turned around out here. And he hoped that gray sky didn't portend more snow.

The rental car had a compass on it. He opened the door and checked the reading just to make sure his sense of direction wasn't deceiving him.

He rummaged in his overnight bag for an extra sweatshirt, took his down coat off and layered the sweatshirt with another jacket before putting the heavy coat back on. He stuffed a couple pairs of dry socks in his pockets for good measure, grabbed the snowshoes out of the back and locked the SUV.

This was it. He checked his phone. He had a strong signal.

Pulling on his gloves, he started through the snow, picking through the places where it was mostly clear. He hadn't gone fifty yards before the only place to take the next step was in a foot-deep drift. He may as well try the snowshoes.

Balancing against a tree, he struggled to fasten the clumsy things to his boots the way Gus had showed him. He'd only tried snow skiing once and it had felt about this awkward. He never had quite figured out the sport. He hoped he had better luck with snowshoeing.

He clomped across a small clearing, keeping his legs wide. The snow had a bit of a crust on it and thankfully, it didn't take long to get the hang of it. Soon, he was making good progress. The shoes made a rhythmic *flop flop* as he walked. He moved along, panning the horizon for any sign of the cabin.

The winding road had descended for the first half mile or so, but he was climbing now. That was a good sign he thought. But it was hard to make out anything against the pale gray sky and it would be getting dark far too soon.

He picked out a couple of outcroppings to keep his bearings by and plodded on. He heard a stream running below him, its music strangely subdued through the cushion of snow. He remembered that they'd heard the water running behind the cabin while lying in the loft bed. He should be getting close.

He'd been walking—climbing, actually—for almost fifteen minutes. The air grew colder and his breath came in puffs of steam in front of his face. Inside the gloves, his fingers were starting to grow numb. He tried not to think about what would happen if he didn't find the cabin or the way back to the SUV.

He should have marked the trail somehow. He felt again for his cell phone. It was there, but it wouldn't be easy to direct someone to his location in this winter wonderland where he was a stranger to the terrain.

The snow wasn't as deep under the canopy of firs and he climbed on, laboring now against the slippery stone and the mash of leaves and pine needles beneath the snow.

He pushed his sleeve back and checked the time. It felt as if he'd been hiking for an hour, but it had barely been ten minutes since he last looked at his watch. Surely the cabin was close. It was hard to tell with snow weighting branches into the path, but the trail he was on seemed barely wide enough for a car to pass. He didn't remember it being this tight a squeeze, but then everything would have grown in the thirteen years since he and Jana were here.

The certainty he'd had of finding Jana here dimmed with every step. What if she'd only stayed here for a night or two and gone on. She could be on the West Coast by now. Still, if she'd been here, maybe the cabin would hold some clue to where she'd gone.

He stopped again to get his bearings. Nothing in his line of vision looked remotely like a cabin. But the river still rushed in the distance. He thought that was a good sign. It was a sound he remembered from before.

He trudged on for a few minutes. Something flashed in the

trail ahead. He squinted, trying to decipher what he was seeing. It looked like a reflection off glass. Windows. The cabin.

He scrambled up the rise toward the glare, losing sight of it, then discovering it again with each turn in the rough trail. The cabin had apparently become overgrown, almost hidden during its disuse.

The trail was rockier the higher he went and the snowshoes became clumsy and awkward. He shed them and tucked them under one arm. Finally he abandoned them under a distinctive copse of trees, planning to come back for them on his way out.

He came to a place where the path seemed to end. He pushed back dense branches to clear the way, seeking the clearing the cabin should sit in, if memory served.

He stumbled and when he reached for a handhold, his hand touched smooth metal. He straightened and brushed snow away from the bulky form. It was an abandoned vehicle. The back fender was creased into a sharp V. With broad strokes of his arm, he whisked away snow. White paint.

Oh, dear Lord. It was a Ford Escape. Frantic, he pushed snow away, searching for the license plates. A husk of snow fell away to reveal Illinois plates. Jana's car. Wrecked.

The unthinkable tugged at hidden corners of his mind. Numb, he worked his way around the car's body to the driver's side. He cleared the window. Holding his breath, he cupped his hands and peered inside. His knees went weak as he discovered the empty driver's seat. He tugged at the door. It was unlocked. He climbed inside and started ransacking the vehicle, scouring every inch for something that would tell him what had happened to Jana, why the Escape was wrecked on this mountain.

Whatever had happened, she'd gotten out of the car. He thought about Larry Harvison's call and shivered. The car sat at an awkward angle, wedged between the trees. He looked up the mountain. The Escape must have rolled. How else had her phone ended up under a log in the woods by the road? He stopped breathing. Could she have been thrown from the car? But the windshield was intact, the windows all rolled up.

He straightened again and pivoted, searching the mountainside. The roar of rushing water floated up to his ears on the icy breeze, chilling him body and soul. What if she'd freed herself from the vehicle, only to be claimed by the icy river? Had these mountains become her grave?

He dropped to his knees in the snow. "Please, God. Don't let her be dead." His voice cracked and he wept silently, his tears freezing on his face. His life with Jana seemed to pass before him. There they were on their wedding day, faces glowing with the promise of a future together. He envisioned her in the hospital bed at Mount Sinai, laboring to bring Ellie into the world. Had he thrown away everything they'd had for his stupid restaurant? "Please God... Please don't let it end like this. Don't take her—"

He put a fist to his mouth. The idea was unspeakable. The love he'd once known for Jana overflowed his heart. It had been so long since he'd felt those emotions for her.

And now it was too late.

His teeth chattered with the cold and with the terror of his discovery. He had to get out of the elements. He had to find the cabin.

He gazed into the snowy panorama, searching every inch within his vision. Where was the cabin? He must have taken a wrong turn somewhere. Something wasn't right.

He started to climb on, past the car, then turned to look back. He didn't remember the cabin being this high up. He'd come too far. But how could he have missed it? And why would Jana have driven up here?

He felt certain now that he'd climbed too far. Besides, if by some miracle Jana had gotten out of the car after wrecking it, she wouldn't have climbed higher. She would have started back *down* the mountain.

He did likewise. As he picked his way around snowy outcroppings and boulders, the sun poked through the gray haze overhead, revealing blue sky. It wouldn't be blue for long, though. It was nearing five o'clock. It would be getting dark soon. Too soon.

Chapter Forty-Three

Mark picked his way down the trail, stopping every few minutes to turn three-hundred-sixty degrees, seeking anything that might lead him to the cabin.

At one point, he could see down to the ribbon of road where his rental car was parked. He rounded a curve and lost sight of the trees that camouflaged the Escape. But then the vista opened up, and below him, popping up through the trees was a steeply pitched roof. The A-frame cabin. He was sure of it now. He must have veered too far south and bypassed it somehow.

If he was going to make it back down by nightfall, he'd have to hurry. He'd already learned how hard it was to judge distance in these mountains.

He rubbed his hands together, trying to find some sensation in his fingers. The temperature had dropped in spite of the momentary sunlight. Long shadows fell across the craggy trail now. He had to keep his eyes on his feet to avoid stumbling.

The snowfall had diminished to a few sparse flakes and his own footprints coming up the trail were still distinct. At least the snow wasn't accumulating.

He glanced to the right and stopped short. Alongside the imprint of his hiking boot was another shallow track. A dog? It was a big dog if that's what it was. The print was probably close to four inches across, and rounder than any dog tracks he remembered seeing. It looked more like a cat's paw, but he sure didn't want to run into any cat these tracks might belong to.

Something made him turn and look back up the mountain. A shadow streaked across the snow to his left. His heart pounded in his ears. A sleek feline shape bounded down the mountain parallel to the trail. Mark stood like a statue, desperately needing air, but not daring to draw a breath.

Without turning his head, he traced the animal's path as it flew down the mountain and out of sight. Dread crawled up his spine.

He seemed to remember reading somewhere that wildcats avoided humans whenever possible? The cat had surely seen him—or caught his scent. It was probably trying to get as far away from him as possible. He bent and put his hands on his knees, trying to catch his breath.

A memory returned to him: a report he'd heard on the radio a while back about a hiker who'd been attacked and killed by a mountain lion. He thought that had happened in California, but these mountains were no doubt home to similar creatures.

His mind scrambled with options. Cats were nocturnal. Did he dare go on down the mountain and risk that a hungry mountain lion would be waiting for him at the bottom? Yet, he couldn't stay here. He'd be a sitting duck—for the storm *and* the cat.

He turned and looked back up the peak. It was probably a ten-minute hike back to where the Escape sat. If he went that way, it pretty much guaranteed he'd spend the night on the mountain. He didn't relish the thought.

And he couldn't be certain the mountain lion—or whatever it was—didn't have a hungry companion waiting for him at the top. Did wildcats travel in pairs? If only he'd humored Ellie all those times she'd begged him to watch Animal Planet with her.

He squinted, trying to catch sight of the creature again. Nothing. He was out of his league here. He'd been a fool to come on his own. He knew nothing about these mountains. He should have waited until morning and hired a guide. Maybe no guide would have been stupid enough to make the trek in this weather.

But he hadn't wanted to risk getting snowed out. He felt in his pocket for the phone and the card with Gus's number on it. The old-timer would know which was the safer option. Maybe he could send help.

Mark pulled off a glove and dug in his pocket for the phone. His fingers touched the icy metal of his keys, and it hit him that he had a key to the Escape on his key ring. If the engine hadn't been damaged, maybe it would start and he could run the heater, warm up a little. That option was beginning to look attractive, but it was a huge gamble. What if the Escape wouldn't start?

Holding Gus's card up to the waning light, he memorized the number, then pulled out the phone and flipped it open. His fingers had lost most of their feeling. He might as well be wearing boxing gloves.

He entered three digits, then hit a wrong key. Nerves on end, he stopped to listen and search the panorama of the surrounding woods one more time.

He thought he saw something in the shadows below him, but he knew his imagination was working overtime. He sought a steadier foothold, and started to enter the number again, but a stone gave way beneath him and he lost his footing.

Clinging to the phone, he grabbed at a fir bough heavy with snow. It slid through his hands as if it were made of butter and sent a spray of snow cascading over him.

Clawing desperately for something to break his fall, he grasped only icy air.

In an instant he was tumbling, thrashing for some lifeline to hang on to. Gravity finally took over. Unable to do anything else, he grabbed hold of his head and tried desperately to form a helmet for his skull.

Chapter Forty-Four

Jana stilled, listening intently. What *was* that? A wail like this morning's wind, but different somehow. This sound had come from a living creature. A wolf? She thought of the cougar sightings and shuddered. Her mind knew she was safe and reasonably warm locked inside the cabin. But something about this storm terrified her. For the first time, she regretted throwing away her cell phone.

She got up from the sofa and paced the cabin, a restlessness unlike she'd known in many days overtaking her. *Please, God. Don't let those feelings come back. Please, Father.*

She began to sing softly, the words from Isaiah that had been such a source of comfort to her. "'Thou wilt keep him in perfect peace, whose mind is stayed on Thee. Thou wilt keep him in perfect peace, whose mind is stayed on Thee…'"

"Keep my mind focused on you, Father," she whispered. She went to the table and touched the letters lined up there. One for Mark, one for Ellie, and another for her father. She'd written all morning long, scribbling, revising and recopying. There was so much to say, and her words seemed wholly inadequate.

Her heart welled with love, thinking of the precious family God had set her in. And again, she was forced to come face-to-face with profound regret. If only she could go back and do things differently.

Oh, Father... Please, somehow, let them know how sorry I am. The prayer had become a litany. One she prayed each time as if it were the first time, as if her grief over abandoning her family were just awakening within her. And each time God seemed to answer back: *I love you, my child. You are forgiven. Be at peace.*

She had no struggle believing the words from God. But oh, could Mark and Ellie find that same grace toward her?

She went to the window again and willed the sky to remain light. She'd grown to find a quiet peace in the sunset. To accept it as the beginning of a restful night's sleep. A restorative sleep. But she couldn't seem to find that calm tonight.

Something she couldn't name had churned up her thoughts and tested her faith.

So many weeks she'd spent wishing, longing to die. Now all she wanted was to live, to have another chance to be Mark's wife and Ellie's mom. To have a lifetime to make it up to them. Instead, she was helpless. Unable to even let them know her feelings, except through the feeble attempts of her pen.

She picked up the letter she'd written to Mark and skimmed the first page again. She'd poured her emotion into every word. Yet, when she read them now, the words were impotent. Empty. Could Mark possibly feel the depth of her love through mere words she'd written? Ink on paper. Could it possibly convey all she longed for him to know?

It was almost five o'clock. The sun had officially set. Soon the sky would be black.

She moved to the kitchen and refilled the kettle with water. She placed it on the grate and hefted another log—the biggest one from the pile—onto the fire.

Igniting a long sliver of kindling wood, she carried it around the cabin and lit candles. She'd used the candles in the cabin sparingly, not knowing when she might truly need them. Tonight, the added light and warmth seemed a necessity.

She had just wrapped up in the sleeping bag and settled on the sofa with Defoe's *Robinson Crusoe* when something shook the cabin. Almost imperceptibly, but she was certain she hadn't imagined it. The wind must have picked up again. She stilled and listened. But all seemed quiet again.

A minute later she felt it again, this time stronger. Maybe the wind had blown a branch onto the deck. The rocking came again, this time accompanied by footsteps. Someone—something— was on the deck.

In all the nights she'd slept in this cabin, she'd spent many moments quaking with fear at her own failures and inadequacies, fear even, that she might harm herself. But never had she been afraid of the elements—of anything immediately outside the walls of this cabin.

The footsteps came again and a shadow flitted across the window. The hair on the back of her neck stood on end.

She got up on her knees, crouching in the corner of the sofa. Maybe the hikers she'd heard on the mountain a few days ago had been camping and gotten snowed in. But the nights were too frigid for any sane camper.

Jana blew out the candle on the end table near the sofa. Watching the smoke curl toward the vaulted ceiling, she felt silly. As if snuffing out one candle's light would hide her from a Peeping Tom, when a fire blazed bright in the hearth.

She disentangled herself from the sleeping bag and went to the door, standing out of range of the window's view. "Is anyone there?" Her voice came out in a weak warble.

A *boom boom boom* on the door sent her heart straight to her throat.

"Who's there?" She forced her voice to sound authoritative.

"Jana! Jana? Is that you? It's me. It's Mark… Are you in there?"

Mark! She fumbled with the lock and threw the door open.

Mark stood there—at least she thought it was him—bundled in torn, wet winter gear. She searched the eyes that stared out at her from inside the jacket's hood. It was Mark. Her Mark. She pulled him inside and shut the door against the cold.

"Jana… Thank God! You're safe." His voice splintered and he studied her. "Are you okay?" Something like anger tinged his voice.

She nodded, numb.

He turned and the light from the fireplace illumined his face.

She gasped. "You're bleeding! Mark? What happened? How did you get here?" She moved to untie his hood. "Oh, Mark, you're bleeding badly. Sit down."

She reached to pull out a chair.

"Tell me! Are you okay?" He glared at her.

"I'm fine. I'm all right. You're the one I'm worried about."

He stumbled and slumped to one side. She helped him into the chair and worked at the knotted string on his hood with trembling fingers. The tie was frozen and sticky with blood. She picked at it frantically, alarmed by the amount of blood soaking his clothes.

Finally the knot gave way and she loosened it and eased the hood back. Blood oozed from a deep gash at his temple. She ran to the hearth and brought the steaming kettle back to where Mark sat. She grabbed a soggy dish towel from the kitchen counter and dampened the corner, swabbed the wound.

He winced.

"I'm sorry."

"No…it's okay." He looked up at her from beneath the towel. He spoke her name, the anger draining from his voice. "You're sure you're all right?"

"Oh, Mark." She dissolved into tears. "I'm so sorry." She cradled his head, unable to believe he was actually here with her. But the warmth of his skin, the pulse of his temple beneath her fingers, had never been more real.

She stepped back and looked at him. He was pale and shaking with cold—maybe in shock? "We need to get you out of those wet things. Are you bleeding anywhere else? We need to get you to a doctor."

He looked at her as if she'd grown a second head. "We're not going anywhere. Have you looked out there?"

"How did you get here? What happened?"

Gingerly, he raised two fingers to the wound on his head. "I— I sort of fell down the mountain."

"Down?"

He fumbled with the zipper on his coat and she came to his rescue, helping him out of the down coat and the jacket and sweatshirt layered underneath. "The road was blocked. I had to walk in. I found the Escape. I thought you were dead... I thought—" His voice cracked.

"What were you doing up there?" Had he actually climbed the mountain in this storm?

"I must have taken the wrong trail."

Her thoughts tumbled over each other. Surely she was dreaming. Mark had come after her. He'd found her.

A chilling thought intercepted her elation. What if he hadn't come to rescue her? What if he didn't want to be with her anymore? She had done a horrible thing, leaving him the way she had. She wouldn't blame him if he hated her. She had to know.

Kneeling in front of him, she locked her gaze with his. "Mark... Why are you here?"

He placed his hands on either side of her face. They were still icy, but she didn't care. She read the emotion in his eyes, asking permission. He must have seen her answer in her face because he bent and kissed her. Tender at first, his lips warm and seeking. Testing, then matching the urgency she felt.

Finally he drew away and pressed his fingers to her lips. "I'm here because you are my wife and I love you."

Chapter Forty-Five

Mark touched the makeshift bandage at his temple. He had a headache the size of Texas and every breath brought pain. But he was here. And Jana was safe. In fact, she seemed better than he'd dared hope possible.

She came from the cramped kitchenette carrying a steaming mug. "Here. Let this cool a minute while we get your boots off." She set the mug on the coffee table and knelt at the foot of the couch pulling at the frozen laces from his hiking boots. She tugged at the heel of one boot and he tried to scoot to a sitting position. She yanked, and he cried out as a knife of pain sliced through his rib cage.

"Mark?" There was stark fear in her voice.

He caught his breath and held up a hand. "I'm okay. I think I might have broken a rib." He inched back to a reclining position on the sofa, wincing with each motion.

"Oh, Mark. You're hurt." Her forehead wrinkled with concern. "Do you have any other broken bones?"

He tested his muscles from his shoulders down. "I don't think so. I feel like I've been run over by a truck, though."

She handed him the mug and came to sit beside him on the edge of the cushion. "Here, drink this." She put her hands around his on the cup and guided it to his lips.

He bent forward to sip, but another stab of pain took his breath away. Leaning back against the arm of the couch, he tried to collect his strength.

"We need to get you to a doctor." She propped a couple of throw pillows behind him and held the mug while he took hungry sips. The warmth of the sweet cocoa spread through his belly. He wasn't sure anything had ever tasted so good.

"I'm okay for now. We're not going anywhere in this weather." He reached for her hand, his heart miserably heavy. Where did they start? It had been so long and there was so much to say. So many things to sort out before they could ever be right again.

Jana closed her eyes. When she opened them again, tears spiked her lashes. She bit her lip and looked away. "How is Ellie?"

"She's fine. She misses you. We both do."

"I'm glad she's all right." Some nameless emotion flickered across her face, dulling her eyes. "How did you know I was here?"

A thread of anger threatened to choke out the kindness he'd felt toward her earlier. He wanted to lash out at her. Make her feel the agony she'd put them all through. But he didn't know how fragile she might be. He'd determined that he would do whatever it took to win her back. Whether it was easy or not.

"What happened, Jana? I don't understand." He held up a hand, realizing that it sounded as though he were placing all the blame on her. "I know I have a lot to answer for, too. I should have—"

"Shh." She shook her head and held a finger to his lips. "I'm the one who needs to explain. And… I don't even know if I can. I'm not sure I understand everything myself. For a while I was so mixed-up. So confused. But, oh, Mark, God has been so good. He's been with me every minute." She reached for his hand. "I feel like I'm finally beginning to heal from—whatever it was that had hold of me."

"What *was* it? Why couldn't you tell me? We could have worked things out. Why didn't you come to me?" As quickly as the words were out, he knew the answer and it tore him up. "Oh, dear Lord." It was a prayer. *Give me the words, Father.* "Jana, I'm so sorry. I know I wasn't there for you when I needed to be. I got so wrapped up in the restaurant. I underestimated what it would take—the sacrifice it would be for you…and for Ellie."

"It was more than just that, Mark."

"Tell me. I'm here." He looked past her out the wide window at the snow settling on the windowsill. "I'm not going anywhere."

She smiled softly and tightened her grip on his hands. "First we need to make sure you're okay."

"Jana. My wounds are physical. They will heal. What about you? Are you okay, really? You seem…different."

She studied him. "In a good way?"

"A very good way." It was true. This tenderhearted, gentle woman holding his hand, worrying over his wounds, was the Jana he'd married. But if she'd had a change of heart, if God had worked to heal her emotional wounds, why hadn't she come home to him?

She seemed to read his thoughts. "I'm so much better, Mark. But I needed time. Maybe I still do… To sort things out. To make sure I'm not overwhelmed when I come back to a job, to—" she looked around the cabin "—to the real world."

"What can I do?"

She started to cry. "I don't know. I want to be the wife you deserve. I want to be a good mother to Ellie. But I'm so afraid. Afraid of failing again. Afraid of the future." She took a ragged breath. "What if I have…what Mom had?"

"Oh, Jana." He drew her into his arms. Pain shot through him at her weight against him, but he bit back a moan and held her as tightly as he could manage. "I should have reassured you. I should have done some research. It's very unlikely that you have Alzheimer's. I think anyone might have been overwhelmed at the load you were carrying, and I was never there to help you. That's going to change. I promise you." He eased back onto the pillows, seeking her face. "Will you go to a doctor so you can know for sure what you're dealing with? Maybe you're suffering from depression. Remember before?"

They'd never spoken of it until now. Would she acknowledge that dark time?

She nodded. "Maybe that was part of what I was going through. I don't know. But even so, I will regret what I did forever, Mark. Forever. It wasn't fair to you or Ellie. I should have gotten help. I'm so sorry."

He started to speak, but she shook her head and spoke softly. "God has used this time—here in this cabin—to teach me some things. About myself. About us. But mostly about Him."

The last vestiges of his anger drained away. "Can you ever forgive me, Jana?"

Her voice fractured. "Oh, Mark. I'm the one who should be asking your forgiveness. I don't know what I was thinking. I got it in my head that I was only going to be a burden to you and Ellie—I was so afraid I'd hurt her. I didn't see any way but to leave. I started driving and I couldn't stop." She drew in a halting breath. "Every time I stopped somewhere along the way I thought about turning back, coming home. But I was too afraid. Pretty soon, I felt like I was doing the right thing."

She swallowed hard and continued. "My thinking was so mixed up, so crazy. I don't know how to even explain it." She disentangled herself from his embrace and went to the table in front of the window.

She brought back a thin sheaf of papers, heavy with her handwriting. A cloud came over him, remembering another letter from her. He never wanted to feel that way again.

She held it out to him. "Maybe this will explain…" She shrugged and went to sit in a dilapidated chair near the fire. She dropped her face in her hands before turning to him again.

"What's this?" He rubbed his fingers over the thin paper.

"I didn't know if I'd ever…if I'd see you again. I wanted you to know how sorry I was."

He wagged his head. "You don't have to—"

"Please, Mark. Just read it."

He unfolded the pages. Tilting them to the firelight, he began to read.

Dear Mark,

I've written this letter so many times I've almost run out of paper, but this may be the last time I'm able to convey my thoughts to you and I want to get it right.

Words seem so inadequate for all I need to tell you. But I must try.

I don't know if I can ever make you and Ellie understand how deeply sorry I am for the way I left—the way I abandoned you. I've regretted it for so many days, but finally, I must simply trust that you will someday find it in you to forgive.

The tone of her letter frightened him. As if she'd expected to die. Was this meant to be a suicide note? He stopped reading and looked up at her.

She was watching him with an expression he couldn't quite read. The firelight haloed her hair and brightened her eyes and he felt as if he were seeing her for the first time, realizing all over again how beautiful she was. Inside and out. He felt like a college kid, his heart hammering the way it had that first time he'd seen her in the student union.

She rose from the chair, came to him and took the letter from him. She sank down beside him again on the edge of the sofa. "Let me…let me try to tell you," she whispered. "In person. I've spent too long not talking to you about my feelings. Maybe that's been part of the problem."

He waited, eager and frightened at the same time.

She let the letter slip from her hands and clasped his right hand between both of hers. "When I left Chicago that day, I was so confused and frightened. I felt as if I was losing my mind, and I was terrified I would hurt Ellie. I couldn't have lived with myself if I had ever caused her harm."

"You just had a lot of stress to—"

Her eyes flashed. "Don't make excuses for me, Mark. Please. Just let me explain."

He nodded.

"I was also afraid of losing you, Mark. I know my actions didn't do a very good job of showing it, but I never stopped loving you. Not for a minute. You were and always will be the love of my life."

He let the words soak in, realizing how terrified he'd been through all this that she *had* stopped loving him.

"I was afraid the mental state I was in would cause you to lose whatever love you still had for me." She shifted and let go of his hand. She rose and went to stand near the fireplace, warming her hands over the dwindling flame.

Her eyes never left his. "I couldn't have lived with that, Mark. It would have killed me. I say *couldn't,* in the past tense, because in these last weeks, here in the quiet of this cabin, in these beautiful mountains, I came to know God in a deeper way than I've ever experienced before. He showed me, in His amazing grace, that He is all I need. I was trying to find fulfillment in so many other things, in so many other people—you and Ellie and my father… I lost sight of the truth."

He waited, longing to know what it was she'd found here. What had changed her so.

"I felt so weak, Mark. But I learned that when I was the weakest I felt God's presence the most. Oh, Mark…I'm so grateful God gave me you to lean on, but when you weren't able to be there for me—or when I wasn't willing to tell you what I needed from you—I fell apart. I should have turned to God all along. My greatest fear is that because of my mistakes—my sin—I've destroyed our family forever. If I've let that happen, I'll never forgive—"

Mark didn't let her finish the sentence. With agonizing effort, he struggled to his feet and started across the room.

She met him halfway, clucking like a mother hen. "Lie down. You'll hurt yourself."

Pain made him obey, but he beckoned her to his side.

She seemed to consider it, then rose and came to sit on the edge of the couch again.

She reached out her hand and he took it, pressed it to his heart. Her bottom lip quivered.

He drew her in and she clung to him, her cheeks wet. He kissed them, tasting the salt of her tears.

"Jana, listen to me. You haven't destroyed our family. If anything I'm the one who's responsible."

Her eyes spilled over again. "Let's not argue about who was wrong." She drew back, trailing her fingers down his arm, searching for his hand.

He laced his fingers with hers. "Can we start all over? Go on from here?" He risked his next words. "Will you come home with me?"

A slow smile came to her face, and a radiance that had nothing to do with the firelight playing off her features.

"Oh, Mark..." She made a pillow of his chest, her head heavy against his ribs. "Now that you're here I *am* home."

His pain floated away on her whisper.

Epilogue

The spicy aromas of bratwurst and burgers mingled with the sultry August air and Jana moved her lawn chair upwind from the grill Dad and Mark tended. She swallowed hard and closed her eyes, leaning her head against the back of the chair. The sun warmed her skin, and for a split second, she was carried back to the cabin in Colorado. Inhaling the scent of wood smoke, she could almost hear the logs crackle in the fireplace, see the mighty firs outside the cabin's front window.

It unsettled her a bit, and yet, it had become almost a healing memory for her. A reminder of how far she'd come. And a marker of the way her husband had come to take her home.

She lifted her eyelids and watched Mark through the fringe of her lashes. How she loved this man.

The past months had been a struggle. It still hurt to see how Ellie had suffered because of her choices. Slowly, one step at a time, she'd regained her daughter's trust, and the bewildered, insecure child had been replaced once again by a happy-go-lucky little girl.

She and Mark had endured their own struggles. New issues presented themselves almost daily when they'd first returned to Chicago together, and old resentments had to be dealt with. Still, not once had she abandoned hope.

Mark had taken charge, insisting she take some time off from working. He still put in long hours at the restaurant, but he'd made a real effort to cut back. Wednesday nights were once again sacred family nights, and Dad and Julia took Ellie the first Saturday of every month so she and Mark could have some time alone.

Within a week of coming home, Mark had scheduled a slate of doctors' appointments for her, and he'd held her hand in each waiting room as Jana underwent a barrage of tests. They ruled out Alzheimer's almost immediately. And every other physical or chemical reason for what they'd come to call her "breakdown." Physically, she'd been awarded a clean bill of health. She was left with a clinical diagnosis of Major Depressive Episode that was apparently in full remission.

Her doctors had warned them that her symptoms might return. Sometimes the possibility filled her with dread. But if that happened, there were plenty of options they hadn't yet explored. She was learning to trust the future to the God who'd been with her in the darkest time of her life. There was always hope.

She and Mark had begun seeing a counselor from their church twice a month and she'd learned to talk out her fears before they overwhelmed her. Mark had become a tender confidant, and she suspected their counselor would soon dismiss them, since recently, their allotted hour had been mostly wasted in laughter and small talk.

Sometimes it was hard to believe the confused woman on that mountain was the same bright-eyed woman she'd seen in the mirror this morning. But she didn't ever want to forget. Agonizing though it was to remember sometimes, she'd gained too much in those months alone with God at the cabin to ever deny His power over her life.

"Look, Mommy! Look what I can make!" Ellie's silvery voice drew Jana back to the present and swelled her heart with love.

She sat up. "Let me see, sweetie, what have you got there?"

One pudgy hand gripped a bright blue bottle—"bubble juice" Mom had called it. *Oh, Mom, if only you could be here.* She still missed her mother every single day.

"It's bubbles! Go-Go gave 'em to me!" Ellie dunked the plastic wand in and out of the bottle, then puffed out her cheeks and blew. A stream of puny bubbles dribbled from the wand. Ellie's face fell and she stomped her foot. "I can't do it like Go-Go does."

Julia appeared at the edge of the patio cradling a salad bowl in her arms. "Did I hear my name? Come here, sweetie, let Go-Go help you."

A flash of jealousy tried to edge its way into Jana's heart, but she let it go as quickly as it had come. Julia had earned the right. She had sacrificed so much for Ellie—for all of them. And instead of resenting Jana for the pain she'd caused and the foolish judgments she'd made, Julia had lavished love on her.

A wave of gratitude coursed through Jana. God was good. So good. And she was so undeserving.

"Mommy, will you help me blow bubbles?"

Julia put the salad on the picnic table and turned to the men. "Are the burgers about ready?"

"Two more minutes." Mark handed the spatula to Jana's dad. "Mind taking over here?"

"Go right ahead."

Mark crossed the lawn and scooped Ellie into his arms. "Let Mommy rest, punkin. Bring me those bubbles."

Jana started to protest, but Mark gave her a knowing wink, and Ellie grinned wide and ran over to him.

Jana placed a hand over her belly and closed her eyes again, smiling to herself. They were announcing their secret today.

Dad would be worried sick about how she would handle the added stress of a new baby. Julia would rejoice with them, excited to be "Go-Go" to another little McFarlane. And Julia would calm Dad's fears. Help him see the blessing in this new little gift from God.

Frankly, Jana was a little worried herself about how she would handle it all. The restaurant was still struggling, but Mark was determined she wouldn't have to work during their children's preschool years. They hadn't planned on a baby quite so soon, but they had a strong support system in place, and she could hardly wait to introduce Ellie to her new little sister—or brother. Mark had his hopes up for a boy.

Mark lifted Ellie to his shoulders. She wrapped her legs around him and held on to his head. He dipped the plastic wand into the bottle of bubble solution. With a wink at Jana, he said a thousand sweet words. Then he lifted his head and blew into the center of the wand.

A confetti-spray of bubbles took flight, glistening in the sunlight. Jana watched as the shiny orbs floated down around them, some of them bursting before they hit the ground, others resting on the grass at the edge of the patio.

Ellie reached out and caught a golf-ball sized bubble in the palm of her hand, squealing with delight. "Look, Mommy!" But just as quickly the bubble burst.

"Uh-oh…" Jana waited for the tears to start. Instead, Ellie's smile never wavered. She rubbed her hands together, then held them to the sky where Mark had blown a new batch of bubbles. "It's okay, Mommy. God can make me a new one."

Ah, Ellie. Such wisdom from the mouth of a child. Jana's eyes stung and she held out her own hand. She'd been given another chance. God had made her a new life.

And His mercies were new every morning.

* * * * *

QUESTIONS FOR DISCUSSION

1. The book opens with Jana McFarlane having an emotional breakdown of sorts. What circumstances brought her to this point? Do you think her breakdown is justified? Have you ever felt overwhelmed by multiple crises seeming to happen at the same time in your life? How did you handle it? What did you find most helpful? Least helpful?

2. Jana chooses to deal with her issues by literally running away. Do you sympathize with her? Why or why not? How does her husband, Mark, handle the crisis? What, if anything, could he have done to change Jana's rash decision?

3. How do you think Mark and Jana's daughter, Ellie, might be affected—in the short term—by what happened? Long term? Did you experience trauma in your childhood that continues to affect you as an adult? If you have children, how do you think they may have been affected by crises *you* have endured? How might you minimize the long-term results for them?

4. Jana's father and stepmother step in to care for Ellie at a time when her parents are unable or unwilling to take their rightful place as parents. Have you ever been in such a situation? If not, do you feel you could make the same decision John and Julia did to care for a grandchild for an extended period of time? Why or why not?

5. Although John and Julia nearly fell into an affair with one another, they married, with God's blessing, after the death of their spouses. Talk about the guilt they dealt with, and the adjustments they had to make in a second marriage. How do you think Jana's situation might have been changed if John and Julia had been honest about their past?

6. John and Julia are relative newlyweds when the McFarlanes' crisis comes to a head, and having Ellie in their home puts a real crimp in their lifestyle. If you have children, what do you imagine the empty nest to be like? How might it affect a marriage to welcome a child who is not your own into your house?

7. Do you feel John and Julia handled the situation in a way that honored both God, and Ellie's birthparents? How might you have handled things differently? What mixture of emotions do you think John and Julia felt when Jana returned home and they had to say goodbye to Ellie?

8. What about Mark? Do you think his decisions honored both his wife and his daughter? What mistakes did he make? How might he have done things differently to lessen the disruption in Ellie's life, and to bring his wife home sooner? During the time Jana was missing, Mark faced a strong temptation to find comfort in the arms of another woman. Did you empathize with his temptation? What "hedges" might Mark have put up to avoid being tempted?

9. Where did Mark's and John's responsibility lie in trying to find Jana when she went missing? Were you satisfied with their efforts to find her? Try to imagine how you would feel if your spouse or adult child ran away. How far would you go and what efforts would you make to try to track them down? Do your thoughts change if you also imagine that your loved one left a note saying they didn't *want* you to try to find them?

10. Jana struggled with deep depression and even suicidal thoughts during the time that she was hiding out in the cabin. Do you think running away helped her sort out her problems? How was her isolation hurtful? Helpful? Have you ever felt like running away from your life? How did you resolve those feelings?

THE AWARD-WINNING CLASSIC NOVEL AND
BESTSELLING MOVIE BY BELOVED AUTHOR

DEBORAH RANEY

"A startlingly honest portrayal of love,
commitment and redemption in the midst
of tragedy." —*Library Journal*

A *Vow* TO
C H E R I S H

AUTHOR OF *Over the Waters*

DEBORAH RANEY

When his precious wife of thirty years received a devastating
diagnosis, John Brighton's world fell apart. He desperately
needed a confidante in his dark time, and a young widow
named Julia Sinclair seemed to understand his pain as no
one else could. As John struggled between doing what was
right and what his heart told him to, he soon discovered that
the heart can't be trusted where true love is concerned.

Steeple
Hill®

A *Vow* TO
CHERISH

Available wherever books are sold!

From Christy Award winner

Vanessa Del Fabbro

comes the third installment in
her South African–set series.

A Family in Full

Follow the stories of the two heroines of
Sandpiper Drift as they complete their families
in the fictional small town of Lady Helen,
South Africa.

Steeple
Hill®

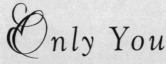

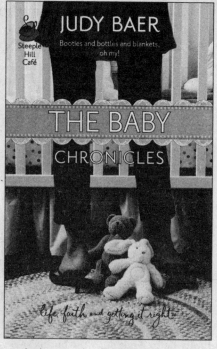